Taste of Honey

Julie Castle

Warning: Not intended for persons under the age of 18. May contain coarse language and mature content that may disturb some readers. Reader discretion advised.

Cover Art Design by: Kelly Moran/Rowan Prose Publishing
Photo Credit: Adobe Images
First Printing
ISBN: 978-1-961967-34-2

Rowan Prose Publishing, LLC
www.RowanProsePublishing.com
Published in the United States of America

Taste of Honey (series) Reviews

"THE GIFT is a very erotic tale of dominance that turns into love. [Castle] has written such a tantalizing story."
-Fallen Angel Reviews
"[Castle] has written a very interesting erotic love story. There's a fine line between engaged and frustrating me as the reader. This is an enticing BDSM love story."
-Erotic Romance Reviews
"The interaction between them makes for hot reading. You can feel the sizzle these two make."
-Fallen Angel Reviews
"Keep ice water near. This is one read that will make you sweat."
-Coffee Time Romance

Taste of Honey
Book 1
The Gift
JULIE CASTLE

Chapter 1

It was ten o'clock in the morning when Penelope Hart saw the package. She and her co-worker Joan were heading for their favorite table in the library's break room.

"Hey, girl, looks like somebody's got a birthday." Joan smiled. "Why didn't you tell me?"

Penny joined her at the table, looking at the gift wrapped in expensive silver paper. "It can't be for me. It's not my birthday."

Joan picked the box up and shook it. Something inside rattled. "It's got your name on it, Penny."

Penny grabbed the box from her, smiling. "Then hand it over, please. I wonder who would leave this here?"

The box was flat and square. Her name was printed on the tag in crisp handwriting. Was it a book? As a librarian, people were always giving her books. She tore it open to find something red nestled inside. A ping-pong paddle? How odd. She didn't play ping-pong. Lifting it out, she realized it was bigger than that and covered in red leather. A little padded.

She turned it over in her hand, showing it to Joan, who giggled. "What on earth is this?"

Joan pulled a sheet of paper out of the box. "There's a verse, Penny. *'How should librarians be spanked? Hard and often! Will you cry when I paddle you? Weeping tears of sweet submission before I make you come? Soon. X'.*"

Penny gasped, her cheeks flaming along with her bottom. She buttoned the top button on her prim white blouse, tucking an errant wisp of her strawberry blonde hair behind her ear.

How could anyone mistake her for a loose woman?

Joan grinned. "Why didn't you tell me you were getting some nookie, girlfriend?"

"I'm not...I don't..." Oh Lord, her panties were getting damp.

"Yeah. That's right, your last date was Paul, the thirty-second man," Joan said, sympathetically. "This means you've got a secret admirer, Penny."

"A secret sadist, you mean." She flipped the paddle over. "The stamp on the handle says Missy's House of B&D."

Who the hell could have sent this to her? She was the least sexual person she knew. Mr. Barto from the AV room? She glanced at him as he made his way to the free coffee for what had to be the twelfth time and shuddered.

No. Not even if someone paid her.

Someone bumped into a table, and she looked over to find Miles Crenshaw. There must be another emergency board meeting. How many emergencies could a library have? Since Vick Deveroux took over, plenty.

Joan waved a hand in front of her face, regaining her attention. "Sorry."

Joan smirked. "Nothing wrong with sizing up the competition. Now, if I weren't married, I might give Miles there a tumble."

"Not my type," Penny mumbled, suppressing a shudder, wondering if she really did have a type.

"As I was saying, B&D is short for bondage and discipline, Penny. Mr. X wants to tie you up and spank you."

Penny's cheeks flamed hotter. Her bottom tightened at the word 'spank,' but she refused to react. It was an intriguing proposition, not that she'd admit it. She read the books, but could she really do the deeds?

"I know very well what it means. Our BDSM downloads are flying off the shelves, so to speak." She ran her hand over the smooth leather. "As if I would let him. As far as I'm concerned, if he's not man enough to face me, he doesn't deserve me."

"I do it," Joan admitted with a giggle.

"What?" Penny gaped at her, noting the twinkle in her brown eyes.

"Every year on my birthday, for sure." Joan took a deep breath. "The first year it happened, we got in a fight. I was being a bitch."

Penny grinned, refraining from comment. Her pal could be hell on wheels.

"Anyway, Doug got really pissed off, pulled me over his knee, and paddled my ass—*hard*. I screamed, I cried, I bit him, but he wouldn't stop, and the strangest thing happened. I started to get really turned on. You know, wet down there. Well, after he spanked me, he gave me the screwing of my life. I could hardly walk, to say nothing of sitting down, the next day."

Penny blushed. She could just picture Doug, a burly auto mechanic, paddling Joan's round bottom. Now some man wanted to do the same thing to her. A little frisson of fear and excitement zinged through her. Shooting an embarrassed glance at grouchy Mrs. Bates, the returns clerk who was passing through the break room, she hoped they hadn't been overheard.

"Nothing but sluts and hooligans," Mrs. Bates muttered to herself.

Penny and Joan both burst out laughing, earning a scowl from portly Mr. Powel, the day manager, who manned the Check Out desk up front.

"Shh."

Biting their lips, they subsided.

"Oh, crap, keep it down," Joan muttered, adding nervously, "Here comes Vlad."

Tensing, Penny looked up. Victor Deveroux was indeed coming their way, here early for the board meeting, she decided. She took in his raven black hair, piercing blue eyes and dark suit, her heart skipping a beat. He was handsome, rich, austere, and way out of her league. Joan, of course, had dubbed him Vlad—the vampire.

His gaze lit on the paddle she held. One of his raven dark brows arched in surprise, and she thought she saw his sensual mouth twitch in amusement. Blushing, she slipped the paddle under the table, letting it rest on her lap.

He nodded. "Ladies."

Her pulse raced. Was he going to comment, or reprimand her? But he passed on by without another word. She stood, tossing her cool cup of coffee down the drain. She didn't need the caffeine buzz today.

"Back to work." She walked to her desk and slipped the paddle into the bottom drawer, then locked it.

"So, you're not going to go to the cops with Exhibit A?" Joan smiled.

"And say what, some anonymous sex maniac wants to spank me?" she said, trying to act casual. "I'll just forget about it."

"Right," Joan said, laughing.

The next two days went by normally. Then, while heading to her desk after lunch, Penny noticed another package.

"Oh!" Joan squealed. "Open it. I can't wait to see what he sent."

"I can." Penny sighed with trepidation. Did she want to get turned on again? It seemed so naughty.

Cautiously ripping off the blue wrapping paper, she opened the box, and gasped. Shiny silver handcuffs were nestled inside. She pulled them out, shivering. They were lined with soft fleece. And there was something else in the box. Black leather. A blindfold. Her knees were rubbery and her panties damp again.

She sagged into the nearest chair. "Oh, my."

Joan started reading, "*'You will call me master when we meet. You will beg sweetly for my pleasures, and my punishment. Devotedly, X'.*" She fanned her face with the letter. "Hot stuff."

"Kinky stuff," Penny protested. She wasn't that kind of girl. Heck, she'd only had sex a few times, and she hadn't found it all that satisfying. If this 'X' thought he could turn her into some kind of sex slave, he had his work cut out for him.

"Same thing. Hey, he sent sweets for the sweet." Joan pulled a red lollypop out of the box and handed it to her.

Penny blushed. It was shaped like an erect penis. She took the gifts and put them in the drawer with the paddle, not that she meant to ever meet him.

The following day, near the end of her shift, there was another package.

"This is getting silly," Penny protested, opening the red box. She lifted out a silver-colored metal chain with clips on either end. It was heavy enough to be real silver. She looked at Joan for clarification.

"Nipple clamps," Joan whispered, so Mrs. Bates wouldn't hear.

She took it from Penny and opened one clasp. "He gets your nips nice and hard, then he clamps these babies onto 'em. The chain adds weight, tugging at your tortured nipples."

Penny gasped, fascinated. Her nipples tingled, beading. "Have you used them?"

"No." Joan softly ran her fingers over the chain. "But, I'd like to borrow them."

Penny snatched them back. "No way. I'm not adding to your lude behavior." *Or giving them up*. She added the nipple clamps to her drawer of naughty things, her nipples jutting, tingling. Her panties were damp again, damn the man. How could he do this to her?

"There's another note," Joan said.

"Of course." She groaned. "What now? You will grovel before me some day? Promises, promises. So far, he's been nothing but a tease."

"*Meet me at the Grand Hotel, room five seventeen, at noon Saturday. X*'." Joan giggled. "Girl, you're gonna get it now."

"Well, I'm not going to do it," Penny firmly protested.

Still, she was dying to know who X was. He knew her movements, had access to the library. The only man that worked here was Mr. Powel, and she had it on good authority the rotund gentleman was gay. She thought about Vlad for a second, her nipples tingling. Now, he *was* good looking. But, he was also stiff and formal, not to mention snooty. And he wasn't here that often, being the new head of the library's board of trustees. Besides, he wouldn't have the desire to send such things to her.

It couldn't be him. No, it was somebody else, probably one of the library's patrons. It wouldn't hurt to check out Missy's House of B&D. They might be able to tell her who he was and put her out of her misery.

After work, she drove to the parking lot at Missy's House of B&D. It was a good thing she'd researched its location on her home PC this week, because it was hard to find. They didn't advertise, but her dogged determination had paid off. A small sign reading 'Private Club' told her she was in the right place.

The restored Victorian mansion was charming, like something out of a fairytale. Was the Big Bad Wolf waiting inside, ready to paddle her?

Not likely, she decided, tamping down her excitement while plucking her courage. When she entered the building, the first thing that hit her was the silence. It was plush, decorated in jewel tones, and empty. Where was everyone? She'd half expected to walk in on an orgy. The curtains parted in a doorway on her left, and a man walked out. He was older, and well dressed in a blue shirt and tan chinos.

She let out a sigh of relief, no black leather or whips.

"How may I help you, pretty one?"

Pretty? Her? "Um, well, I'd like to talk to Missy please."

"You're talking to her Dom, love. My name is Samuel."

She blushed. "Her Dom?"

"Her dominant master. Missy is my sub's name. It's homage to her, so to speak."

"Sub?"

He smiled, his eyes twinkling. "Yes, submissive, dear child. You're new, I see."

The very word *submissive* made her tremble. She needed to correct him quick. "Well, I'm not...that is, I don't..."

"Sit." He pointed to a chair behind her.

She frowned. "No, thank you."

"Sit," he said, gruffly, raising a brow.

Gasping, she sank into the chair.

He patted her on the head. "Obstinate, but quite trainable. You're a true submissive, love."

Trainable. She shuddered, her nipples peaking.

"Now. What is it that you want?"

"Some things were sent to me—some obscene gifts." She gulped as his interested gaze pierced her. "I demand to know who sent them."

"Oh." He smiled. "You must be Penelope."

Shocked, she gaped at him as his voice lingered over her name. "How do you know about me?"

"Simple. My friend is the man that sent the naughty gifts to you, love. Meeting you, I can now understand why he's crazy about you."

He's crazy about you. But who was he? She tried not to focus on the teasing way Samuel said *naughty*. She wasn't naughty, or crazy about a secret stranger. "Who?"

He shook his head. "I can't reveal that, love." He pulled back a curtain. "But I've got more goods for sale, if you want to send something to him."

Penny rose, unable to stop herself, as she walked into the back room to look. She gazed at a row of nipple clamps on display, clasped to the mannequins' plump nipples, and gulped, her mouth going dry. She noticed the silver ones that X had sent her. Sterling and heavy, as she touched them, her nipples began to tingle, jutting out against her thick cotton bra. Appalled, she stepped back, hunching her shoulders, so he wouldn't see.

"You should meet him," Samuel said behind her.

He knew about their proposed rendezvous. How embarrassing.

She turned to go, but a man and woman entered the building. When they walked past, she noticed the woman's wrists were cuffed in front of her, her nipples hard, her eyes shining with excitement. The man, walking fast behind her, carried a black paddle.

Penny looked at Samuel. "What goes on here?"

"Anything that two consenting adults want to happen. The rooms are sound-proofed." He added, softly, "So, no one will hear you beg for it."

She flushed. As if she would. "I have to go."

Chapter 2

Penny stood outside the hotel room Saturday, half an hour early. Not that she meant to submit, but she wanted to see X, *was aching* to see him. She had to know who he was.

Letting herself in with the key the desk clerk had handed her, she felt like she was doing something forbidden. Naughty. But she wasn't going to submit. She'd come to tell him just that, and to snoop. He wasn't here yet, or so the desk clerk had said. Did the desk clerk know why she was here?

She walked through the suite of rooms. Someone was staying here, she noted, eyeing his books on the coffee table. His slippers sat by the king-sized bed. Mr. X had big feet. She tried not to think about the size of his penis. She moved on to the exercise equipment in the corner—a weight bench and a rack with a pulley system—how odd.

She strode into the bathroom, featuring a big whirlpool tub and walk-in double shower. His toothbrush was by the sink. It seemed wrong peeking at his things, but she needed to know something about him.

She made her back to the bedroom, looking at the book on his bedside table. His choice in reading was interesting. Mythology. She turned, looking at the king-sized bed. It was covered with a silver velvet throw. Old fashioned yet traditional. She ran her hand over it, shivering. It was sensual to the touch.

She paced the bedroom's thick carpet, looking for something with his name on it. She didn't have much time. Her hands shook. She wiped them on the skirt of her dress.

Then she noticed the gifts from her naughty drawer laid out in a row on top of the dresser—her nipple chains, blindfold, handcuffs, and paddle. Her breath caught in her throat. How had he gotten them? They were still locked in her desk. Next to them was a big box of condoms—king size. She gulped.

The door opened, and she turned. Her eyes locked with his piercing blue ones, and her middle turned quivery.

"Vlad," she said with a gasp.

"You may not speak until your master gives you permission, Penelope."

Her bottom clenched as she stepped back, stung by his masterful tone. It was no-nonsense, determined, and hot. He stood there, staring at her, handsome as sin, but formal in his dark tailored suit.

She hunched her shoulders so he wouldn't see her budding nipples. "But you're not my master. Why should I obey you?"

"Then why are you here?" he demanded.

She bit her lip. Why *was* she here? To snoop? Maybe see him—and more.

"Strip," he commanded.

She jumped, startled. Her hand went to the top button of her dress.

Wait, why was she obeying?

"That's good," he praised.

As his dark raspy voice poured over her like honey, she sighed, acknowledging to herself she secretly wanted this.

Stripping off her dress, she stood, trembling, in just her panties, bra, and shoes. His hot gaze roved over her, and her nipples tingled.

"Kick your shoes off and come here."

With a gulp, she did as he commanded, feeling like a wanton. She'd never paraded in her undies before a man. Did he like her figure? She looked up at him, curious and turned on.

"Eyes down," he said.

Tearing up, she looked down. He was angry, strict. Would he use the paddle? She blushed, her bottom heating as she thought it. Finally, she stepped into his space, halting before him, smelling his sandalwood cologne. She'd noticed it before at the library. How long had he been watching her, thinking about dominating her, having sex with her? Shivering, she waited for him to say something.

He reached out to stroke her hair, undoing the clip at her nape, fingering a strawberry-blonde curl.

"What a good girl," he praised. "Your hair is lovely, Penelope. I want you to wear it down like this, but only for me."

She shivered, getting wet, excited and scared.

He reached behind her, unfastening her bra. She stood frozen, embarrassed as he slipped it off her. His hands were on her breasts, warm and rough. His fingers teased her nipples, making her blush harder, as she bit back a moan. It was so good, so sexy. She leaned into his touch, wanting more.

"Such beautiful breasts," Vlad murmured. "And so responsive."

Her face flaming, she pushed them into his hand, and he pinched her nipples.

"Oh." It hurt and felt good.

"No talking," he warned. "That's one demerit."

Demerit? She wasn't a child.

She glanced at the paddle on the dresser, and shuddered. Would she let him use it? Did she want him to discipline her? His fingers, pinching and tugging at her nipples, made her gasp. Then, his hands moved to the waistband of her panties, pulling them down, exposing her curls. Her hands moved to cover them.

"No." He smacked her bottom.

"Ouch!" His red handprint throbbed on her bottom. Her hands fell away from her curls.

"Better," he said, rubbing her ass.

Penny couldn't help it, she leaned into his touch.

He eased back, and she stepped out of her panties.

"Go lay down on the bed, Penelope," he ordered, suddenly gruff.

Shimmering with excitement, she did as he commanded, climbing on top of the velvet spread. It tickled against her back.

"In the center."

She inched over. He was going to make love to her, bring her pleasure. She could hardly wait. Although, she wasn't sure she had what it took to be the sexual wanton he thought she was. Still, she was willing to give it a shot. Her sex was wet, quivering, her nipples tingling. When he looked at them, they jutted out harder.

"Give me your right hand."

She reached out to him tentatively. Holding hands wasn't exactly what she had in mind.

Instead, he pulled a handcuff from the nightstand drawer and slapped it on her wrist, quickly fastening it to the headboard.

Shocked, she could only gape at him for a moment. Licking her dry lips, she whimpered, "No...I don't."

"Quiet, slave."

Penny's mouth snapped shut as his suddenly hard tone stung her. She shivered as he methodically cuffed her other wrist. He wasn't kidding about this bondage stuff. As he stood, looking down at her, she couldn't help wriggling. Excitement and terror warred inside her.

He reached for her blindfold.

"No!"

He turned, scowling. "Don't make me gag you. I want that pretty mouth free."

Free for what? His cock? Samuel's words came back to her. *He's crazy about you.* She shuddered. She'd never had oral sex or given it.

He lifted her head, sliding the blindfold in place, tightening it so it shut out all light. Beneath it, tears stung her eyes. It was frightening to be blinded like this.

She waited. Why wasn't he touching her, taking her?

Then, he spread her legs, tied them to something so they were lewdly splayed open.

"You've got the most beautiful pussy, Penelope," he said softly. "It's pink and perfect for me."

She was mortified.

The bed sagged as he sat next to her, his finger caressing her labia. She sighed, straining toward him. This was what she wanted, what she craved. He kept circling her sex, playing with her, driving her mad. Why didn't he take her?

"Speak. Who am I?" He tickled her clit.

She gasped, arching toward his teasing finger. "Vlad. Um...I mean, Mr. Deveroux."

"No." He flicked her clit hard.

"Ow," she cried as pain shot through her. She wouldn't call him Master. No way.

"Who?" he demanded, smoothing over her clit.

"I'm not calling you that." She sobbed in frustration.

He spanked her mound. "Who?"

"Ouch." Pain rippled through her.

"Do you want me to fuck you?" he asked, sticking a finger into her wet pussy. "Speak."

How could he make her ask him? It was shameful. She didn't talk like that, didn't use those kinds of improper words. He shoved another finger into her, and she gasped with pleasure.

"Yes, I want you to fuck me," she bit out.

Then, he pinched her clit. Pleasure—pain—*goodness me*.

"Not until you ask me properly, naughty Penelope," he said, rubbing her clit.

She whimpered when he pulled away.

"Speak," he demanded.

Sobbing with need, she cried out, "Fuck me, please."

"Please, what?"

"Please, Master." Her pussy clenched, aching for him.

She heard his zipper, felt the bed sag again as he moved between her spread legs. He was still dressed, his pants rubbing against her naked thighs. How naughty. The head of his cock butted against her mound. He was hard and wide, definitely extra large.

She whimpered, wondering if she could hold him. Instead of taking her, he bent to suck and nibble on her nipples. She arched, rubbing against his cock, crying out.

"Shh," he demanded. "No sound, four demerits."

She whimpered silently as he sucked and nibbled on her nipples, drawing them deep into his hungry mouth. His cock thumped against her, teasing her, but not taking her.

"Please, Master," she sobbed.

"Five demerits," he growled, moving to suck the other nipple.

She shivered, the sucking making her hotter, driving her wild. She tugged against her restraints, writhing under him. "Please, Master, fuck me." She wailed.

"Six demerits," he growled.

She felt the broad head of his cock entering her. "Oh!" He was huge.

He kept filling her, relentless, stretching her.

"Seven demerits," he bit out, shoving farther inside.

She whimpered as he thrust his big cock the rest of the way. He lay on her, flattening her, breathing hard.

Vlad the Impaler, indeed. If Joan only knew.

He drew out, slamming back into her. She saw stars beneath the blindfold, her pussy rippling as he slammed into her again.

"Don't you dare come," he ordered with a growl. "Not until I give you permission, slave."

Permission to come? He couldn't ask that.

She shuddered, crying out, as he pumped inside her.

"Shh." Holding her bottom tight, he thrust in and out of her.

Her pussy clamped onto his cock, milking it hard as she came, screaming.

When she recovered, he was still pumping in and out.

"Bad slave," he grumbled. "No self-control." He pumped into her again, coming.

His weight lifted from her and his cock pulled out.

What a mind-blowing experience. She'd never come so hard.

He lay down beside her. Why wasn't he undoing her restraints? He ran a hand over her breast, pinching the well-sucked nipples. She arched toward his hand, feeling the pull deep inside. She gasped while her pussy rippled and grew wet again.

"Oh, my. Twice?"

"Shh. You've been a disobedient girl, Penelope." He pinched her nipple. "How should I punish you?"

"You can't. I won't let you."

Spank!

His palm slapped her mound, and she shrieked. *It hurt.*

"Wrong answer, naughty slave." His hand soothed her spanked mound, tickling her clit.

She sighed, arching toward to him. *More fucking, Vlad*, she wanted to beg.

His finger slid to her anus, tracing it, tickling it.

She tensed. *Not there!*

"Have you ever had anal sex, naughty Penelope?" He wet his finger with her juices and slid the tip of his digit into her ass. "Speak."

"Oh," She moaned at the strangely pleasurable sensation, tightening against him. "No, that's dirty."

"Nice and dirty." He chuckled. "It's where bad slave girls get fucked. But, don't worry, Penelope, we'll work up to that. I'll introduce it to you slowly, like a good master should. Would you like that? Speak." He spanked her mound again.

She yelped at the flash of pain, her ass tightening around his finger. "Yes, Master."

"Excellent," he said, tickling her anus and clit at the same time.

Her hips rose from the bed at the filthy, good/bad feeling. She shouldn't like it, or allow it, she told herself while quivering against his probing digit.

He bent down, his finger still partially inside her bottom. His warm breath caressed her mound. He was breathing fast, she realized. He licked at her pussy, her labia, sucking them into his mouth.

Nobody had ever...

He nipped them lightly—first one, then the other.

She moaned, thrashing, overcome with pleasure.

He licked her clit, and she screamed.

"That's eight demerits," he said against her.

His warm breath made her tremble. He went back to sucking her clit, drawing it into his mouth, nipping at it.

She whimpered as pleasure-pain washed over her. Vlad was a perfect nickname for him, she decided. He was a vampire, a pussy vampire. His tongue thrust into her, licking. She came, muffling her shriek, her clamping on his tongue.

Then, he did it to her again, licking, sucking, making her come again.

When he finally pulled away, she was limp, drained. She felt her head and shoulders being raised, as the bed sat up electronically. It startled her, and she whimpered. Her cuffed wrists were pulled back, her legs still restrained.

"Open your mouth for your master," he commanded.

She'd never given oral sex before, but there was no denying her master, she knew.

Penny opened her mouth, feeling the blunt head of his cock brush her lips. Tentatively, she reached her tongue out, to lick him. Salty, sweet, male—her tongue swept around the velvet head of his cock. She licked a drip of come off the slit, and thought she heard him sigh.

If only she could only see him while she was doing this wanton act. Opening her mouth wider, she took the head of him in her mouth, feeling it twitch. Sucking, she slid up and down it, as far as her bonds would let her go. His hands gripped either side of her head, holding her steady, as he pushed into her mouth. She gurgled, him push deeper.

"That's it," he husked. "Open your mouth wide for your master, Penelope."

She shuddered, him pumping between her lips, trying to please him. He was pulsing, tightening, getting bigger.

"When I come, I want you to swallow it," he said tightly. "Don't spill a drop, you hear me?"

She could only gurgle as he fucked her mouth faster. He came in hot salty spurts. Sucking and slurping, she gulped his cum, feeling it drip down her chin, and onto her breast. When he pulled out of her mouth, she sighed.

"You spilled." He smoothed the cum around her nipple. "How shall I punish you?"

She kept silent, bottom tightening, waiting for it, at his mercy. The bed shifted as he got up. He undid her wrist cuffs and her leg restraints.

"Give me your hand," he ordered.

What was he going to do, rap her knuckles like the nuns had in elementary school? Trembling, she held out her hand.

He grasped it, giving her a tug. "Come."

She wiggled to the side of the bed. Standing beside him, her knees buckled. She'd never been so well fucked in all her life. She reached up to remove her blindfold.

"No," he snapped.

She let her hand drop, tears stinging her eyes at his hard tone. Why was he so mean? She'd done all the things he'd said.

He tugged on her hand again, and she followed him, padding barefoot over the carpet. Where was he leading her? When they stepped on the cool tile, she knew it was the bathroom. She heard water running, smelled jasmine bath oil.

He was going to give her a bath? While the water ran, he abruptly sat down on something, tugging her over his knee.

She screeched, startled.

"Quiet!"

She could feel that he was still dressed, while she was naked, over his knee. Her butt, raised up in the air, tightened. His hand slapped her ass.

Spank!

She screamed.

"Quiet, or I'll gag you."

She sobbed, whimpering against him. Joan was crazy if she thought this made her hot.

Spank!

His hand smacked against her ass again. She bit her lip, stifling her cry, her mound pressing against his wool pants. But there was a small spark of pleasure.

"Better," he praised, rubbing her ass. "Four more."

Her bottom tensed as tears wet her blindfold. "Sadist bastard."

Spank!

His hand slapped the bottom of her ass, making her jump forward as she squealed.

Spank!

She whimpered as his palm flattened against her left cheek.

Spank!

Her right cheek. He was playing with her, enjoying it. And damn, her pussy was getting wet again. Her legs inched apart. Maybe Joan wasn't making it up.

Spank!

She screamed as he hit her harder. She lay over his knee, crying and aroused. He gently rubbed her bottom, making her sob, his caress tender now.

"I knew you'd cry," he said softly. "Was it a good spanking, Penelope?"

She stiffened. She couldn't answer that. It was too personal.

His hand cupped her mound. "You're wet, naughty Penelope. Speak."

She shook her head, sobbing.

Spank! He spanked her mound. It quivered, as pain tightened it.

"Yes," she cried out.

"Good slave," he said, rubbing away the hurt. He pushed her off his lap to land on the floor.

Startled, she yelped, and started to rise.

"No. Stay."

She settled back down. She heard him walk away to turn off the taps and then came back.

"On your knees," he ordered, pulling off her blindfold.

She rose onto her knees, blinking at the suddenly bright light.

"Spread your knees apart"

She did, acutely aware of her nudity. He was still wearing his shirt and tie, for Pete's sake.

"Good. Eyes down," he barked.

She dipped her gaze, peeking at him from under her lashes. He was handsome, her master.

"Put your hands on your knees, palms up."

She did, trembling. How must she look, naked, spanked and well fucked?

"You are in your first submissive position, naughty Penelope."

Submissive position. Her pussy fluttered.

"Up," he said. "And into the tub."

She stood and walked toward the whirlpool tub, embarrassed. She'd never bathed with a man before, never done a lot of things before.

She was astounded when he took her hand, gently helping her into the tub. She eased into the swirling water with a sigh. It immediately soothed her spanked bottom. When he started scrubbing her shoulder with a sponge slathered with jasmine body wash, she blushed. Staring up at him, she watched his blue irises contract when he scrubbed her breasts, paying extra attention to the nipples. They jutted out for him, tingling. He moved down, scrubbing her tummy, down to her curls. She squeezed her legs together, earning a black scowl from him. She opened them, and he scrubbed her pussy, rubbing the clit, over and over, until she came, crying out. She opened her eyes to find his sensual mouth tightened, sweat on his brow.

"Turn over, onto your knees."

She blanched. Was he going to spank her again? Biting back a sob, she did as he said, getting on her knees, holding onto the edge of the tub. The sponge was on her ass, scrubbing hard, swirling around her spank marks, making her whimper. He sponged down between her legs, rubbing her pussy.

Then, he moved to her anus, making her tighten and pull away.

He swatted her wet bottom.

She sobbed, stilling.

He soaped her anus, working a soapy finger inside, swirling and scrubbing. Her ass tightened around his finger, and her pussy rippled.

He laughed and pulled his finger out. "Bad slave." He smacked her wet bottom again, playfully this time. "Up," he said, yanking the plug.

She stood, a bit wobbly, and took his hand as he helped her out of the tub.

He dried her with a plush towel, then led her to the vanity.

"Bend over," he said, roughly.

She bent over, hands on the sink, bottom thrust out. What would he do to her now? Her cheeks clenched.

Waiting, she heard him disrobe. He was getting naked? Why? Then he was behind her, sucking on her neck. His big hands squeezed her spanked bottom.

She moaned, pressing against him, getting hotter. He reached between her legs, touching her pussy, running his fingers over her labia, toying with her clit. She shivered against him, growing wetter. He pushed one, and then two, fingers into her, stretching her.

She humped his hand, groaning.

"Shh," he admonished.

His cock brushed her pussy—hard, throbbing. She whimpered, needing it so bad.

"You're so wet, naughty librarian. Are you ready for your Master to fuck you?"

"Oh yes, Master," she cried. "Fuck me, please."

She felt every hard inch of him slide into her, her pussy hugging him. He surged into her, driving her against the sink, and she moaned with pleasure. Grasping her hips, he pulled almost all the way out, then surged into her again.

She was shivering, gasping for breath, as he took her hard. "Oh please, Master. Yes, Master," she repeated.

He reached for her clit, pinching it, and she came, tightening around his cock.

He came, thrusting hard, and holding her tight. He sagged against her, his breathing harsh.

When he pulled out, she collapsed against the sink.

Vlad was insatiable.

He turned the shower on. "Come," he barked.

She stood, turning to look at him, her pussy still rippling. "What?"

"One demerit," he growled, reaching for her. He pulled her into the big double shower with him.

She looked at him, seeing him naked for the first time. He was handsome, even more handsome naked. Powerful upper body, washboard abs. He worked out, she surmised. Strong legs, big feet. Of course, his cock, even limp, was enormous.

"Wash me," he ordered.

Well, he'd washed her, it only seemed polite to reciprocate. She reached for a sponge on the ledge and a bottle of body wash. Sandalwood scent. She added some to the damp sponge, and approached him. He stood there, stiff as a statue, watching her. Wasn't he even going to help?

Frowning, she lathered first one arm, then the other, and moved on to his flat stomach. Looking at his cock, she panicked and dropped to scrub his feet, soaping both legs. She came to his cock, eye level, and blowjob level. Blushing, she scrubbed it, and watched it grow before her eyes.

Peeking up at him, she took in his smile as the water rinsed the soap away.

"Open your mouth," he ordered.

She did, tongue flicking out to taste him, taking the head of his cock inside her mouth. It grew, twitching as she sucked on it harder, longer. He slid in and out of her mouth, holding her head steady while he fucked it, making her gag a little on the deep strokes.

Pulling away, he tugged her to her feet and entered her while standing up.

"Wrap your legs around my waist, Penelope."

She did, his hands gripping her bottom while he thrust hard into her, slamming her down onto him, making her take more until she came.

He held her that way for a long time as she sobbed, overcome by emotion, water pounding on them.

He turned off the shower and stepped out, him still inside her. Dripping wet, he carried her into the bedroom.

She moaned with every step as his cock rubbed inside her. Her pussy rippled against him.

He laid her, still wet, on the edge of the bed, and rammed into her over and over until he came, and she exploded with him.

When he pulled away, she lay there, panting.

"Stay," he ordered.

She lay still, too tired to argue, and heard the water in the sink running. He came back and washed her pussy.

She blushed, closing her eyes. Would she ever get used to that?

He dried her with a towel, and pulled back the covers.

"Come," he said.

She crawled between the sheets. He covered her up, and she fell asleep.

When she woke hours later, it was already dark outside. How long had she been here?

He wasn't in bed. She sat up.

The lights came on, making her blink.

She looked at the wet bar in the sitting room. He was sitting there, watching her. He was dressed again, this time in a robe and slippers.

"Up," he ordered.

She got up, but sidled away from him, acutely aware of her nudity. "Vlad, it's been fun—mind-blowing actually—but it's time for me to go."

"No."

She froze. "What did you say?"

"You heard me, naughty slave. Now, assume the position."

Her cheeks flamed. "I'll do no such thing. A few games are okay, but it's gone far enough."

"Do you want a paddling?"

Her bottom clenched. "No." She looked around. Where were her clothes? "This is illegal, Vlad."

"Do you want to call a cop?" he asked politely.

"No," she said with a frown.

"Then don't make me repeat the command. Down."

She sunk to her knees before him, her legs spread, head bowed, as she shuddered.

"Very good," he praised.

She watched him pour himself a drink. He stood there, watching her, like she was an exhibit or something. His plaything. Her knees hurt, her nipples tingled, her pussy clenched, growing wet.

"Come," he said.

She stood and walked to him. When he held out his glass, she thought he was offering it to her. A black scowl when she reached for it made her drop her hands, along with her gaze.

"Better," he said.

He rubbed the cold glass over her left nipple, and she gulped as it got harder, stinging. He bent to suck on it, drawing it into his hot mouth. She trembled, her middle melting, as he sucked harder. Then, he held the glass to her right nipple, swirling it, making her shiver as she moaned.

"Shh," he scolded, then sucked her right nipple.

Her knees wobbled as he drew it hard into his hot mouth. She whimpered when he stopped. He put down the glass and reached up to pinch both nipples, rolling them in his fingers, tugging on them. Gasping with pleasure, she leaned toward him.

"Who's playing with your pretty tits, slave? Speak."

"M-m-master," she stammered with a cry when he pinched them.

"Very good," he said, his hands dropping. "Come." He turned and walked to the dresser.

She followed him, her nipples hard, aching points.

"Are you ready to wear your jewels, naughty librarian?"

She shivered at the nipple clamps in his hand. Could she take it? At his frown, she murmured, "Yes, Master."

He reached for her left nipple, pinching it, rolling it.

She closed her eyes and shoved it out at him, moaning. It felt so good. Cool metal clamped down, pinching it, extending it, making it sting. Gasping, she looked at him.

"You will wear it to please your master."

She shuddered as he played with her other nipple, getting it ready. Yes, she'd do it to please him. Moaning with pleasure, she pushed the other nipple out at him as he tugged on it. The cool clasp clamped down, making her squirm. It hurt, but not as much as she had feared. She opened her eyes to look down at her tits. The silver clasps pinched the nipples, jutting them out even more. They were swollen, red. She whimpered. He dropped the chain and she gasped. It hung, tugging on her poor tortured nipples, pleasure/pain shooting through them.

"Walk for me," he ordered.

She took a few cautious steps, the chain swinging. She looked helplessly back at him.

"Over to the table. Sit."

She slowly walked over to the table and chairs, nipples tortured, biting her lip. The table was set for two. Light glinted off champagne glasses. A bud vase contained a single red rose. She sighed. The chain moved, tugging on her nipples. Tears welled in her eyes.

He pulled out her chair, ever the gentleman. Blinking back tears, she sat, letting him push her chair in.

Someone knocked on the door.

She startled, blinking at him.

He was watching her. "Dinner," he said, walking to the door.

She panicked. She couldn't let the room service person see her. She started to get up.

"Sit," Vlad said sharply.

Wincing, she sat back down.

He opened the door and stepped out into the hall.

She heard him talking, joking with the deliveryman. This was her chance. She could jump up, cry out. She heaved in a shaky breath. Her nipple clamps tugged, her pussy contracted, raw from his loving, but still randy. She stayed put.

How had he turned her into this shameless wanton?

He came back into the room, shutting the door behind him, locking it.

"I have to go home."

"No. I want you to stay for the weekend and take your preliminary submission lessons. An obedience course, if you will."

She gaped at him. He sounded serious and strict. He set a plate before her. Quiche, salad, strawberries, and chocolate mousse. All her favorite foods, how did he know? Her stomach rumbled, but she waited, minding her manners. He carried his plate to the table with the same foods.

Sitting next to her, he nodded. "Good. You may eat everything but your dessert."

He couldn't tell her what to eat.

Gazing at his determined expression, she decided that he could. She nibbled on her salad, and caught him watching her mouth. She moved on to her quiche, which was delicious. Heaving a sigh of relief when he started to eat, her nipple chain tugged, and she gasped. Luckily, he seemed not to hear.

She wouldn't put it past him to tug on that cursed chain. She speared a plump strawberry, bringing it to her mouth, nibbling it. She felt him watching her. It was exciting. Emboldened, she ate another, licking the juice off her lips. A peek told her he was aroused, his cock stirring under his robe.

Suddenly, she was nervous.

He stood, taking off his robe. He was naked, and hard.

"Position one, now," he demanded.

Blanching at his harsh tone, she stood, walked over to him, and sank to her knees.

He scooped his finger into the chocolate mousse and held it in front of her. "Suck, it off."

Shocked, she took his finger between her lips, sucking the dessert off. She was trembling, her arousal peaked. When he pulled his finger out, she sat back, gasping as her nipples tugged. She watched him spread chocolate mousse on the head of his hard cock, and gulped.

"Suck," he ordered.

She hesitated—it was so naughty. Flicking her tongue out, she tasted him and the mousse, then opened wider, slipping the head of his cock into her mouth. She sucked. He began to move in her mouth, over and over, deeper and deeper.

"Open your mouth wider, Penelope."

She complied as he pushed deeper, holding her head, fucking her mouth. She didn't want him this way. It was demeaning. Still, she grew wet, her pussy twitching as she gagged on his huge cock.

"When I come," he hissed, "swallow it all. Don't miss a drop, or I'll have to punish you, naughty librarian."

He came, spurting into her mouth. She swallowed, feeling cum run down her chin.

She'd be punished. She started to cry.

He pulled out of her mouth, and she dared a look up at him.

He was frowning, his blue eyes dark and dilated. He touched the cum on her breasts, lifting it up on his finger for her.

She licked it off, shuddering, dreading her punishment.

"Up," he said. "Into the bedroom."

Blinking away tears, she walked toward the bedroom. Would he paddle her? Would it be worse than the spanking? Her nipples tugged, and she shivered.

He walked over to the funny exercise equipment—the frame with pulleys.

He took her right hand, and pulled it up, manacling it to the top of the frame. She whimpered at the tug to her clamped nipple. He did the same to her left hand. She gasped at the pull when both her breasts lifted. She was stretched, taut, and scared. He bent down to secure her ankles. Her legs spread. Her pussy got wet again. Was he going to take her like this? It was an exciting possibility. But he'd promised to punish her.

She watched him walk to the dresser and pick up her red paddle. Her bottom clenched. Oh, no!

He stepped beside her, and kissed her shoulder. "Time for punishment, Penelope."

She shuddered, her nipples tugging.

He rubbed the paddle on her bottom. "Ready?"

"No," she cried, shuddering.

He drew the paddle back, and she moaned in anticipation.

Smack!

She shrieked.

"No sound," he grumbled, covering her mouth with his hand.

She cried muffled sobs into his hand.

Smack!

"Oh," she yelped.

Smack!

"No, ouch," she cried into his hand.

Sobbing, she heard him drop the paddle. What other tortures did he have in mind?

"Tears of sweet submission," he said, brushing a teardrop off her cheek.

She cried harder. When he held out his finger, she obediently licked the drop off.

He went behind her, kissing her neck, sucking on it, biting. She shuddered, her pussy getting aroused. His hot lips ran down her spine, making her shiver as he knelt behind her. She felt his lips on her paddled bottom, kissing, licking, soothing the fire from her paddling. He nipped her, and she trembled.

His hands spread her ass cheeks and he licked her anus.

She shrieked, tightening at the unexpected touch of his hot tongue.

"No," he said, and stabbed his tongue in her ass again.

She cried as his rough tongue pushed at her tight bottom, burrowing inside. She gasped, her pussy and bottom rippling.

Then he drew his tongue out, and she felt his finger, rubbing, probing. It had something cool and sticky smooth on it.

"I'm lubing your bottom, naughty slave." He stood and walked to the dresser.

She groaned, her bottom still rippling. When he came back, carrying what looked like a short, stubby, thin dildo, she shook her head. He wasn't going to...

He stepped closer, showing it to her. "This is your butt plug, naughty librarian." He smiled, holding it up to her lips, and she kissed it, reluctantly. "Very good," he praised with a smile.

He walked behind her.

She tensed while he parted her cheeks. The plug touched her anus, and she jerked away.

"No," he said. "I'm opening your ass, naughty slave."

Shuddering, she stilled. She felt it entering, stinging and stretching as he wedged it firmly inside her.

He backed away.

The butt plug stayed in place, holding her open, feeling too big, too invasive.

She cried quietly as he stood, then walked around to face her. She stood captive, stretched, bottom plugged, and peeked up at him. He was smiling, satisfied, because he'd done this to her. She shuddered, her nipple chain tugged, and she gasped.

He stepped closer, nearer. Was he going to kiss her? She blushed. With all they'd done, he'd never done that. His mouth brushed hers, and she sighed, closing her eyes. Her pussy got hotter as he thrust his tongue inside her mouth. She sucked on it, earning a groan. He touched her tits, tugging on the chain. She yelped into his mouth at the pleasure/pain that zinged through them, making her pussy contract, her anus ripple around her butt plug.

She felt him pinch her nipple and gasped. What was he doing?

He released her left nipple clasp. Pain rushed in, making her whimper. But then his mouth was there, sucking the tortured nip into his mouth. Sucking hard, he made her squirm, laving it with his tongue when she moaned with pleasure. It was almost enough to make her unaware of the chain dangling heavily from her right nipple. Then he released that nipple, too.

The chain hit the floor as he moved to suck on her right nipple, drawing hard on it while he pinched the left one. She shuddered, putty in his hands.

His mouth left her tits, and she whimpered in protest. He knelt, spearing his tongue into her pussy. Flicking it at her clit. Teasingly, sucking on the lips of her labia. She was writhing, groaning, when he stabbed his tongue into her again. He reached back to swirl the plug in her anus, and she came, shuddering, hanging limply afterward.

He stood and kissed her.

She tasted her own juices on his tongue, sucking it obediently when he stuck it into her mouth. Then, he pulled back. She watched him walk away, carrying her nipple chain. He was smiling. She was stretched, her butt plugged, and she was shaking. When would he come back and release her?

When he didn't, she started to ache.

After a while, she called out, "Vlad, um, Master, untie me, please."

He came back in, frowning. "Quiet." He walked to the dresser, and pulled something out of the top drawer.

He unrolled one of the things, and she realized they were two of his ties—one blue, the other red.

"Open your mouth," he commanded.

Was he going to kiss her again? Some of her aches receded at the thought. She opened her mouth. He pushed the rolled up blue tie inside her mouth. She gasped, her eyes widening, he wouldn't dare! Her eyes flashed fire at him, as he secured the makeshift gag with the unfurled red tie.

"Sadist vampire," she tried to yell. "Stop that."

"Subs must be quiet and respectful to their masters," he explained, pleasantly. He kissed her shuddering shoulder and left the room, saying, "One hour gagged for speaking out of turn."

She shuddered, her stretched ass burning, aching as the minutes ticked by.

Crying, she watched the clock. How could he be so cruel?

At the end of the hour, he came back, removed the gag. Her lips were dry, swollen. He bent to kiss them, and she let him, crying softly. The fight was beaten out of her, for now.

He unfastened her feet from the bonds, then her hands. She sagged against him, crying at the sensation of pins and needles that shot through her limbs. Lying over his arm, she felt him pull out her butt plug, and blushed. In all her agony, she'd almost forgotten about it—almost. Her bottom twitched, gaping.

He picked her up, and carried her to bed. Then, he climbed in behind her, naked. Was he going to...

"Go to sleep, naughty librarian, you've got more obedience lessons to learn in the morning."

She felt him tuck his semi-erect cock between her cheeks. His hand cupped her breast possessively and she fell into a deep sleep.

Penny woke Monday morning when her bottom was smacked. Wincing, she sat up, blinking at Vlad.

Her Master wanted her. He was already dressed.

"Get up, breakfast is ready," he said.

She climbed out of bed, naked again. He'd kept her naked all weekend. Tying her up, spanking her, stretching her ass with the butt plug, fucking her until her eyes rolled back in her head from the repeated orgasms. It had been a hell of a weekend. She was pooped.

Obediently, she walked to the table, waiting for him to pull out her chair. Poached egg, English muffin, and strawberry jam—more of her favorites.

"You may eat everything but the jam," he said, joining her.

She blushed, knowing what he wanted her to do with the jam. She ate her breakfast, careful not to touch the jam. Sitting back, she looked at him.

"Come," he ordered. "Position one."

She got up, her pussy contracting, and knelt before him. At his nod, she unzipped his black pants. She reached in, her hand slipping through the opening of his briefs, to pull out his cock. It throbbed in her hand, growing. It bobbed before her, but she waited for the command. She watched him spread jam on the head of his cock, making it redder.

"Suck," he said tightly.

Her lips closed over him, sucking, as she bobbed her head forward. His hands gripped her head as he slipped in and out between her lips.

"That's a good, slave Penelope, servicing your Master." He groaned.

Penny moaned as his cock surged deep into her mouth.

"Swallow my cum," he ordered. "Don't let it spill, or you'll be punished."

She shivered, but knew their weekend was almost over. It was an idle threat. He came, in great salty spurts, more than ever before. She sucked, swallowing, feeling it spurt, drip down her chin onto her breast, her belly.

When he pulled out, she peeked up at him. There was a stern but satisfied look on his handsome face.

"Up," he ordered. "Shower and dress."

Penny rushed to the shower, glancing at the clock. She didn't want to be late for work. She showered, a bit surprised he didn't strip and join her. It was their last morning, she would have liked one last fuck by his magnificent cock.

When she walked out to the bedroom, he was waiting, clothes laid out on the bed. But they weren't hers.

"Where are my things?" She gazed at his hard face.

"I like these better."

"But, I can't let you." Tears stung her eyes. "Like payment for services rendered."

"Don't you dare say that," he growled, stepping forward.

She blanched seeing his anger, and hung her head. "Sorry."

"Put them on," he said, handing her the panties.

She held the cocoa satin and cream lace thong panties in her hand. She'd never worn anything so sexy. She slipped them on, shivering with excitement. They were high cut. The thong nestled between her cheeks, leaving her paddled bottom bare. She reached for the matching bra, slipping it on. Its satin and lace cupped her breasts, pushing them up. She could see her beaded, tortured nipples, plump against the light fabric. It was sexy, erotic.

She looked at the clothes he had bought her. A pink silk blouse. She put it on, marveling at the sensual feeling as she slipped into it. Could she really go to work this way? Looking up at his hot expression, she knew he'd insist on it. She pulled on the skirt, black and tailored. It enhanced her figure, she thought, cupping her bottom before flaring out. He'd even brought her shoes, she saw. Black pumps. She slipped her feet into them, feeling her breasts thrust out, her bottom sway. She was used to wearing flats.

"Sit," he ordered, pointing toward the bar.

He came up behind her, brushing her hair, pulling it back, fastening it with a new black clip. Then, he put pink quartz earrings in her pierced ears. She sat there trembling as he dressed her, turning her into his own private doll to dress, fuck, and punish.

She was thinking about saying goodbye. He hadn't said anything, and she didn't know quite how to bring it up. Would he even miss her?

"Come." He helped her off the stool. "Time for you to go. Your car is gassed up and ready. The valet has it waiting for you downstairs. It's been fun, naughty Penelope."

He didn't even kiss her goodbye.

She blinked back tears, walking away. He hadn't asked her to stay or said anything about seeing each other again.

Maybe it was for the best.

Chapter 3

Penny felt like a changed woman when she walked into the library. Was she a slut, a wanton woman, to have enjoyed most of it? She'd had Vlad every way. Well, not every way. He hadn't fucked her ass—only opened it. But still, she'd been very naughty.

Deciding to put her troubled thoughts on the back burner, she walked up to the time clock. Joan was standing there, waiting to punch in.

"Hey, girl." Joan did a double-take. "Well, look at you, pretty lady. Wow, I like the new outfit."

"Thanks." Penny blushed, pleased and embarrassed. Did she really look that different? She hadn't had time to look in the mirror after Vlad had dressed her. Her cheeks flamed redder at the thought.

They both punched in and went to put their bags in their desks. Penny could feel Joan watching her, studying her. Did her debauchery show?

"You met him," Joan said with a knowing smile.

"Um." Penny flashed a stricken look at her friend. "I don't want to talk about it, Joan. I can't."

"That means it was something special. You, girlfriend, have the look of a woman who's been done good and hard by her man."

Penny looked away. "Hard, anyway." She wasn't so sure about good. Did she even want to be a sub? It had all happened so fast. Too fast.

"I heard that," Joan said with a giggle.

Penny ignored her, putting her purse in her desk drawer.

Her gaze caught on the naughty drawer. She unlocked it and slid it open. Her erotic gifts were still there. She sucked in a breath, feeling her nipples rub against the satin bra. He had more than one set. Did he have one in the office he used here? She shivered, her panties getting damp.

She was filling shelves two hours later when Vlad walked by.

Formal as ever, he said, "Miss Harris, I need to speak to you. In my office, five minutes."

She dropped the book she was holding. She wasn't sure that she wanted to see him. He was taking her submission for fact.

When he walked away, Joan rushed up her. "Penny, what did you do?"

"Do?" She blinked at Joan's concerned face.

"Yeah, *do*! When Vlad the Vampire calls you on the carpet, he means business."

Penny shivered at the words. She knew that very well. She'd learned it with the paddle and his relentless cock.

"Would you help me out here, Joan? And watch the checkout desk too, please?"

She walked toward his office. Maybe she shouldn't have started up with him. Business and sex didn't mix. She'd heard that said a hundred times. Still, she couldn't help trembling as she neared his closed door. His office was far in the back of the building. No one would hear her beg for it.

She shivered and tapped on the door.

"Come," he called from inside.

She opened the door and entered.

"Close it," he ordered.

She did.

"Lock it and come here, Penelope."

His rough tone made her shiver. She locked it and took a few steps his way. Did she want to submit? It was too hard. She should just call a halt to the whole thing before he broke her heart.

She stopped in front of his desk, nervous, as his hot gaze ran over her.

"Around the desk," he said, adding, "now."

Her nipples peeked. "Um. Vlad...it might be better if we didn't get involved. Office sex and all."

"Are you saying you don't want me?" he asked softly.

"No." She felt her nipples bead, watched him focus on them. "It's just that—"

"Come."

She walked around the desk.

He swiveled his chair to face her, then stood. "Bend over my desk, naughty one."

With a sigh, she did as commanded, powerless to resist him and her secret desires.

Shuddering, she felt him pull her skirt up. His hand ran over her bared bottom in the thong panties.

"Very sexy," he grumbled.

Her pussy got wet. His stroking hand was the touch she'd come to crave.

"We need some rules," he said, patting her bare bottom. "At the library, you will call me Mr. Deveroux, not Master, or

Vlad. I will call you Penny. We will continue your submission lessons here, at my hotel, and finally, at Missy's B&D when you progress. Do you agree?"

She whimpered, excited, when he reached down to touch her damp mound. Pressing against his firm hand, she gasped. "Yes, Mr. Deveroux."

"Good. Now I'm going to punish you. No noise," he added gruffly.

Trembling, she waited.

Spank!

His hand smacked her ass. She screeched into her palm.

"Quiet," he snapped.

Spank!

She muffled her cry, her ass stinging as his hand slapped it.

"Better," he praised. "Now, two more."

She sobbed, her butt was already on fire.

Spank!

She groaned, his hand slapping her bottom.

Spank!

"Oh," she gasped as he caught her on the mound. Lying across his desk, she cried silently, her ass burning, her pussy wet.

Then, out of the corner of her eye, she saw him open a desk drawer and pick up a condom. His zipper opened, the foil packet tore. In a second, he was pulling her thong aside, slipping his cock into her pussy. She pushed back with a needy sigh, taking him in. This was what she craved. Her breasts flattened on his mahogany desk as he pumped into her. She cried out, his cock thrusting harder, deeper.

"Quiet," he snapped. Grabbing her hips, he rammed into her.

Penny silenced her pleasured moans, muffling them in her hand, as he fucked her harder. It was so naughty, so forbidden, doing it here.

Her pussy milked him as he slammed into her. He was reaching down, pressing her clit while his other hand covered her mouth. She came, screaming into his palm. He jerked hard into her, coming.

They were both breathing hard. She was trembling as he pressed her flat against the desk. Then, he pulled out.

"Freshen up in my bathroom, Penny."

Pussy still rippling with after spasms, she stood and walked into his private bathroom, shutting the door behind her. She needed a moment to compose herself. Glancing at her image in the mirror, she saw that she was glowing, her face flushed, her nipples still semi-hard. Even her mouth looked too full.

Fucked good and hard indeed. No wonder Joan had guessed what she was up to.

Splashing cool water on her face and running it over the racing pulse in her wrists, she tried to slow down, look un-fucked.

When she left the bathroom, Vlad was zipped up, back at work. He glanced up at her, his gaze warming for a moment.

"I'll talk to you later," he promised.

She scurried from his office and back to work, rushing past Mr. Powel. He made a point of looking at his watch, indicating she was wasting library time.

I was busy fucking my Master, she thought with a secret smile.

Mr. Powel shook his head and walked away.

She tried to avoid Joan's scrutiny the rest of the day, knowing she'd be able to tell.

Vlad avoided her the rest of the day, being curt and stiff, which hurt her feelings. Did he regret their time together? It wounded her pride.

She punched out, said goodbye to Joan, but lingered, hoping to see him. When he didn't appear, she sighed and walked to the parking lot.

Vlad was standing by her car. He frowned when he saw her. "What took you so long, Penny?"

"Um. I was…"

He opened her car door for her. "Follow me to the hotel. It's time to begin phase two of your obedience training."

"Yes, Mr. Deveroux." She slipped into the car, her bottom tingling.

Chapter 4

Penelope went up to the suite with Vlad, blushing at any glance turned their way. She was acting far too guilty, she knew, but still, she couldn't stop herself from feeling like a naughty girl.

What would he do to her, she wondered with a shiver as he opened the door to his suite. What did phase two mean? It would probably be harder. Her bottom tensed at the thought. But, when he held open the door for her, she entered, giving him a shaky smile. He shut and locked the door behind her, but she couldn't work up the courage to face him. She'd tacitly agreed to her training by following him here. Now she really was in his clutches, at his mercy.

His hands were on her back, softly skimming down her arms. Making her shiver with delight, he nuzzled her neck, kissing it. It was making her hotter, making her forget her fear, until she was sagging against him.

"Don't worry, Penelope," he husked. "I'm a good master. I'll train you well. I'll give you all the pleasure and discipline you need."

She trembled at his words, her nipples hardening.

He reached around her, unbuttoning her blouse, tugging it off of her. Next, he unzipped her skirt, letting it fall.

She stood still, embarrassed and turned on.

"Stay," he ordered, backing away.

From the corner of her eye, she watched him strip, gulping when she saw his hunky body. Goodness, he was a walking advertisement for hot, steamy sex, although he probably wouldn't thank her for saying it. She decided to keep that little tidbit to herself. It was a good thing slaves weren't supposed to speak unless spoken to.

Walking boldly in front of her, he sat on the bed and leaned against the headboard. She could see that his cock was growing. He was already semi-aroused, ready for her. Still, he didn't call for her. Lowering her gaze, she stood there nervous, not knowing what to do with her hands. She settled for putting them behind her back, feeling incredibly wanton standing there in her brand new panties. They were sexy, blatantly sexy. She could feel his hot gaze on her, but didn't dare glance up.

Why didn't he reach out, grab her, toss her on the bed and ravish her? She licked her dry lips. It would have been so much easier on her pride. Instead, she knew he watched her, could feel his hot gaze roaming over her.

"Look up, Penelope," he commanded.

Slowly, reluctantly raising her head, she could feel her cheeks flame as she gazed at a spot above his head. Knowing she had no choice, she slowly lowered her gaze to lock onto his deep blue eyes. She knew he noticed her embarrassment. He noticed everything.

"Turn around in a circle for me, Penelope. Slowly," he ordered, adding in an intimate rumble, "show me your beautiful body."

She turned, acutely aware that she was on display—blatantly sexual in her scanty panties and bra. Her panties got damp as her excitement peaked. She spun, doing a slow catwalk turn, hardly believing herself capable of such behavior. Turning back to face him, she found a fevered look in his eye and shivered deliciously.

"Take your bra off," he ordered.

Blushing, she reached back to undo the hook and slowly let the sexy garment slide down her arms. Emboldened, she teased him, seeing him take a deep breath, his nostrils flaring. Finally, she let the bra drop from her fingers to the floor.

"Play with your tits," he ordered thickly.

Shocked, she blinked at him for a second, then slowly obeyed. Cupping her breasts in her hands, hiding them, she softly ran her fingers over the swells. She'd never touched herself like this before. Was she turning him on? His intense gaze said yes. Fanning her fingers over her nipples, she felt them stiffen, jut out, and sighed at the sweet sensation.

"Good," he said with a low grumble. "Now, slip off your panties. Slowly."

Biting her lip, she hooked her fingers into the waistband, pulling them down. Instinct made her turn to the side so he could see her bare bottom. His quick intake of breath told her he liked what he saw. Encouraged, she let the panties drop to the floor and stepped out of them, turning to face him.

"Play with your pussy," he demanded. "Get it wet for me, Penelope."

Shy, hardly believing she was obeying, her index finger went to her strawberry-blonde curls. She'd done this before, but never with an audience. Her fingers parted her labia, and touched her clit. It was already stiff, sensitive, but it got stiffer when she rubbed it. It was so naughty what she was doing, so wicked. Her breath came in little pants, her legs trembling as she pleasured herself. Her pussy started to spasm.

Almost there...

"Stop," he snapped.

Groaning, she tore her hand from her throbbing pussy, and opened her eyes. Shaking as she gazed at him, her pussy ripples subsided. Why was he teasing her this way? It wasn't fair.

"Climb up from the foot of the bed," he ordered her in a firm tone.

Oh no, he was going to make her come and get it, not just give it to her. Shuddering with unfulfilled need, she climbed on the foot of the bed.

"Come," he commanded, never taking his gaze from her.

She crawled toward him, feeling his intensity. He was in a strange mood tonight, ever since she'd tried to deny him at the library. Would he satisfy her need now? Or, would he tease her some more, taking her to the brink, but not letting her fall over? Tears of frustration stung her eyes at the thought. She'd been so close, teasingly close to coming. Creeping closer, she saw that he was fully aroused, his hard cock sticking up, and she shivered in anticipation.

When she got to him, he pulled her down on top of him, kissing her deeply, pinching her nipple. His hand unerringly found her clit, rubbing it rougher and harder than she had.

Breaking the kiss, he demanded, "Come, now."

She exploded, coming on command. She pressed against him with a pleasured cry. He flipped her onto her back, making her reel at the urgency. He settled between her legs, ramming his cock into her, fucking her hard. She whimpered with pleasure, her hips snapping up to meet his thrusts. His hands reached down to cup her ass, pulling her higher, thrusting deeper.

"Now," he shouted, pounding into her.

With a cry, she came again, her pussy clamping hard on his cock as he shuddered and ground into her.

She lay under him, gasping, his weight pushing her into the mattress.

Then, their breathing slowing, he rolled off her, tucking her to his side, and she fell asleep.

When she woke, she was on her stomach, and her hands were above her head. She tried to pull them down, but couldn't.

Wriggling, she realized that her wrists were manacled to the headboard. Her legs were tied, too. Why had he restrained her facing down? Anal sex, or a whipping, she decided with a whimper. Both prospects frightened her.

She saw him coming closer, carrying something. It wasn't big enough to be a paddle, and she heaved a sigh of relief. It was shaped like a small penis. A vibrator.

Oh no, how humiliating. She couldn't have a man do that to her.

"Good, you're awake."

"And tied up," she grumbled, glaring at his handsome face. "It's not fair to do this."

"Who's your master?" he asked sharply.

Seeing the flash of annoyance in his eyes, she blinked back tears, saying grudgingly, "You."

He smiled, patting her bottom. "Excellent, Penelope. Therefore, everything I do to you is fair."

She shuddered, her objections subsiding as he slipped a pillow under her belly, raising her bottom higher. He kissed her shoulder, and she felt him part the globes of her ass. She whimpered, trying to clench them against his motions. She'd assumed he was going to use the vibrator on her pussy, not her bottom.

"Please," she cried, as he applied cool lube to her anus. She inhaled hard when he wiggled the tip of his finger inside. "It's not right, not proper," she protested as he pressed something against her pucker. It was bigger than the butt plug, but not as big as his cock. She thanked her lucky stars for that, but she tightened, anyway.

"No. Loosen up," he said in a strict tone, giving her a hard spank on her ass.

"Ouch." She whimpered, trembling, struggling a bit to no avail. She couldn't get away.

"It's time to open your bottom again, naughty Penelope. I'm going to use your small vibrator. Be good so I don't have to spank you."

Shivering at the grumbled warning, she tried to mind him as he pushed the head of the vibrator into her. An invasion. Sobbing, she felt him slowly slide it deeper than the butt plug had gone. She was stretched, burning. She whimpered, but didn't pull away as he pushed it the rest of the way in.

"Very good," he praised. "You took it all up your bottom." He sat beside her and started to move the vibrator in and out slowly, without turning it on.

She stifled a groan. It felt dirty, too tight, but it made her pussy ripple again. She was getting wetter as her arousal revived. She gasped when he moved it faster.

He chuckled. "You're learning. Who's opening your saucy bottom, Penelope? Speak."

His delighted laugh poured over her like warm honey. "Master," she said, panting when he switched on the vibrator. Her ass and pussy twitched, clutching at the vibrator.

"Excellent, now don't come until the seventh stroke," he insisted.

One, her bottom clutched.

Two, her pussy rippled.

Three, four, five—he jerked the vibrator in and out rapidly and harder, making her whimper with discomfort, driving back her orgasm.

Six, he did slowly, her excitement reviving.

Seven, he thrust it into her, and she came, shuddering.

Chapter 5

A week later, Penelope walked behind the library counter, doing her stint as checkout person. She was wearing another one of her stylish and revealing outfits chosen by Vlad. This one was a rayon aqua dress with a sweetheart neckline that she was amazed to find did good things for her eyes and complexion. She'd always stuck to neutrals or black, but he was adding color to her life, in more ways than one. Her bottom was red half the time from his spankings.

She bent to add a book to a bin and looked up. Several men suddenly switched from Mr. Powel's line to hers. The first guy in line was tall and burly, wearing workman's clothes. The one behind him, thin and pale with a prominent nose. They were both staring at her. She felt them ogling her and blushed, wondering why.

Looking down, she saw swell of her breasts as she bent over, her cleavage showing. Oops. She wasn't used to this much male attention. It'd been happening all week, to her discomfiture.

Joan had noticed, joking that she was library bait, an excuse for the local guys to read.

Penny was embarrassed, but she was starting to feel her feminine power. With a smile, she checked out their books—a how-to for the burly guy, mystery for the thin man. After that, she went on break.

Sitting at the table where Joan was sipping her cola, she said, "I thought I'd never get away."

"Library bait," Joan said, with a sly smile.

Penny shook her head, refraining from comment.

"So, tell me about Mr. X, girlfriend," Joan said with a sly smile. "I assume he's the one who's got you dressing better at last."

She wasn't sure how Vlad would feel about her revealing his name. He hadn't forbidden it, but still, she held back, embarrassed to talk about him.

She frowned at Joan, trying to change the subject. "Dressing better, huh? Does that mean you think I dressed poorly before?"

"You said it, not me." Joan offered an apologetic smile. "Stop changing the subject and spill it, Penny."

She looked around to make sure they weren't overheard. The break room was clear.

She turned back to Joan, admitting softly, "All I can say is that it hasn't been easy. He's lived up to all his promises, and then some."

Joan winced. "Your bottom must be red then."

"Sometimes," she said, standing up and turning away to hide her embarrassment. "I think it's time to go back to work."

"So, how is he?" Joan stood to follow her out of the room.

"Magnificent," she admitted, with a soft sigh.

Entering the hotel suite after work, her words came back to her. He was magnificent, but also hard and demanding.

He seemed cross tonight. She'd noticed it on their silent ride in the elevator. And at the library, she'd seen him frowning at her once or twice today. What had she done to displease him so?

"Strip," he ordered in a clipped tone of voice.

She shuddered. There would be no tender strip tease today. No playing with herself.

Obediently, she stripped off her dress and undies. Standing there naked, she shivered. How had she angered him, she wondered, feeling his critical gaze on her.

"Kick off your shoes and come here."

She stepped out of her high heels and padded over to him, acutely aware of her vulnerability. She was naked before him, again.

"Position one, slave," he snapped.

She sunk to her knees, blinking back tears. He was coldly furious. What had she done? Why was he so stiff and formal again?

"Tell me, Penelope, have you enjoyed teasing other men this week?" His tone was gruff. "Flirting with the library patrons?"

"Teasing men? Flirting?" she repeated, confused, licking her lips.

"Yes. Teasing men, the library patrons. You're library bait. I heard you and Joan Anders joke."

Her heart skipped a beat. Vlad the spy, he knew all. Was it possible he was jealous? Or did he just not want his slave girl acting up? She had to know.

"Well, Vlad, you're the one that dressed me that way."

His eyes narrowed and his mouth tightened, and she wished she could call the defiant words back.

"Take out my cock," he demanded.

She rushed to obey before he had time to change his mind and paddled her bottom instead. Unzipping his pants, she started to reach inside.

"Pull them down," he ordered.

This was new. He never stripped for oral sex. She tugged his pants down to reveal his black briefs, his growing cock stirring beneath them.

"Take my shorts down."

When she reached up, he grimly shook his head. "Use your teeth, bad slave."

Stung by his anger, she blinked back tears and caught the edge of his briefs in her teeth, her nose brushing his groin. He was furious. She shouldn't have teased him. She tugged his briefs down with some effort, and waited, breathing fast.

"Suck," he commanded her dryly. "Show me you remember your place."

What was her place in his life? She wondered as she drew his stiff cock into her mouth. Sucking, she bobbed up and down on his engorged cock, taking it deeper into her throat, feeling it twitch in her mouth.

"Good girl," he praised, holding her head steady.

She opened wider, him pumping deeper between her lips. She gagged trying to be good, trying with all her might to please him.

"When I come, swallow it all, or else," he bit out, surging into her mouth.

His balls tightened, twitched. He was coming, spurting into her mouth in salty spurts. She sucked, draining him, feeling a little drip down her chin onto her breast.

When he pulled out, she let out a whimper of despair. She'd be punished for sure.

He pulled up his pants, zipping them. "Come," he ordered, walking toward the bed.

Her wet pussy quivered with anticipation as she stood. The bed not the rack. Maybe she was going to get fucked, after all. How wonderful.

"Climb up on the edge of the bed, naughty librarian."

Feeling his watchful gaze on her every step of the way, she hurried to obey. Why was he standing there, still fully clothed? Wasn't he going to take her?

Biting back a cry of disappointment, she climbed up on the edge of the bed.

"Face and tits down," he ordered, pressing her upper body onto the bed. "Bottom up. Higher in the air, now," he added in a harsher tone.

She arched, her bottom high and out for him. She was suddenly glad her blushing face was hidden by the velvet spread. She shuddered, this was a spanking position, and she'd have to hold still for it, without restraints. She didn't know if she could do that.

"You are in your second submissive pose, Penelope." He ran a hand over her butt. "Your head is down respectfully, your bottom is out for your master's correction."

She shivered, waiting for the first spank. Why wasn't he punishing her yet? Was he drawing it out, toying with her? Peeking over her shoulder, she saw him walk to the dresser. When he came back, he was carrying a double-pronged vibrator and her lube.

She wasn't waiting for a smack on the bottom. She was in position for him to insert that device on her bottom.

"Oh no," she gasped as he stopped beside her.

"Oh yes," he insisted.

Her cheeks clenched, but she didn't run away. She couldn't. She needed him, was wild for him.

He bent to drop a kiss on the rounded curve of her buttock.

"What a good girl," he praised.

Shivering, she held still as his praise soothed her fears. She felt him reach under her to tickle her clit. Her pussy fluttered. Oh, what a magic touch he had. She sighed, getting wet, starved for him.

"Such a wet pussy," he teased, inserting the vibrator's big front prong in her pussy.

She gasped, contracting, clamping down on it, as he moved it in and out of her playfully. If only he'd turn it on. She didn't dare ask him to. She didn't want to make him angry again.

He lubed her anus. She tensed, but he distracted her by moving the vibrator faster in her pussy. She let out a pleasured sigh. This was what she needed. The back prong was pressing into her pucker. She forced herself not to tighten and move away, letting him slide it in, parting her, opening her. She whined, totally stretched, burning, both her pussy and ass filled.

Oh my, she couldn't take it. "Too big," she panted.

"Hush," he said, leaving it lie still inside her, buried to the hilt.

Biting back a cry, she slowly made her body relax around the double invasion. Vlad was opening her, and she had little choice but to obey. He started to move the double pronged vibrator in and out, slow at first and then faster. She moaned as pleasure swamped the pain.

"Oh my."

"Hush." He moved it faster and deeper. "I'm going to turn it on in a minute, Penelope, and I want you to control your orgasm. Don't come until I tell you to. Speak."

"Yes, Master." She moaned, her pussy quivering, her ass clamping on the vibrator as he thrust it deep.

"Good," he said, and flicked on the switch.

She cried out, arching her back, letting him press the humming vibrator deeper. Her whole bottom half was rippling.

"I'm going to count to five. Count the strokes. Then, you can come."

She panted, feeling him ratchet it in and out of her. She couldn't wait, but she tried.

"One," she breathed. "Two." She whimpered. She couldn't wait. "Three." Her ripples started. "Four." She all but wailed when he thrust it faster. "Five," she shouted.

She exploded, her pussy and ass, clamping down on the vibrator, tugging it deeper.

Chapter 6

Penny was perched on Vlad's lap in the suite a few days later. She was naked, of course, while he remained dressed in his robe. It was after supper, and they were settling down for the night. She held the book he handed her and turned to chapter three of 'Phoebe the Sex Slave' with a blush. It seemed so bold, reading him erotica. What would the people at the library say if they knew?

Library bait indeed.

She licked her lips, and his hand slid down her back, gentling her frayed nerves.

"*Phoebe knelt waiting for her Master's correction. It'd been three weeks since Phillip had bought her at the slave auction—a lifetime away from her former life. Her boyfriend had stranded her penniless in a foreign land, and she'd been approached by a man who told her about the auction. She could put up with anything for three months, she'd told herself. When the time was* over, she'd walk away with a fat check and fly back to the States in style.

Naked, bent over, bottom up, she tried not to cry as she waited for her whipping. She'd been bad, slapping one of her Master's friends when he touched her breast. Phoebe cried, knowing that it was too late to run. She'd been bought and paid for, and she'd signed a contract. Now that she was a bed slave, she had to get used to it. But it wasn't easy fighting both her Master and her own growing sexual appetite.

Would her submission now please her Master? Or was it too late to get back in his good graces? She knew the other bed slaves laughed at her, calling her an American princess in a mocking tone, pretending to curtsy to her. They thought she was spoiled, and maybe she had been, but being put up on the auction block had soon knocked that out of her. Now she was a bed slave, the lowest of the low in this house of loose women. And she'd been bad.

Hearing his footsteps approach, she shivered. Punishing her excited her Master. She knew that because he usually took her quite forcefully afterward. He was there, admonishing her, correcting her form, widening her stance, having her arch her back so that her bottom stood out. Trembling, she waited for correction.

"You've been a very bad slave," Master Phillip said, harshly.

She shivered. "I'm sorry for being so bad, master."

"Apology accepted," he said, swinging the cat of nine tails.

It stung her bottom, its leather straps spreading across her ass, finding their way between her legs. She yelped with a cry.

"Bad slave," he said, flogging her again.

She whimpered, trying to maintain her form, trembling uncontrollably as he whipped her. Kneeling behind her, he slipped his hard cock into her pussy, driving her hard. She moaned, unable to stop the thrill that surged through her as he fucked her. She started to come, and he pulled out, making her cry out in protest. She sobbed. Why was he withholding it from her?

"Go apologize to my guest, Master Anthony," he ordered.

Whimpering with unfulfilled need, she stood and reached for her gown.

"No. You'll have to earn your clothes back, bad slave."

She shuddered. He wanted her to earn them back by performing sex acts, she knew. Could she do it? Naked, ashamed, she walked out to the solarium where she'd last seen the Master's friend, Anthony.

He was still there, short and burly, with a Roman nose, dark hair and eyes. His eyes flashed angrily when he saw her.

Phoebe hesitated, alarmed. Jodi, a blonde slut of a bed slave came up to him, cooing at him as she caressed his slapped face.

Phoebe bristled seeing them together. She couldn't stand Jodi.

She walked to stand in front of Anthony, chagrined seeing her red handprint on his face. "I'm sorry, sir," she said quietly.

"Are you now, mi amore? We shall see. Come," he said, turning away.

Phoebe followed Anthony and Jodi down the hall to a guest suite. Oh no! She couldn't do it in front of Jodi. But she knew refusal would bring harsh punishment.

She walked into the bedroom, stopping next to Jodi as Anthony shut the door with a click. She couldn't help shivering. Beside her, she thought she heard Jodi sigh with excitement.

Anthony leaned against the door his steamy gaze running over the women. "Kiss," he commanded.

Phoebe couldn't believe her ears. She'd never kissed another woman. Jodi was facing her, leaning in to touch her mouth with soft, gentle lips. She shuddered, shocked that it felt good, and kissed her back, her arousal returning.

"Get her ready for me, Jodi, dear," Anthony said.

Phoebe wondered what that meant until Jodi touched her breast, whisper soft fingertips gently fanning her nipple. Phoebe moaned, she couldn't help being aroused.

Then Jodi's hand was on her pussy, tickling the clit, making Phoebe shiver with excitement. Her pussy started to spasm, and she came.

Coming out of it, she opened her eyes to see Anthony standing before her. His hand on her shoulder, he pushed her down to her knees. She shivered, excited in spite of her fear. He wanted oral sex, she assumed.

She watched Jodi strip his clothes off, silently, like the obedient little slut she was.

Phoebe shivered when she saw his cock. It was thick, purple-headed, with red veins.

"Now, mi amore, you may demonstrate your contrition," he said, cupping Phoebe's naked breasts in his hands, rubbing them, pinching the nipples hard.

Phoebe winced, but didn't pull away.

"Good," he praised. Then, he stepped closer. Sticking his cock between her breasts, he pressed them together to cradle his dick between them.

She gasped, shocked. She hadn't expected this. He was thrusting, squishing her boobs tighter around his hot cock. She was on fire, wanted this hard purple cock inside her, but he wouldn't give it to her. Jodi was dribbling baby oil over her breasts, it trickled down onto his cock, helping him thrust faster.

"Lower your head and stick out your tongue, mi amore."

Phoebe did as he said, embarrassed. Her tongue flicked the head of his cock as he thrust. He was spurting, filling her open mouth with his cum."'

Penny finished the chapter with a blush, and closed the book. Vlad was still toying with her breasts, watching her. She could feel his curious gaze.

"Well?" he asked.

She slipped to her knees, knowing what he wanted.

He stood, stripping off his robe, already hard. When he weighed her breasts in his hands, she shivered, excited. His hard cock was slipping between them. He squished her breasts together, sandwiching himself in the middle of them.

He began thrusting in and out. She was excited, pussy clenching. It was just like the book, except for the whipping, thank goodness. Bending her head, she stuck out her tongue, licking the head of his cock each time he thrust upward.

He shuddered and came, spurting into her mouth.

Chapter 7

Penny watched Vlad's office door two days later. It was slightly ajar, but he didn't look up.

She'd made several trips down the corridor, hoping he'd catch a glimpse of her, call her inside and make love to her. It was lovesick and foolish, she knew, but she was desperate. He'd barely made time for her at work the last several days. Sure, things were hot and sexy at the hotel, but what about here? Was he growing tired of her, or was he just simply taking her devotion for granted?

She didn't like the feeling of being cast off one little bit.

"Excuse me, miss," a male voice rumbled behind her.

She looked up, finding the guy who'd been by to check out how-to books five days in a row. What now? He'd already poured over the whole section.

"Yes, sir, how may I help you?"

"I can think of lots of ways." He winked, accompanied by a macho smile.

Her jaw fell in shock. He wasn't after how-to information.

"Library bait," she said under her breath.

Men were still noticing her, and despite Vlad's grumbles, he was still dressing her sexily. Today, she was wearing a white *crepe de chine* blouse and a tailored gray linen skirt with cute black heels.

Embarrassed, she wasn't sure how to respond. Darting a glance at Vlad's office, she saw he was watching her with a pensive frown on his handsome face.

Bold, not believing she was doing it, she turned back to the reader. "Really? Maybe you'd better tell me about them." She could hardly believe she was flirting. Was she even doing it right? Apparently, she was because the guy flushed a brick red while pinning her with a leering look.

"Anytime, sugar. What time do you get off? How about we meet at Red's?"

She flushed when he suggested a rendezvous at a nearby bar. It'd gone too far. Stupid as it may be, she was loyal to Vlad. "Well...um...I'm busy. Maybe some other time."

She watched the guy walk away smiling.

"Penny," Vlad called out, clearly.

She looked toward his office door. Of course, he had heard. And now he was angry. He was probably going to punish her good.

She scuttled toward his office, glad they were out of earshot of the rest of the staff. She didn't want them to hear what might occur. She walked into his office and shut the door behind her.

"Yes, Mr. Deveroux?"

"Come here, now," he bit out.

Blanching, she walked forward. From his tone, she knew she was in for it. Her bottom twitched as she anticipated a spanking. But she didn't deserve it, she thought defiantly, glaring at him.

His eyes narrowed and his sensual mouth tightened.

She sighed, giving in to his silent demand, even though he'd never made any kind of commitment to her, never even called her his girlfriend. Walking around his desk, she stopped before him. Gone was his playful mood of a few days ago. She looked into his troubled eyes.

He stood. "Over the desk, immediately."

She bent over, tearing up. Why was she obeying?

Because she was crazy about him, she realized, shaken. He'd come to mean much more than hot, kinky sex. His touch was like a drug she needed.

He lifted up her skirt and bared her bottom, covered in peach lace thong panties.

She sniffled into her hand, trying not to cry.

Swat!

She yelped as his palm landed without preliminaries. He was furious, she realized. Spank after burning spank rained down on her bare bottom. She sobbed, muffling her cries, trying to hold still for it and failing.

He jerked her thong out of the way. Thank goodness, this was what she needed, to be fucked. To be...loved. But instead, he lubed her anus.

Oh, no. She wasn't ready for that, was she? Something touched her pucker, but it wasn't his cock. She felt her bottom being parted as a butt plug pushed inside, and she groaned. Undeterred, he pushed the plug all the way in and slipped her thong back in place.

"Stand," he said, adding angrily, "and turn toward me."

She stood, whimpering, feeling her ass burn as the plug shifted inside her. Stretching her, it was so naughty. She turned toward him, keeping her gaze lowered, trying to be good. His hands were on her blouse, quickly opening the pearl buttons. She shivered, realizing there was no playfulness in his touch. It was ruthlessly efficient. He pulled her blouse wide open, baring her breasts in the peach lace bra. Then he tugged down the bra cups, fingering her nipples. She moaned as he rubbed them, getting hot despite his anger. Her nipples jutted out for him. She winced when cold metal clamped onto her right nipple.

Not her nipple chain.

She opened her eyes to realize it was different. A single clip, silver, with an engraved floral design on it. Shivering, she watched him pick up a matching clip. She stood still for him while he fastened it to her left nipple. Then, he put thick pads into the bra cups and slipped them into place. He buttoned her blouse all the way up.

She looked down. The pads hid the fact that her nipples were clamped, but she could feel it down to her toes. He couldn't mean to leave her this way, could he? It wasn't decent. It simply wasn't right. This was the library, for goodness sake. A glance at his determined expression told her that was exactly what he meant to do.

"Back to work," he said in a stern tone. "If you're good, I'll remove your bad slave toys when we get back to the hotel."

He did mean it. But could she do it? Could she go around for an hour until punch-out time like nothing was happening to her body?

Yes, if he demanded it, she'd try to comply.

Biting back a whimper, she walked out of the office, acutely aware of the butt plug riding inside her anus, the clips pinching her tender nipples. They ached, she ached. Oh, why hadn't he fucked her? It would have made this punishment easier to take.

She walked back to her cart to finish restocking the shelves. Mr. Powel made a point of looking at his watch, and she scowled at him, until he scurried away.

Damn it all, she was plugged here, wasting time was the least of her worries. What would Vlad do to her back at the hotel? She shivered, half afraid, half turned on. As usual, since she'd called him Master, her libido was raging out of control. Her pussy was wet, her ass clamping around the plug, and her nipples ached for him to take the clamps off and end this sensual torture.

Flinching, she bent down to put the last book on a low shelf, feeling the butt plug rub inside, her ass twitching on it. She glanced at the clock. Break time, thank goodness. A cool drink might help quench the fire that raged within her. Or, at least, take her mind off it.

She got a cola out of the machine and joined Joan at their table. As usual, Joan got there first.

"Hey, girlfriend."

"Hi." Penny let out a little gasp when she tried to sit. She realized with a stifled groan that it wasn't going to be easy. Her whole ass was pulsing, clamping around the plug as she perched gingerly on the chair.

"What's the matter?" Joan asked, looking her over with a frown.

Penny realized she undoubtedly looked a sight. Her face was flushed, she knew, and there was, no doubt, a turned-on gleam in her eye. On top of that, she was perched very lightly on the chair. "Um...nothing. Don't ask, okay?" She looked away, knowing Joan could read the signals.

"The way you're sitting reminds me of my birthday paddling. Oh, my gracious. Penny's just had a spanking!"

She blinked at her. Did it show that much?

But she had worse things to deal with, like the plug stretching her ass and the clamps pinching her poor nips. She resisted the urge to rub them.

Joan's eyes widened. "I'm right. I can tell by your guilty expression. Oh God, it's Vlad, isn't it? Vlad is X."

She just sat there and blushed, unwilling to confirm or deny it.

Joan grinned. "Wow. He's so hot, girlfriend. But I always thought the man had ice water coursing through his veins."

"He does not." She'd leapt to his defense, and then bit her lip at Joan's knowing chuckle. Damn, she'd walked right into that one.

Joan fanned her face, murmuring, "You and Vlad, who would have thought it? Be still my racing heart."

Penny knew just how she felt. She couldn't quite believe it herself. She was having a full-out, raging, kinky affair with Vlad the Vampire.

Riding to the hotel an hour later in Vlad's passenger seat wasn't easy. Her butt plug was still in place. Her anus quivered around it whenever she moved, and her nipple clips were driving her crazy. To add insult to injury, he had insisted she leave her car in the library parking lot and come with him. He didn't trust her not to remove the clips, she surmised. Her pride hurt. Still, she knew better than to push her luck by arguing the point. Anyway, that cat was already out of the bag as far as Joan was concerned. She'd figured out their affair, but Penny knew she'd keep mum, and was grateful for her tact. She still wasn't sure how to broach the subject with Vlad and tell him Joan was aware of their secret.

"Stay put," he said, putting the car into park. He waved the valet away from Penny's door.

She was stricken by his clipped tone. Why was he making her wait? Was he planning on dumping her? She couldn't take it if he did. In fact, she'd fight him on that.

He got out and walked around to her door, opening it. He reached in to help her out and immediately clamped a hand on her upper arm, not hurting, but not letting her go.

She shivered, realizing he was still upset. But at least he wasn't breaking up with her. She brightened a little at that thought.

She let him steer her through the lobby and into the elevator, keeping quiet. She didn't know what to say, anyhow. How did one tell a man, *I'm crazy for you, please spank me?*

The elevator opened, and suddenly, he was towing her toward their room. She hurried to keep up with his faster pace, and waited, breathing hard, for him to open the door. He did it one handed, never letting her go. She wasn't sure whether to be comforted or scared, and settled for a little of both.

She let him march her into the room. After kicking the door shut and locking it, he marched her to the rack, shivering.

She shuddered, *not that.* She needed to be touched and reassured. Instead, she was to be punished more. But, when he let go of her arm and stepped in front of her to briskly undress her, she didn't object.

Off went her skirt and blouse. Then he unhooked her bra, pulling it and the pads away. Her nipples instantly throbbed, and she whimpered.

But he didn't touch them, soothe them. Instead, he jerked down her panties. She stepped out of them, shivering, and knew better than to object when he cuffed her wrists high above her head. She stood, stretched tight, as he fastened her ankles to the side posts so that her legs were spread. She trembled, whimpering, her ass rippling on the butt plug as it shifted.

His hand smacked her bottom, making the plug jerk inside her, and she cried out. He stepped beside her, his hand covering her mouth as he rained hard spanks on her ass.

She sobbed against his open palm, her ass on fire.

Suddenly, he was untying her, marching her into the bedroom. Pushing her onto the bed, he rammed his cock into her starved, wet pussy. She was stretched too tight, her butt still plugged.

Aroused, she matched his thrusts. When he reached down to take the clamps off her nipples in mid-thrust, she gasped.

They throbbed.

They ached.

They stung.

He pinched her nipples, rolling them in his fingers while he fucked her hard. Making her even hotter, making her squirm as he ratcheted in and out of her.

She came, a shower of stars seeming to go off inside her.

Later, much later, he took out her butt plug.

Chapter 8

A week later, Penny was doing her stint at the check-out desk, and she was lonely. Vlad had been gone for five days. He'd been out of town on business for a week, or so he'd said. She couldn't help worrying that he was spending time with another woman, another sex slave. It was petty of her, but she couldn't help it. The feeling of abandonment was so strong.

She checked out another patron's books, ignoring his roving eye. She was wearing another one of the outfits Vlad had bought her—a cream silk twin set with a low scooped neck and a fitted chocolate brown skirt. The matching cream high heels and the red satin bra and panties underneath made her feel sexy, but for whom?

She turned to drop a book into the bin.

"Hey there, sweetheart, you must be new here."

She groaned at Paul's voice behind her. The thirty-second man, Joan had dubbed him when she'd told her co-worker about their terrible previous date. Oh nuts, why hadn't she known the copier repairman would be here today? She'd have managed to be elsewhere.

Joan grinned at her from the backroom. Darn her little matchmaking heart. Had she called him because Penny was moping around with Vlad gone?

She scowled at Joan, who looked unperturbed, and turned to face Paul. "Hello, Paul," she said as flatly as she could. What had she ever seen in him? He was nice looking enough, she mused, if one went for boyish blond surfer types.

She didn't anymore.

His eyes widened. "Penny?"

"Yes." She enjoyed his discomfiture just a bit more than she probably should. Let him see her in a different light. He'd had the nerve to call her the 'ice queen,' even though he didn't have the drive or the equipment to thaw her out.

His gaze roamed over her approvingly, his jaw dropping a bit. Good.

"You look so different," he murmured.

"Do I?" She turned her back on him. "You know where the copiers are. I'll let you get on with your work." She didn't look back, didn't give a rip what he thought or did.

She pushed the cart out to the Fiction section and started putting back the returns.

Joan walked up to her. "Well, what about it, girl? You feel better after seeing TS, don'cha? I figured it might be a boost for the old ego. It's better than you dragging your depressed butt around here."

"TS?" Penny asked, confused.

Joan grinned. "Sure, you know, thirty-second man."

Penny nodded, getting it. So, that's why Joan had set up this meet, to give Penny an ego boost. "Thanks for trying, but I'm not interested in TM."

"That's TS, and I didn't think you were, but I bet it made you feel better for him to realize what he missed out on. I can see that fire in your eyes again."

Her friend had a valid point. "Yeah, you're probably right. It did make me feel good to not give him the time of day now. Paul practically had his tongue hanging out. It was too funny after the way he treated me last month."

"So?" Joan asked.

Penny frowned at her. What more was there to say? "What?"

"He wants to take you out for coffee after work." Joan said with a wicked smile.

Startled, she wrinkled her nose at the thought of dating the dud again. "And how do you know all this?" she asked, suspecting more matchmaking.

Joan shrugged. "He asked me to ask you."

"What, are we back in junior high?" Penny rolled her eyes. "He's a grown man. Can't the guy look for his own dates?"

"He as much as said you're out of his league now." Joan giggled. "You intimidate him. But he said he has a problem, and he really needs to talk to you about it." At Penny's frown, Joan backed up a pace. "Hey, don't blame the messenger. I'm just relaying it."

"So, do you buy his hard luck story?"

"No," Joan said with a shrug. "But then, he's not trying to sell it to me. I'm a happily married woman. Who knows, maybe surfer boy is in deep trouble and you're his only hope? Can you turn that down? Besides, you got nothing better to do with X out of town. How many days has it been now?"

"Five," Penny admitted, feeling dismal.

Maybe helping TS would make her feel better. Having him look at her like she was eye candy wouldn't hurt her pride, either.

Penny blanched when Paul slid into the booth beside her instead of the empty one on the opposite side. The fact they were in a bar instead of a coffee shop should have been her first clue that it wouldn't go well, and the coffee he ordered turned out to be Irish, laced with lots of booze. She could almost hear the wheels turning in his mind as he leaned closer.

She poked him in the chest. "Get over on the other side, and stop crowding me," she demanded.

"But I don't want people to overhear what I've got to say." He slid away from her a few inches. "Is this better?"

"A little." She arched a brow.

She had a strong suspicion he was up to no good, but she decided to hear him out to satisfy her curiosity. What could be so private that he didn't want to be overheard? Oh crud, he wasn't going to tell her about his sexual problems, was he? She wrinkled her nose, looking at him as he took a big swig of his Irish coffee, then coughed. Boy, he was downing the booze fast. It must be bad.

He put down his mug and turned to look at her. "You're so pretty now, Pen. Sexy, even."

Had she been ugly before?

Her eyes narrowed. He wasn't here to talk about his personal problems. He was here to put a move on her. There was no way she'd even consider dating him again, and she hated the way he always called her "Pen," like a frickin' office supply.

"My name is Penelope, and I'm not interested in whether you think I'm pretty or not."

"Now, Pen, don't get mad." He reached out to touch her shoulder. "We were good together once. We could be again."

She shrugged away from his hand, frowning when he fingered her silky sweater. "I'm not interested, Paul. Do I make myself clear?"

"Aw, come on," he said with a slur. "Don't tell me you're still the Ice Queen. Not dressed in this tight sweater."

His hand was back, this time brushing her breast.

Furious, she leaned in closer. "Paul, next time you manage to get it up, I want you to do something for me."

He gave her a leer. "And what's that, Pen?"

"Go fuck yourself." Raising her hand, she whacked him in the balls.

Smiling, she watched him fall over with a groan. He tumbled out of the booth and onto the floor.

His hand curled into a fist as he glared at her. "You bitch," he bellowed. "You really are the Ice Queen. I'm gonna kill you for that."

She glared down at him, ready for the fight.

All around her, the bar patrons murmured, but she ignored the buzz, concentrating on the man she'd just felled. If he tried anything else, she'd kick his butt.

Just then, a man's foot came down on Paul's fist, pinning it to the floor.

Shivering, she recognized that wing tip shoe. Vlad! But how? He was supposed to be gone for two more days.

She looked up.

Grim anger glared back at her. Furious, actually.

Paul yelled, "Get off my hand, you asshole."

Vlad pressed harder with his foot, making Paul yelp. "Apologize to the lady," he demanded.

"Sorry," Paul said with a whimper of pain.

Vlad took his foot off Paul's hand, and held out his hand to Penny. "Come, Penelope."

She slipped out of the booth, taking his hand. Her racing pulse kicked up a notch. Vlad had saved her. Her hero! Not that she couldn't handle a worm like Paul, but she appreciated the gallant gesture.

Walking out of the bar, she cut a sidelong glance his way, noting Vlad's rigid expression. Did he think she was deliberately cheating on him?

"I wasn't—"

"Not another word," he commanded.

Falling silent, she waited for him to open her car door and slipped inside. Was he simply angry? Jealous? Hurt? Had he missed her?

He slid behind the wheel and started the car, driving toward the hotel. When he didn't turn on the radio, she reached for it. A stern scowl from him made her drop her hand.

She fidgeted, wringing her fingers in her lap, nervous. They'd been apart for five days and nights—a long time. And to top it off, he'd caught her with another man. That couldn't be good. He wasn't letting her explain, either.

"Be still," he snapped.

Tears stinging her eyes, she obeyed. Had she just ruined everything, pushing Vlad too far by going out with Paul? Why had she listened to Joan? She'd met with Paul partly because she was curious about what he wanted, and partly because she was lonely and bored without Vlad. Now, she had to pay the price. She hoped it wasn't at the expense of their relationship, but she knew if they continued their affair, there'd undoubtedly be lots more infractions. She had to push the boundaries, it was her nature. It was up to him to make the next move.

Once at the hotel, she kept silent, following him up to the suite.

He opened the door to his suite, turned, and scooped her up in his arms.

She let out a squeak, startled. What was he going to do?

His mouth was on hers, his tongue thrusting into her open mouth, and she stopped worrying. She kissed him back as he carried her into the room, and he kicked the door shut.

Then, they were moving again. She didn't even open her eyes, trusting him completely. Feeling the velvet strength of his strong body, tasting the coffee he must have drunk, she trembled in his arms.

He laid her on the bed, her skirt riding up. He tore her panties off while continuing the torrid kiss. She was burning, sucking on his tongue, while she heard him unzip his pants. He surged into her, filling her. Her hips snapped up to meet his thrust. He grasped her ass in a tight grip, lifting her to take more.

Her pussy rippled around his cock, contracting. She came with a shiver as he pounded into her.

He suddenly pulled out.

"Up," he demanded, tugging her to her feet.

She stood, sagging against him, limp for a moment.

He steadied her, setting her back on her heels.

"Take your clothes off, Penelope," he demanded.

At his tight tone, she knew he was far from done with her. Trembling with delight, she took off her twin set and skirt, then peeled off her bra and panties. Naked, she stood there, all but panting for him.

She looked at his cock, still hard. She needed it.

"Position one," he commanded, his voice stern.

She sagged to her knees, tearing up. He was still mad at her.

"Suck," he said.

Sighing, she leaned forward and took him into her mouth. She sucked, bobbing up and down as she took more of him into her mouth.

He grasped her head, steadying her as he thrust. She slackened her jaw as he fucked her mouth, deeper, harder, like he couldn't get enough.

"I'm going to come," he said with a groan. "Don't you dare spill a drop, or I'll paddle your ass."

She shuddered at the blunt warning. He came in salty spurts. She tried not to spill it, but failed when some dribbled down her chin. She'd be punished, she knew.

When he pulled out of her mouth, she blinked up at him, crying a little.

"Tears of sweet submission," he said, lifting a teardrop from her cheek and tasting it.

She waited, kneeling before him, watching a hint of a smile on his face. Was he satisfied? She wasn't. She needed him. Her pussy was wet, aching. But she stayed still, trying to obey him.

"Get up on the edge of the bed, Penelope. Go into position number two."

Rising, she walked toward the bed, her excitement building. Was he going to take her again? Or was he going to punish her?

Trying not to speculate, she got onto the bed and in position, her bottom up. She wasn't restrained, she could say no, get up and run. But she didn't want to. She was his to play with or punish.

He stepped up beside the bed.

Spank!

His open palm hit her butt. She yelped.

Spank!

Spank!

Spank!

He punished her with rapid-fire smacks.

She sobbed, crying into the velvet spread.

He parted her cheeks, spread lube on her anus, and partly inside with his finger. She shivered, but stayed.

Then, something broad pushed against her pucker. It was too big to be her plug, and it was warm. *His cock.* Could she even take that monster inside her tight passage?

Whimpering, his head pressed inside her ass, her pucker stretching, spreading as he inched inside. It burned. It hurt. But, yet...

"Oh," she gasped.

"Do you know what's pushing into your tight little bottom, naughty librarian?" He groaned.

"Ah." She moaned with mingled pain and pleasure. "Yes. It's your cock, Master," she panted.

"That's right." He hissed, pressing in a little more. "I'm opening you, bad Penelope. This ass is mine. You're all mine, and don't you forget it again." Slowly, he thrust the rest of the way inside her, until he was leaning against her spanked bottom.

"Yes, Master," she said, straining.

His throbbed inside her. Her ass clenched around him, milking it, as she tried to adjust to being wide open. She was shocked by the too-full, dirty, good/bad sensation.

He eased halfway out and rocked back into her. She shuddered, gasping, as her bottom and pussy rippled in tandem. Grasping her hips with his strong hands, he fucked her bottom, slowly at first, then harder, pulling her back to meet his strokes.

She panted, beads of sweat on her brow. Tension built in her belly. Heat radiated.

He reached down to play with her clit, rubbing it, making her moan.

"Come now," he demanded, pinching her clit.

She exploded with a shriek, clamping hard around his cock.

He slipped two fingers into her pussy while pressing her clit, and she came again. Spasmodic, quivering, he drew out her orgasm, taking all she had to give.

He rammed harder into her, coming, spurting deep inside her ass.

She was his—all his.

Chapter 9

Penny sat in Vlad's car, silent and tense, two days later. Her handcuffed wrists rested uneasily in her lap as he drove to Missy's House of Bondage & Discipline for her graduation.

Graduation, did that mean he was almost through with her? She got misty at the thought, but decided to worry about it later. First, she had to get through tonight. She was a naughty slave to be fucked and paddled.

Her bottom twitched at the thought. Her nipples beaded, but she sat still. Her red paddle lay on the seat between them. No doubt, he knew about her previous venture here. Knew she'd seen the other woman cuffed, knew it would get her hot, make her a little scared. Vlad, the spy, knew everything about her. Her favorite foods, books, flowers, and music. How she liked to be caressed, her bottom rubbed after a spanking. How she liked to be softly cuddled, tucked next to him so she could fall asleep.

She knew a lot about him, too. How he sighed when she took him in her mouth. How he snuggled against her, smiling, when she read to him out of their favorite erotic books. How angry he got when she paid too much attention to another man. He was her man, her Master, and she loved him.

He parked and got out, taking the paddle, and walked around the car. Opening her door, he leaned in to unbuckle her seatbelt, and helped her out. "Come, Penelope."

She stood, walked up the steps, his hand on her arm.

He opened the door, and she entered the foyer quietly.

Tears stung her eyes, but she didn't cry. She wanted Vlad, her Master, to be proud of her.

"Hey there, pal," said a male voice.

Penny looked down, trembling, when Samuel stepped out to greet Vlad. How humiliating to be standing here cuffed, submissive.

When Vlad stopped to chat with him, she stood, embarrassed. Clasping her cuffed hands together, she peeked up, looking around, to make sure the lobby and gift shop were empty.

A man was testing riding crops in the gift shop, thwacking them on a leather bolster.

She shuddered, looking down again. Not that. She couldn't take that.

Vlad was moving. He patted her bottom lightly with the paddle, signaling her to walk.

"Head up the stairs, Penelope," he murmured.

She rushed forward, the paddle caressing her bottom. They all knew she was going to get it. She shivered a little in anticipation. Her pussy was already damp, her nipples tingling and her ass hot, expecting a paddling.

"Have fun, naughty Penelope," Samuel called out pleasantly.

Would it be fun or scary? Whatever she encountered, she trusted Vlad to take care of her.

She hurried up the stairs, Vlad right behind her with the paddle. Still, she couldn't help being nervous, even a little frightened.

He'd seemed so tense this week, so easily irritated. How hard would he paddle her? Even worse, was this the end? Graduation, he'd called this. Did that mean he was tired of her? Her eyes misted again at the thought. She wasn't ready to give him up.

He urged her down the hall, swatting her bottom playfully, and she cried, quietly overcome with emotion. She loved him, loved Vlad her Master, even when he spanked her.

He opened the door to their room, and she entered slowly. She was a bit scared about what she might find, but her panties were getting wet with excitement, anyway. She needed his cock, his punishment—craved it.

She glanced around, noting with relief and a bit of a letdown that it looked like a regular hotel room. Then she noticed the rack in a far corner. Next to it was a wide, padded bar with a row of paddles, straps, and even a riding crop.

A spanking bar, she realized. Her bottom heated as she trembled in anticipation.

Vlad shut the door, locking it behind him. She stood in the middle of the room, frozen, eyes down, peeking at him from below her lashes. His firm expression made her tense. Was he angry?

He stepped closer and into her personal space. Inhaling his sandalwood cologne, she relaxed a little. He was her Master. They'd been down this road before. Staying still, she waited for him to tell her what he wanted.

Instead, he reached up, unbuttoning the straps of her yellow sundress. It fell to the floor, baring her breasts. Next, he silently jerked down her panties, moving her to the side to step out of them.

Why wasn't he speaking? Had she angered him again?

"Leave the shoes on," he ordered, his voice clipped. "Go, bend over the spanking bar."

Biting her lip, she complied, recalling Samuel's words. *The rooms are soundproof. No one will hear you beg for it.*

She bent over the padded bar, bottom out, and grabbed for the lower bar.

He walked around to the front, pulling her handcuffs over a hook. She was stretched out, naked for him to paddle. It was shameless, wanton, she knew. Her ass tensed, anticipating her paddling, while her pussy clenched, getting wetter.

Did he even care for her?

"Very good," he murmured, stepping back, and walking toward the rack of spanking implements. "These are your graduation presents, Penelope," he said a bit roughly, pointing to the straps, paddles, and crop. "But, I think, for old time's sake, we'll use big red." He picked up her red paddle.

She whimpered, knowing it would hurt, as he rubbed the red paddle softly across her bottom. She leaned into the caress anyway.

"I'm going to paddle you now, Penelope," he said, his tone softening a little.

His sensual tone relaxed her a little, but still she trembled, tensing, waiting for the first smack.

But instead, Vlad kept rubbing her with the paddle.

"Do you want me to?" he asked in a brisk tone. "Will you allow it?"

She froze, shocked by the question. He'd never asked permission before. How could she say yes? It hurt and made her feel depraved. It was naughty. It would be worse to have to ask for it.

When he kept rubbing, making her squirm, arousal and fear warring within her, she sighed. "Yes, Master."

"Good," he said with a low rumble.

Smack!

She yelped, stung by the paddle.

Smack!

"Ouch." She whimpered, biting her lip.

"Three more," he growled. "Stick your bottom out farther, Penelope."

She arched, sobbing. Her ass was on fire, her pussy clenching.

Smack!

She yelped, the paddle catching the bottom part of her ass near her thighs, making her jump.

Smack!

"Oh." The paddle drove her hard against the bar.

Smack!

"Ouch." She sobbed against the bar.

He dropped the paddle on the floor. Lube was applied to her anus, up and inside.

She shuddered. Would it be the plug, the vibrator, or his cock? Something was touching her anus. It wasn't her plug, it was his cock. She shivered, dreading it, even though it made her horny. She was still slightly tender from two days before.

The broad head of his cock butted against her pucker.

"Do you want me to fuck your ass?" he asked hotly. "Will you allow it, naughty Penelope?"

He was so big, but she was so hungry for his possession. "Yes, Master," she said with a whimper.

His broad head slowly pushed inside, opening her again. She tried to relax, to breathe through the initial discomfort, feeling naughty and stretched to the hilt. Her body was already clenching around him, her pussy spasmodic. And he was only part way in, she whimpered.

"Push back the rest of the way onto my cock, Penelope," he bit out. "Show me you want to be fucked."

How could he ask that of her? It was so shameless, so wicked. But he was her Master, as well as her lover. He could ask anything of her.

She moaned, pushing back, impaling herself, feeling it push deeper inside her tight passage, spreading her as it filled her with its hot length.

"Oh." She gasped. "It's too big." Still, she kept going until he was buried to the hilt, throbbing inside her.

"Excellent," he said in a tight tone.

She shivered. She could tell from his strangled tone how turned on he was. She, however, hovered between pleasure and pain. He was just so dang big, she was aching and throbbing along with him.

He pumped slowly, fucking her ass gently, letting her feel every inch sliding in and out of her ass, and pleasure won out. Her pussy and ass both rippled with pleasured tremors.

"Who's fucking your ass, Penelope?"

"Master," she panted, as he fucked her faster.

"Good." He growled, driving even harder.

She gasped as he thrust. Her ass and pussy spasmed, gripping at his cock.

Reaching down, he rubbed her clit, pinching it, and she came with a scream of pleasure. He stiffened, ramming hard with a groan as he came, his cum spurting deep inside.

She gasped for breath, him still inside her.

He pulled out and zipped his pants.

She couldn't resist peeking over her shoulder at him. He caught her and smiled. Then, he got a damp cloth and cleaned her. She tensed, half expecting to get it again for peeking. Instead, he walked in front of her, undoing her handcuffs.

"Come," he said, grabbing her hand.

She stood, feeling a bit wobbly, and followed him to the bed.

He handed her a gift, done up in silver wrapping paper. Was it another naughty present, she wondered, intrigued. She opened it.

A beautiful silver bracelet was nestled inside on pink tissue paper. She looked up at him.

"It's my slave bracelet, Penelope," Vlad said in a tight tone. "Will you wear it, be my submissive?"

Her heart skipped a beat as all her secret wishes came true. His gruff voice told her he wasn't sure of her answer.

She smiled at him, trying to reassure him. "Oh, yes," she cried, adding softly, "I love you."

He smiled wider at that. "I love you, too, Penelope." He sobered, his smile fading as he added in a clipped tone, "You'd better think about it. I will be your Master, as well as your partner. I will punish you and give you pleasure as I see fit. Once you give your answer, there's no changing your mind."

She smiled. He was worried she didn't want him! She almost laughed, she was so happy, but she restrained herself. It was nice to know she had some power in this relationship, too.

"I'm sure, Master." She lifted the sterling silver bracelet from the box.

He took it from her and slipped it on her wrist. He shut the sturdy clasp with a loud *snap*.

She looked at the beautiful bracelet, warmed beyond belief. It was a symbol of their love.

She belonged to him, forever.

Taste of Honey
Book 2
The
Commander's
Club
JULIE CASTLE

Chapter 1

Courtney Fox stood outside the Commander's Club, her stomach twisting with anxiety. Her pulse raced as she visualized all the kinky things that had to be going on behind this brownstone conglomerate's innocent-looking ivy-covered walls.

She'd have to go along with the program, maybe even submit to a Dom initially in order to find Laura and save her. Yesterday, her summer intern had vanished, leaving behind a cryptic text that she'd get their story. Damn, if only she hadn't let on how obsessed she was about this story, Laura would still be safe, unemployed when the summer can to an end, but safe.

But no, she'd exploded when her editor had handed her baby over to some unsavory freelancer. A sexy biker in black leather who'd dazzled the other reporters.

She sighed, remembering Law's troubled glance as he shut the door in her face. She'd done her homework, researching the Commander's Club through the back channels, gaining access to their website where they put the girls on auction to the highest bidder. The pictures she'd fanned through made her squirm in her seat. Women in various stages of undress, some being caressed, and others were bound and gagged with hot gleams in their eyes. The last one of a spread-eagled vamp, tied to a frame, while a man approached her with a huge dildo. Remembering it now almost made her knees buckle.

Consequently, here she stood, on the club's doorstep, scared and embarrassingly on the edge of arousal. No innocent virgin, she figured she could handle anything they'd throw at her. She was wearing a wire, of sorts, a discrete lapel cam set to record all. In addition, her weapons were secreted in her bag—her real phone, an upgrade from the ones civilians usually carried, and a panic button for her backup.

Uncle Stan, who wrote the financial column for the Banner, wasn't much of a backup, she had to admit, but he was the best she could do in a pinch. She was also packing heat in the form of a taser because guns scared the crap out of her. Clear plastic, they would go through any metal detector. She knew, she'd put them to the test. She was going to rescue Laura the only way she knew how, by infiltrating the Commander's Club as a submissive.

Her clit twanged at the 'S' word. *It won't be like that. They'll assign me to some hulk with bad breath, and I'll hate every minute of it.* She shuddered at the thought, but moved forward, jaywalking to the hoot of taxis. Her pulse raced as she approached the sex club with mingled trepidation and, she was ashamed to say, excitement.

With a mixture of bravado and nervous energy, she strode into the building and made her way toward the sultry looking woman behind the reception desk. The blonde's pert round breasts were clearly outlined by her silky red dress. A little preview of what lurked upstairs, Courtney decided.

She glanced at the smoky bar on her left. A couple danced slow in the corner to some sultry jazz coming from the jukebox, him in a business suit, her in lingerie—a black thong and bra, to be precise. Courtney gulped, shocked, despite the fact that she'd done her homework. The couple was entwined, the man's hands roaming all over his voluptuous partner's body, moving down to cup her ample bottom and squeeze. The woman laughed, and Courtney's face heated.

She trembled and looked away as she imagined some man doing that to her. Her gaze drifted to a group of men sitting at a corner table, smoking cigars and laughing. *God, please don't let them know what I was fantasizing.* Two of them stared back, their intentions clear.

Shit, this was suddenly scary real.

Courtney broke eye contact with them, comprehending in a heartbeat that there was something eerily familiar about one of the men. Tall with gray hair and cold gray eyes. She froze in her tracks, her blood icing over. Arthur Stringfellow, in the flesh, but it couldn't be. Her editor had said he was gone. Unless he'd gotten details wrong.

She should have felt better, but she didn't. *Oh God, if Stringfellow recognizes me, I'm dead.* She'd dressed semi-casually by her standards, looked nothing like the staid photo in her byline. She'd even let her hair down. When his gaze flicked indifferently over her, she let out a breath.

"Yes, may I help you?"

Courtney almost jumped out of her skin at the receptionist's mocking voice and spun toward her. Seeing the woman's eyes narrow with disapproval, she forced herself to relax, look submissive, whatever the hell that was. A blush, the curse of redheads everywhere, heated her face again.

The receptionist smiled, and although she didn't know what the other woman was smiling for, Courtney let out a relieved breath. That was more like it.

"Hi. My name is Tiffany Andrews, I have an appointment with Mr. Malone," she said, recalling the code words she'd memorized.

The male buzz of conversation in the bar cut off abruptly.

Courtney froze, knowing they were watching her—probably on the hunt for new submissives, she figured. She tried to ignore them, she really did, but she couldn't help notice the entire cluster of men turning to stare at her en masse, Stringfellow included. It was more than a little overwhelming.

Keep your cool, you can do this.

Stringfellow smiled, and made a low voiced comment, making the others laugh, his assessing gaze roving over her like he already owned her.

Ice encasing her heart, she clutched at the reception desk to steady herself. *Damn it, you're stronger than this, Courtney. Don't let him see that you notice. He's a predator, and predators need prey to chase. Don't be that prey.*

She straightened her spine, saw that her knuckles had gone white on the counter, and made herself let go. Part of her almost hoped he'd go for her so she could take him out. But then, she wouldn't be able to find Laura, much less search for evidence against Stringfellow. But she knew that her personal vengeance had to take a back seat. She sighed, letting it go, and some of her burden went with it.

God, she'd lived and breathed that vengeance for years. How could she just abandon it? But the realization she could was freeing in a way. Oh, she'd see that Stringfellow got what was coming to him. He'd pay for destroying her family, but she'd be smart as she went about it.

The receptionist smiled. "May I have your invitation, driver's license, and phone?"

Courtney readily handed over the appointment slip she'd wheedled out of a contact, and the fake driver's license, and the new phone she'd purchased for this. There was nothing on it to give her away, and plenty of fake tidbits to sell her story.

"Go up to the second floor. It's the third door to your right."

Courtney nodded and slipped into the elevator, trying her best to ignore the men's assessing stares following her every move. *They don't matter. Nothing matters, except finding Laura.*

Her gaze swept contemptuously over Stringfellow, and he glared back at her. *Stupid, she scolded herself. Don't piss off the gangster.*

She quickly jammed her finger on the second floor button, making the doors close. Standing, shaking inside the sleek elevator car, she restated her priorities. Find Cara, and get out. The elevator stopped, and the doors whisked silently open. She stepped out into a dimly lit antechamber and walked down to the door indicated.

The conference room was even darker than hallways at the Banner. A light illuminated the center of the table, but left the rest of the room in oppressive darkness. The atmosphere here was downright chilling, probably on purpose, she figured. *Nothing like scaring the crap out of the girls to keep them compliant,* she supposed, scowling. Well, she was made of stronger stuff, straightening her spine, refusing to let it intimidate her.

Striding into the room, head held high, she sat at the table, setting her bag on the oriental carpet next to her chair. She glanced around the room, impressed by the plush surroundings if nothing else. One thing she could say for the Commanders Club, it was a pretty trap.

The fact that she hadn't passed any other girls was disconcerting. Rescuing Laura might not be the snap she'd thought it would. It meant she was going to have to go along with the program, at least for a little while.

She sucked in a tremulous breath, her body tingling a little. It was all atmosphere—dramatics designed to scare her and keep her in line, but it was getting to her. Darting a nervous glance around the dark shadows in the room, she couldn't help wondering how hard the training would be. Her head bowed as she chewed her lip, coaching her muscles to relax. *It doesn't matter how hard it is, I have to rescue Laura.* Folding her damp hands in her lap, she deliberately slowed her breathing, practicing her yoga.

The door opened. She looked up to see a rather nondescript man heading her way. He was tall and lean with thinning sandy brown hair.

She smiled, tension ebbing away. This was good. He certainly didn't resemble any Dom her suddenly feverish imagination could dream up, like the biker from yesterday. Hell, she didn't even know his name, but he'd still starred in her dreams last night. She figured he'd be eminently resistible, and easy to manage.

"Hi."

"Hello, Miss Andrews." He sat down next to her, opening a manila folder containing copies of her fake ID and invitation. "Let's get on with it, shall we?"

Miss Andrews, was it? Excellent! The realization they'd bought her cover story, her fake name, made her sag into her chair. Damn, she hadn't known how keyed up she'd been until now, but things were looking up.

All business, apparently this guy couldn't wait to sign her up for submissive training, the officious jerk.

She looked his rangy body up and down, and tried not to shudder. He wasn't her type, but that was good, she certainly wouldn't be distracted by lust. She noticed a stack of very official looking documents under the copies of her fake IDs. No wonder it was so hard to prove this was abduction.

The man pulled off the top sheet. "This one explains the terms of the agreement. In exchange for our training and guidance, you will repay us with personal services for a one-year term. But first, you must successfully complete the six day training course."

On the Commanders Club's website sale's pitch, she'd read that their girls were handpicked, and well trained, but she hadn't counted on six days of training. Of course, the minute she found Laura, all bets were off, and they were out of here through her secret escape tunnel, so no big deal.

She took the paper and signed, eager to get it over with. "That's fine."

He picked up the next form. "This is the training contract. You must agree to be molded by your trainer."

"Right," she said, cringing inside, her body tightening as she imagined some sleazy guy instructing her in the finer points of pleasing a man: Blow Job 101. Of course, the fictional man had the face of the biker.

She had it bad, and she'd never see him again. Unfortunately, her sex got slick anyway, and her face heated again. *Get it together, woman! Just looking at the biker isn't enough to thaw you out of a thirty year deepfreeze. Maybe she'd better get her hormones checked when they escaped.* What would thin man think of her stupid blush? He'd think she didn't have enough experience to even set foot in the place, much less have the Commander's Club waste their resources on her.

Oh Lord, she was blowing it. She glanced his way, stunned to see him smiling, and blurted out, "It isn't group training?"

He chuckled. "Not to worry, my dear. We find a one-on-one approach gets the proper results. In addition to sex, you will be trained in dress." His nose wrinkled when he looked at her suit. "Also, you'll be schooled in attitude, and deportment. You will be disciplined as your trainer sees fit. You must be open to his instructions—body, mind, and spirit."

Disciplined? Her face heated as she trembled, squeezing her legs together, trying to stop the inappropriate tingling from starting again. She was turning into one big erogenous zone, and she didn't like it. The pen shook in her trembling hand as she quickly scrawled her signature.

He nodded. "That about wraps it up, young lady." He stood, and when she started to rise, he motioned for her to keep her seat. "I'll take your bag to your suite. Stay put. Your trainer will be right in."

"So soon?" Her spine went ramrod straight at his words, her breath catching in her throat as she watched the man walk away with her weapons, her lifeline. Well, at least she still had her lapel camera. But would it be enough?

I'm professional, I'm prepared—I'm scared to death. Oh shit!

He winked at her. "We do things fast at the club."

Chapter 2

FBI Special Agent Ty Dragon stood stock still, glaring at sexy little Courtney Fox through the two-way mirror. Damn it all, she looked even better than she had at the paper yesterday. Had the little snoop overheard him briefing her boss and his ex-platoon mate on the mission?

Of course, she had. She was a reporter—a natural born snoop. And from her background, she came by it naturally. Coming from a long line of snoops, from her great-great-grand-dad, who'd started the Banner, to her parents, who'd run the operation before they were taken out in a still unsolved hit and run accident. Courtney had been ten at the time, and come out of it, with only a visible scar on her throat. An inch to the right, and she'd have been dead. A chill encased his gut at the thought.

Focus, Marine! She doesn't need you to hold her hand. She doesn't need you, period.

She was probably wearing a wire. He focused on her blazer, picking out the spy camera from miles away. He frowned. He'd have to strip her to take it away from her. The fact that he was enjoying the prospect more than he ought to bugged the hell out of him.

Idiot, you're horny enough to get turned on by anything.

Behind him, the club boss, Simeon Alexander, crunched on another antacid tablet, a sure sign he was thinking about whacking someone. Fuck! Courtney Fox, looking like God's gift to men, was signing on to be his pupil at the Commander's Club. Newest trainer, newest submissive, and thank God for that, or he'd have to kill someone. How in the hell was he going to save her neck without compromising his mission?

This was going to be tricky, seeing that the bosses were already on edge. It could mean death for both of them if she let the wrong word slip. He'd just have to keep her from talking. Maybe keep her bound and gagged. His cock lurched against his leather pants at the thought.

Ty watched Courtney fidget in her conference room chair, flipping her long red hair over her shoulder. She buttoned the top button on her blazer, pulling it snug over her luscious C-cup breasts. He tore his focus off her mesmerizing tits, and focused on her emerald green eyes. They were alive with excitement, telling him she was both scared and turned on by this caper. He knew the telltale signs of a woman's arousal as well as he knew his suddenly rampant one. Despite the danger, Ty's cock swelled, beating an insistent tattoo against his left leg. Did she have any concept of what she was getting into? A lethal combination of courage, balls, and naiveté, she was way over her head, and she didn't even know it yet.

He was aware of the people working behind him. Mario, Alexander's computer tech, running background checks over the web using her ID. Ty held his breath, hoping she'd been clever enough to use a primo false one. The house boss, Simeon Alexander, short, squinty-eyed and mean, impatiently waiting for the results crunching another tablet, his eighteenth cup of coffee on the table beside him. The man was never far from a half-filled Styrofoam cup. The caffeine overload helped explain the mobster's mercurial temper and yellow stained teeth.

"Well, Mr. Dragon, what do you think of her?" Alexander said, stepping up next to him.

Was the man testing him?

Trying to keep his expression impassive, Ty shrugged. "She'll do."

"Hey, we got trouble boss," Mario said. "Her ID doesn't check out worth a tinker's damn. It's fake as hell. Looks like Vick Lassiter's work."

Ty tensed. Damn, why the hell had she used Vick for the fake ID?

Because she didn't think she had any other option. The FBI had stonewalled her, just like the Chicago PD had for years. Lassiter had more bad ink floating around town than anyone else.

Ty iced over when Alexander grunted. Turning to look at the man, he searched for a way to turn this mess around. The mobster was scowling, his squinty eyes all but disappearing in his furrowed face.

"Crap." Alexander stalked up to the PC, scowling at the computer screen. "This ain't good. We can't afford to take any chances since that bitch from the newspaper started making noise about pandering."

Two guesses who that bitch was. The only saving grace was that the bastard hadn't recognized her.

"So," Ty said casually. "Send her home. No harm done."

"It ain't that easy, Dragon. She's been inside. Besides, she might be some kind of spy."

Alexander was more perceptive than he looked.

"Look at her," Ty said, drawing Alexander's attention back to the two-way window. "Does she look like any spy you've ever seen?" He knew Alexander was thinking about cutting his losses, and her throat. "She's probably just hiding out from the law or a boyfriend. If trained properly, you could make a bundle off of her. And what, with your new submissives running off in droves," he added, knowing his team had siphoned out two new girls in the middle of the night, "you're in a bind. Look at that red hair, that body. I'll handle her myself."

He watched the man hesitate, greed warring with caution in his tiny brain.

After staring at her a bit longer, Alexander nodded. "Okay, the lady is on probation. If you think you can handle her, Dragon, I'll go in and make the introductions."

"No. I want to do this alone. It requires privacy."

Ty stood fast in the face of the mobster's fierce scowl. He needed a few minutes of privacy to pull this off. Besides, he wasn't into voyeurism like the slimy mob boss no doubt was.

"That ain't how things work around here," Alexander insisted, crumpling his Styrofoam cup and tossing it into the trash. He slanted a threatening look Ty's way. "I hired you because you came with good references, Mr. Dragon, but if you can't do things our way, there are other trainers."

The menace in the mobster's voice came through loud and clear, but Ty just stared him down. "As she's my first student at the club, you'll just have to trust to my methods."

After a few tense moments, the pudgy thug raised a scraggly brow.

"You don't scare easy, I'll give you that. I'll leave her to you, Dragon. Remember, your standing as a trainer only cuts so much ice around here."

Courtney sat in the darkened room, feeling her tension escalate along with her heart rate. Maybe they wanted to scare her. If so, it was working beautifully because she was terrified.

Her pulse sped as her imagination cranked into overdrive. How bad would it be? How hot would it make her? Based on her reaction to the biker yesterday, she knew she was far from frigid.

She heard a door at a far end of the room open and close, and turned toward the sound. In the pitch dark, she could sense a presence, but she couldn't tell who lurked there. Watching her, waiting.

"Stand up," a low male voice said.

Startled, Courtney peered into the stygian darkness as his commanding voice washed over her, her sex creaming automatically. She bit her lip, ashamed of her body's primitive submissive reaction.

"What?" she said, stalling.

"I said, stand up." It was repeated resolutely.

Nibbling her lower lip, she jumped up, automatically obeying even as she fought against it. He wasn't shouting, but there was a weight of authority in his tone she instinctively responded to, even as it pissed her off. It was like he commanded the room, but damn it, he didn't command her. She had to remember that.

Annoyed by the barked order, and the fact that he was hiding in the dark like a coward, she scowled in his general direction. This had to be her trainer, her own Dom, and he was a jerk.

Her chin raising with indignation, she couldn't stop herself from blurting out, "This is ridiculous."

"Quiet. I didn't tell you to talk."

Her sex clutched at the stern tone even as a shiver went up her spine. What the hell was he going to do to her? Her breath caught in her throat at the thought even as her clit pinched.

Stop it. *This imperious jerk, hiding in the shadows, is nothing like the biker. Stop projecting feelings on him that are only figments of your demented imagination.* So, her lack of decorum was understandable. She'd probably run a mile if she met him in broad daylight. Still, it didn't change the fact that she felt on display, in the spotlight, and under his command.

She couldn't help squirming as a long minute ticked by. Why didn't he say something?

"I'm your personal trainer. You may refer to me as TA or sir, but only when permitted to."

He had to be joking. No fucking way was she calling him Sir.

"Say it," he demanded.

She jumped, startled by his vehemence. Licking her lips she said, "TA." There was no denying him if she wanted to stick around and find Laura. The fact that this was turning her on sexually was a shameful secret she needed to keep to herself.

"Very good," he said softly. "Now, take off your shoes."

She kicked off her shoes, her toes curling into the carpet. *Why does he want me barefoot? Maybe so it's harder to run? Not a pleasant thought.*

"Unbutton your jacket, and take it off."

She froze, disinclined to take orders blindly or lose the lapel cam. Did he know about it? How could he? It was very discreet. Still, she hesitated to remove it.

"Why?"

"Do it."

A chill went up her spine at his clipped, impatient tone. She was blowing this, and all because she couldn't follow the basics. But she froze, her body rebelling at the thought of getting naked in this public space.

"I'll do no such thing."

"You signed a contract."

Her stomach tightened at the unsaid threat. He'd bounce her out of here so fast, her head would spin, then she'd never find Laura. No, she couldn't risk it.

Hands shaking, she unbuttoned her blazer, regretting she was losing her camera, but doing it, anyway. If she folded it just right, she'd get a picture of his no-doubt ugly face.

"Good. Fold it, and place it on the table."

She grinned. Dang, he'd read her mind. She folded the blazer, camera facing out toward him, and laid it carefully on the table.

"Yes, Master," she muttered under her breath.

"What?"

She sobered, instantly regretting her smart remark. Shit, don't piss off the Dom that stands between you and saving Laura. *If I survive this, without being booted from the program, it will be a miracle.*

"Nothing."

She looked down, noting that her pink lace bra was clearly visible through her white silk blouse, and stifled a whimper of shame. It seemed almost obscenely see-through in the strong light. Her nipples tingled, jutting out harder, the strumpets. Surely, he could see it. Crossing her arms in front of her to hide her reaction from him, she glared into the darkness.

"Put your arms down."

"No."

"Fine, you'll pay the penalty for that."

"Penalty?" She instantly regretted her refusal. It was true, self-restraint was never her long suit, and now she was going to pay the price.

"You agreed to be disciplined."

Biting her lip, she nodded, her bottom warming at the word *discipline*. Would he spank her? She swallowed a groan when her sex got slicker, her clit pinching hard. Lord, if TA touched her, he'd know how turned on she was, and she'd be putty in his hands. That couldn't happen, but how could she prevent it? She had to stall for time.

"Yes, but not so soon."

"Come here."

Courtney quaked inside, knowing it was obey his commands, or leave. She couldn't leave. Her blush got hotter, encompassing her bottom, her quivering sex. How could she fight this? By not letting him know he was getting to her, that's how. She could brazen it out. She was professional, she was prepared.

She was scared to death.

Walking toward him into the dark, she felt her way around the table, goosebumps breaking out on her arms despite her internal pep talk.

It was stupid, but she couldn't help being scared, and ashamedly aroused. Feeling her way, using the backs of chairs, she followed his breathing. It seemed to be growing faster, a little ragged.

"What kind of game are you playing, TA?" she mocked, pretending she didn't care.

With a yelp of surprise, she tripped over him. He was sitting sideways in his chair.

His hands reached out to grab her waist, steadying her, and her belly quivered along with her sex as they made contact. Shit, he had big hands, and big hands equated with big...

Don't go there she scolded herself.

"Thank you," she murmured, then bit her tongue. Why should she thank him?

"You're welcome," he said.

With a jerk, he tugged her off balance, putting her over his knee.

She let out a yelp of shock, burning up as her body melted over his hot one. And she thought she'd been burning up before. That was nothing compared to the inferno of his skin against hers.

Embarrassed as his arm looped over her waist, she tried to wriggle off his hard lap. It didn't work. He held her trapped, her futile struggles telling her she was no match for him in a physical fight.

Absorbing the enormity of her blunder, she realized her only option was to outsmart him. That ought to be easy to do. People were always underestimating her.

His lap was rigid under her, his semi-erect cock thumping against her belly, distracting her from her plan to outsmart him. He was wearing leather pants. She gulped, inhaling the lethal-to-her-virtue combination of hot man and leather. What kind of guy wore leather pants?

A real Dom, she realized a second before his big hand spanked her bottom with no preliminaries. No teasing, no tender caresses, just punishment.

"Hey," she yelled, wincing at the pain. "Stop that, you sadistic bastard."

"Quiet if you don't want to be gagged," he ordered. "You will count the spanks."

She sucked in a shocked breath at the order, chilling her.

"No, damn it, I will not." She tried to wriggle away, but his strong arm around her waist kept her restrained in perfect spanking position.

Stinging spanks rained down on her bottom like hot fire. Even through her clothes, they hurt. God, they weren't teasing or playful, these were angry and brisk. And he meant every single one of them.

"Do it," he said.

Spank!

"No." She moaned, squeezing her butt cheeks together. It didn't help.

Thwack! A hard spank flattened her ass.

Okay count, she told herself, needing the distraction. It would make it all more tolerable.

"O-o-one," she stammered.

He went still. "Good girl."

Spank!

She bit her lip, warming at his praise. "T-t-two."

"Good, we go to six."

"Six! God, my bottom's on fire now."

He chuckled.

Spank!

Oh Lord, why had she said that?

"Three," she said with a grumble. "How dare you find this funny, you beast."

"Funny doesn't even begin to describe it," he said grimly, drawing back a hand.

Spank!

What the hell did he mean by that? "F-f-fo-four."

Spank!

"Five," she gritted.

Spank!

"Six."

Draped across his lap, bottom on fire, gasping for air, her sex clenching, she was a shocked mess. His cock was getting bigger, harder, practically thumping a conga beat against her leg. Stunned, all she could do was feel the heat. At least she hadn't come for him. That would have been utterly humiliating.

He caressed her sore bottom through her skirt, and she sighed with pleasure.

She let out a needy little moan, melting against him, one big erogenous zone. His big hand rubbing her ass felt soothing, and shockingly good. She hissed and arched her hips, unable to control herself. Her stiff clit rubbed against his leather-clad leg, and she gasped at the electric sensation, and then did it again, unable to resist the thrill it was causing down below.

Keep it to yourself, woman, he doesn't need to know.

As his hot hand rubbed lower down her smarting bottom, her legs fell apart a little in sensual abandon. His hand inched under her skirt, touching her pink panties, cupping her mound. She bit back a whimper as he held her needy, quivering sex in his big hand, his palm still hot from her spanking.

She groaned, pulsing against the heat.

"Good, you're wet."

So much for keeping it to herself, she thought sourly at his satisfied tone. He meant to drive her insane with lust. She froze, trying to pull her legs together even though it was like trying to stop a tsunami from crashing into the shore. He wasn't about to budge. In fact, he let out a grumble at her attempt to try to shut him out.

He wedged her legs apart with his big hand, and gave her a sharp spank on the mound that set her whole sex fluttering, from stinging clit, to quivering vagina, to puckering anus.

Lord, she was in trouble deep.

"Oh." She groaned at her own unguarded response, pain and pleasure mingling inside her, making her toes curl.

"Full access, student. Remember your contract."

She grumbled at his sharp tone, and was it just a little bit mocking? Like he was pissed off she'd signed the contract, that he'd been stuck with her. That had to be what was making him so gruff.

Damn, here she was, half in lust with him, and he didn't want her.

It's for the best, Courtney, falling in lust with your trainer isn't part of your game plan.

Tell it to my tingling clit. It isn't listening.

Parting her legs farther for him, she whimpered, letting him soothe her, rub the sting away, feed the fire a little more. She hissed with pleasure when he thumbed her clit.

Then, he reached down to slip something leather over her eyes. A blindfold, she realized, stunned.

So, it had begun. She froze as the blindfold closed out the remaining light, but didn't fight him. What would be the point?

"Good girl. Now, get up." He pushed her off his lap.

She landed in a heap at his feet. The hell? She started to stand.

"No, on your knees," he corrected. "Bottom back, resting on your calves, legs spread, arms at your sides."

Courtney moved as he half-instructed, half-pushed her into the vulnerable position.

"You are now in training position number one, and open to my instructions. You will maintain it until I tell you to move and give you permission to rise."

Permission to rise?

Stunned into silence, she trembled, kneeling in front of him, the reality of the situation setting in hard. This wasn't a game. She was his slave in training, at least, until she rescued Laura and ran.

"Good girl," he said, stroking her hair.

She leaned into his touch, was actually warmed by the praise, telling her how far she'd already fallen. How sick was that? No more!

She knelt there, her pussy wet and excited despite her vow, her heart racing, knowing he was watching her, making her wait. And then, he slipped a necklace around her neck. A choker. Jewels from her trainer!

She almost whimpered with relief when he smoothed it across the scar on her throat. She knew the mark was faded, almost invisible, but she still saw it in the mirror every day, dreamt about the crash nearly every night. It was almost like he knew, and he was trying to soothe her. Wishful thinking, she knew. Still, she couldn't resist leaning into his touch, reveling in it.

Then, metal rasped against metal as he attached something to the choker. She realized with a semi-numb sense of shock, she was wearing a collar, his collar, and he'd attached a leash. How humiliating.

"You may rise."

She stood, wobbling against the chair.

"Not very graceful," he murmured.

The words stung like a spank, almost worse than one, actually.

What the hell do I care if I disappoint him, if he finds me less than graceful?

On that firm thought, she tried to peek under the blindfold, but a thump of his finger to her chin told her he noticed. She raised her chin a bit defiantly.

She had to admit, while silently being commanded by his nudge, she couldn't stop herself from muttering, "Stop that."

She was rewarded with a slap across the back of her thighs from the end of the leash.

"Ouch."

"No speaking." He gave a little tug on the leash. "Come."

She followed behind him, stunned by the rapid turn of events. What choice did she have? No choice at all if she wanted to complete her mission and save Laura. She heard the door open, her bare feet padding over soft carpet, then cool tile. Where was he leading her? Did others see her blindfolded, on a leash?

At last, she stepped onto carpet again.

"Stand still," he demanded, his voice hot and gruff. "Eyes down."

"But, I'm wearing a blindfold."

"Insolence again. You really can't help yourself can you, Courtney?"

Courtney. *He knows my real name.*

Fear clutched her heart, and she gasped, taking half a step back as far as the leash would allow. She shuddered, frozen with dread as her blindfold was tugged off.

Blinking at the suddenly bright light, she glared back at the story-stealing biker. What the hell?

He loomed over her, his dark hair falling forward, his ice blue eyes spearing her with fury.

She sucked in a breath as he invaded her personal space, drawing in the intoxicating scents of hot man, chocolate, and leather. What was it about him and leather? Today, black leather encased his powerful body, the vest highlighting his bare chest, his washboard abs, his navel where a whorl of hair went south into his tight pants. The pants fit his massive package like a second skin, putting it all on display.

Her mouth watered, but she still glared from her leash, held in his firm hand, to his angry face. He wasn't the only one who was furious. Maybe he'd had the same idea going inside as a fake Dom, but the spanking he'd administered felt anything but fake. Her backside was still on fire, her sex quivering.

"Who the hell are you, and what the fuck are you up to?"

He raised one imperious raven brow, his sensual mouth tightening. "You little snoop. You have about five minutes to say what you're going to say and get it out of your system. That's about as long as I can scramble any listening devices without making them suspicious."

Her jaw dropped at his words. Scrambling devices meant he was probably a Fed. Useless, in her experience, and the fraud held her leash like he owned her.

"Let me go."

He gazed back at her, immovable as granite. "They're onto you, sugar. Your ID didn't pass muster."

Her eyes widened when she heard the certainty in his voice. Was he lying? Her blazer, with her cam carefully folded to the inside, lay draped over his arm. He saw the direction of her stare and arched a brow as if daring her to complain. So, he'd noticed the camera. The rest of them hadn't, so why was he so hot under the collar?

She wasn't about to play his games. "You're lying. I used the best maker in town."

"Vick Lassiter," he filled in sourly.

She frowned at his tone. "How did you know?"

"Sugar, he's got so much bad ink circulating around town, even an idiot like the house boss could spot it."

"Simeon Alexander," she said, thinking of the clandestine photos she and Laura had taken of the house boss. She smiled, seeing that she'd surprised him. "I did my homework. If what you're saying is true, then why am I here, with you, and not dead in some alley?"

He closed in on her, spearing her with a sharp gaze. "I told them you were probably running from the law. I'll get my tech to phony up a plausible background they should buy."

Pinning him with a doubtful look, she muttered, "So, you and a computer nerd are the only things between me and disaster."

"Got it in one, sugar. Although, I wouldn't call my associate a computer nerd. I talked them into letting me train you."

She trembled at the seductive way he said *train you*. "You need to have your head examined if you think I'm actually going to stay and let you train me. I'm only here to get Laura Evens, my summer intern, out of here. Turn her over to me, and I'll leave."

"Yeah, right. You think they'll just let you waltz out the front door?"

Was that all he was worried about? "Don't worry about me. I've got a foolproof exit plan. Now, about Laura..."

His eyes narrowed. "When did she come in?"

"According to her text, she entered around midnight last night."

He shook his head. "In that case, you're too late."

She sucked in a breath, shrinking away from him, the handler's *'we take things fast at the Commander's Club'* ringing in her ears.

"She couldn't have been sold so soon."

His jaw tightened. "I shouldn't tell you, but you'll just do something stupid if I don't."

She glared back at him, insulted. Although, she had to admit, so far, her actions hadn't worked.

"She must have gone out with the group my team siphoned away in the middle of the night."

She sagged with relief at his words, leaning against him, seeing his eyes widen with what looked like alarm. So, he was comfortable with spanking women, not comforting them. It didn't matter now that she knew Laura was safe.

She smiled at her new hero, wanting to kiss him, but the brooding look in his eyes stopped her short. "Thank you. Now, I'll just leave and—"

"Weren't you listening to a word I said? You can't leave. You don't have a choice in the matter if you want to survive."

"Now who's being over-dramatic? I'm not scared of Alexander," she lied.

"That just proves that you need a keeper." His hand tightened on the leash.

"Of all the insensitive—"

"*I'm* the kind of insensitive, sugar. Ask anyone." When she grumbled, he taunted, "I guess you don't want Stringfellow to get what's coming to him."

She quit arguing, shocked that this Fed was actually telling her about the case. At least, a little bit. "Of course, I want him to go down. Are you saying my capitulation would help make that happen?"

He nodded. "Damned straight, and remember, you're on probation, so watch your step." His eyes twinkled as he added, "From now on, we play by my rules."

"Probation, how ridiculous," she protested.

His eyes narrowed. "It's too late for that. Like I said, they are on to you, slave girl. So, the whole case hinges on you. The club owner is on edge. He said something about a nosy reporter going to the cops a few weeks back. I'm guessing that's you."

Courtney looked away, distressed. She had thrown around a lot of accusations. Who knew it would come back to haunt her?

"What now?" she asked, glancing at him. "Why did you go to the trouble of saving me?"

He smirked. "Maybe I've got a weakness for taming redheads."

Her knees wobbled, but then she remembered he wasn't all he claimed to be. It was all an act, just another day in the life of a spy. "If it's all fake, then you can just tell them you tamed me. You don't have to actually do it."

"Sorry, sugar. It's got to look real, feel real. They have cameras and mics everywhere." He smiled. "Like I said, we play by my rules. That is, if you want to pursue your story."

"Who said I was after a story?"

He rolled his eyes, and she had the grace to feel chagrined. He really knew her.

"Given the carnage Stringfellow has done to your family, of course, you're out to get him. Hell, I would be if I were in your position."

She smiled. Did that mean he was going to help her?

"Just how long were you eavesdropping on us, anyway?" he asked.

"Long enough."

He nodded. "That's what I figured. Behave yourself for the next six days, and I'll find a way to get you what you need. Act up, and I'll keep you bound and gagged."

She trembled as his hot gaze raked over her body like a caress. Her bottom tingled, still hot from her spanking, and her temper boiled over. "I will not behave myself. How dare you spank me!"

He yanked at her collar, pulling her to him so that their noses were inches apart. "Your five minutes of free talk are up. Now, who am I?"

Was there really a listening device? Or was it just a ploy to keep her in line?

Feeling his dominant sexual power wash over her, she realized he wouldn't have to stoop to subterfuge to dominate a woman.

"How dare you spank me, sir?" Her pulse raced with a tremor of excitement that surged through her. She could smell his sandalwood cologne, see the stubble from his five o'clock shadow, the sensual curve of his mouth when she's given in and called him TA. His eyes were a deep blue, and she sank into them while her nipples tightened.

"I'm your Master," he said, inches from kissing her. "It's my duty to bend you to my will. To lash your sweet ass with my paddle and belt, and open you with my cock." Rubbing against her, he murmured, "Don't you agree?"

Something deep inside of her melted at his words, and she trembled. She already knew he had what it took to make her submit. Now, he was saying he was going to turn up the heat.

Fighting the urge to lean in and kiss his tantalizing mouth, she said, "If I'd known it was you, I wouldn't have come."

"Maybe, but it's too late for you to go. We'll both have to make the best of it."

She froze, trembling. Was that regret in his voice? Was he sorry it was her instead of another woman? Did he think her attractive, sexy? It was a stupid thought, but she couldn't help it. How long had he worked undercover for the FBI, training subs? Her nipples tingled, her pussy got wetter. Could he smell her excitement? She saw the dangerous glint in his eyes as he inhaled, and realized that he could.

"I don't think so."

"You lost the option to say no the minute you walked through the door. I'll do the thinking for both of us."

"Of all the egotistical, ass—"

His eyes narrowed. "Don't say it."

Her pussy rippled in response, and she blurted out, "Why don't you just take me and get it over with?"

Oh Lord, she was so damned needy.

He shook his head, his mouth firming. "You haven't earned that privilege yet."

Her jaw dropped at his cocky statement. "Arrogant, aren't you?"

"I haven't had any complaints." He stepped back, dropping her leash so that it dragged on the floor. "Now, strip."

Stalling, even though she was aching to comply, she looked around the room. It was like a deluxe hotel suite, complete with a king-sized bed. Did he mean to make love to her here? A thrill went through her at the thought. Still, she didn't want to give in that easily.

"Every second you delay is another demerit," he informed her.

"Who do you think you are, one of the nuns from grade school?"

"And did they spank my little slave girl?" he asked, amused.

"No. They used to rap my knuckles with a ruler and stand me in a corner." Her cheeks flamed.

He glanced at his watch. "By my count, you've been stalling for five minutes. Care to go for ten?"

Ten demerits couldn't be good. Embarrassed by the situation and her inclination to get naked with him, her trembling hands went to her blouse, unbuttoning it. She slipped out of it, shooting him a furtive glance.

He stood there, watching her as if she were the most fascinating creature in the world. It made her heart race.

"Neatness counts," he added, looking at the crumpled garment in her hands. "Your Master will expect perfection in all things."

The comment dulled her arousal, making her suddenly itch to throw the blouse in his face. His raised brow told her he read her indignation. She walked to the closet and hung her blouse on a wooden hanger, then turned to look at TA.

He smiled. "Now, the skirt."

She slipped out of her pinstriped skirt, keenly aware she was down to her pink lace bra and panties. Her underwear was feminine, girlie even, and admittedly, a little old fashioned. It hadn't been a conscious thought when she'd put them on, but now she was glad she was wearing them. TA was about to go down in flames.

She heard his breathing quicken. It turned her on as she hung the skirt up and turned to face him.

"Good." His sultry gaze flowed over her.

She felt warmed by the praise.

He frowned, pushing off from the dresser. "Come here, slave girl."

She walked to him, intensely aware of the eroticism of the leash dragging on the floor, her hard nipples poking out of the lace bra, the damp heat between her legs. Stopping a few inches in front of him, TA's body heat seemed to make the temperature in the air shoot up. She darted a glance at him. He had a slight smile on his face. He was definitely getting off on humiliating her, or was it part of the act? No, glancing at him, she realized it was real. It made her mad and turned her on at the same time. What a quandary. He wanted her in a very primitive, caveman, sort of way. Her heart fluttered. He was the only thing standing between her and disaster, and she was itching to see him naked.

"I've got to take care of your punishment, and I'm fresh out of rulers and dunce caps," he said with a slow shake of his head. "Five demerits, wasn't it?"

"Asshole," she muttered, telling herself she was better off staying away from him.

He stepped close, taking a handful of her hair, gently but firmly tugging her head back to nuzzle her neck, her ear. "You'll pay for that, sugar."

She shivered, his warm lips slipping up her neck, making her crazy. Did he know how close she was to coming? He nipped at the tender skin on her neck, and she gasped, her pussy fluttering.

"Soft," he whispered.

She leaned into his touch, both alarmed and excited. What was he going to do with her? Did he like her? Was he attracted?

"But so naughty," he added, setting her back on her heels.

She flinched as his voice went from sexy to firm. Did he mean to spank her again?

He walked to the armoire, opening it wide, and pulled out a big black paddle.

Fascination and fear warred inside her as she watched him walk back toward her, paddle in hand.

"What are you going to do with that?"

"Discipline you, of course." He sat down on the edge of the bed. "You take your paddling over my knee."

"No." She shook her head and watched his eyes darken.

He couldn't expect her to meekly lie over his lap and take her punishment. She glared at him, only to see him quirk one imperious brow. That was exactly what he expected. It would be so much easier if he just grabbed her, spanked her, fucked her, put her out of her sexual misery. But he wasn't going to make it easy on her.

As his sultry gaze roamed over her, she decided that the girlie undies might have been a mistake. Red leather, now that might have showed she was in charge. She couldn't let him think her a weak, frightened female.

"Fine, spank me, big strong Master."

He patted his lap. "Come here."

She approached him like one would any other lethal weapon. She didn't know what might set him off. Her face heated, sending a shock wave through her body. Her pussy rippled again, and her bottom heated in anticipation.

Biting back a humiliated sigh, she gingerly draped herself across his lap, trying not to make too much contact with his body. The feel of his leather pants against her almost bare belly and thighs was shocking. Her whole body seemed to flush with heat, quivering in anticipation.

TA's big hand splayed across her bottom, pushing her down so that she was pressed tight against his thighs. She blinked back tears, appalled by how vulnerable she was.

"Now, slave girl," he said, casually rubbing her bottom through her lace panties. "Why are you being punished?"

Her bottom warmed as his hand caressed her. "Because you're mean."

He chuckled. "Come now, don't stall for time. You're going to get paddled, and that's that. Now, speak. Why are you being punished?"

She shuddered as he rested the paddle against her bottom. "Because I stalled, and then I called you an asshole."

"Very good. And am I?"

"Yes," she hissed angrily.

His hand stopped rubbing her tingling bottom and she instantly regretted her outburst.

"No," she quickly bit out.

He started rubbing again. "What's my name?"

"Sir."

He toyed with the edge of her panties. "I love these baby doll panties. Feminine and perfect, like you."

When he started to pull them down, she felt herself blush, but she didn't try to stop him. He pulled them all the way down to tangle around her knees, baring her round bottom. She felt the restraint acutely. It increased her fear, her excitement.

"Very nice," he murmured resting the paddle on her bottom. "You've got beautiful breasts, slave girl. But most of all, I like your saucy ass. It just begs for my attention."

She tensed when he drew back the paddle, smacking it down onto her bottom. She let out a yelp, grinding against him, her ass burning, her pussy clenching.

"That's one," he said. "You'll take six."

"No." She whimpered. She couldn't take five more. She shuddered, leaning into him as she grew wetter.

He drew back the paddle and smacked her bottom again. "Two."

Tears started falling from her eyes as she lay bent over his knee.

"Quiet. Now's the time to learn some self-control. Don't you dare come. You're being punished."

And then his paddle came down on her again, *hard*. "Three."

She gasped, this time not shrinking away. Her butt throbbed and she leaned into him when he rubbed it. She couldn't take three more. She shuddered, leaning into him, her vaginal walls twitching.

"Very good, naughty girl. Such a nice ass to punish."

She cried, her pussy as hot as her bottom as he gave her four, five, and six in rapid succession.

Sobbing while his palm caressed her throbbing ass, cooling the sting from the paddle, she lost herself in his touch. And then his fingers slipped down between her legs to touch her hungry sex.

She gasped, her pussy clamping onto his teasing fingers as he played with her. She moaned, arching her back, trying to take his big finger deeper while on fire.

"Nice," he praised.

She whimpered, out of her head with desire.

He dipped his little finger into her pussy juices and then slipped it into her anus. She'd never allowed a man to try that with her.

Amazed by the naughty but nice sensation, she let out a ragged breath. It made her hot to be taken that way, too. She pressed her ass against him, but he withdrew.

She felt bereft. Her pussy was pulsing again, along with her anus, and her poor spanked ass was on fire. She lay draped across his knee, frustrated, fuming. He was a bastard—a ruthless bastard, to treat her this way.

"Why don't you just take me?" she whispered.

"No. You'll come when I say so, and not before. Now, get up." He helped her to her feet.

She stood there, wobbly, her panties down around her ankles.

He tugged her leash, making her hobble forward a few steps. She was humiliated, turned on, and embarrassed. She glanced up at him, watching her, his eyes a stormy blue, and there was an undeniable bulge in his pants. He'd gotten off on spanking her, but not enough to take her. Probably some dumb FBI code or something.

"Take your bra off."

Her eyes widened. Maybe she was going to get some attention, after all.

She reached behind her for the bra's clasp and unhooked it. Shrugging out of the delicate garment, her breasts fell free. The pink nipples were hard, jutting, just begging for his attention. She was so turned on, she was tied up in knots. Gazing at him, she decided she hated him for doing this to her, even while she burned for his possession.

"Excellent." He took the bra from her, putting it in the top dresser drawer. He turned back to rake a hot gaze over her. "You've got beautiful breasts, slave girl." He reached out to run his fingers over her swollen flesh.

Her nipples puckered harder, and she bit back a moan. Instead of taking what she offered, he dropped his hand. There was a grimly determined look on his face, which she couldn't quite interpret.

"Now, the panties."

She stepped out of the panties, picked them up, and handed them to him like she was offering him a gift. There was an intense gleam in his eyes as he accepted them. Folding them, he tucked them into his shirt pocket like a handkerchief. They carried her scent, her arousal. Did he want to remind himself? She couldn't help being curious. She knew so little about him, her trainer.

"This is the new order of things. You, naked." His hand ran down her arm, making her lean into his touch "Spanked, and very responsive. You've never had a man paddle you before, have you, sugar?"

She didn't much like the grudging amusement in his voice, but she had to be honest. There would be no lying to him.

"No," she admitted softly.

"It's a start. Go fetch your paddle and put it away."

She was shocked by the order, but found herself obeying. She walked back to the bed and picked up the paddle. It might have been her imagination, but it still felt warm from her spanking.

She looked at him, standing there with the armoire wide-open, waiting for her. There was a sultry but understanding look on his face. She could tell she wasn't the first woman he'd introduced to submission. It made her angry, jealous even, although that was ridiculous. Still, her heart raced as she walked to him carrying the paddle.

When she went to hand it to him, he shook his head.

"You put it away. The next time you're to be punished, you will go fetch it."

She couldn't help bristling at his masterful tone, but her bottom heated as she leaned in to put the paddle on its holder, right next to the strap and riding crop. She paled just glancing at them, and the bevy of vibrators, lotions, and sex toys on the shelves. There was even a huge dildo like she'd seen online. Did he mean to use them all on her? He pussy flooded with heat. What she wouldn't give to have him use one of the vibrators on her right now. She needed something to fill the aching void between her legs. She'd use it on her herself if that's what got him off.

He reached for something that looked like a thick stubby penis with straps, and several pairs of restraints. Good grief, what was he going to do with them?

"This is your penis gag," he said, turning back to her. "Open your mouth."

Shocked, her mouth dropped open, and he pressed the gag into her mouth. He fastened the straps behind her head and she sucked on the rubber penis. She really had no other choice.

"A slave can be made to suck her penis for hours," he explained, matter-of-factly. "Kneel on the floor."

She sunk to her knees, trembling. Was this it, was he going to fuck her? Instead, he attached restraints to her wrists and ankles, shackling her until she was positioned kneeling, head down, bottom up in the air. How humiliating. Her whole body trembed as she sucked on her the rubber penis.

"This is submissive position number two. Behave yourself," he ordered, patting her bottom.

Chapter 3

Dragon turned to go before he gave into the wicked temptation to fuck Courtney.

The look in her eyes still burned him to the core and made
his cock ache. He could slide into her hot cunt, doggy style,
or maybe open that tight little bottom of hers. After her hot
response to the paddling, he knew she was perfect for him. Too
perfect. She was sexy, feisty, and despite her search and destroy
mission, hot for it, and he knew he was toast. But he didn't have
to let her know she could twist him. How in the hell was he
going to sell this to his team? His AIC, Nick Harrison, was not
going to be amused, to say nothing of his team members. He'd
be a laughing stock when this got out.

But that was okay as long as he took care of Courtney.

His gut tightened. He couldn't even consider failure. As it
was, he walked a tricky tightrope—make her training convinc-
ing enough to mollify Alexander, while the agency moved in for
the kill. His choices were clear—train her, or lose her. There was

no way he was losing her, even if it cost him his damned job. The trick was not to get attached.

He groaned, pushing away the feeling. She'd brought this trouble on herself. He had to keep that thought in mind. Was her story about coming to rescue Laura true? He huffed a breath. He'd find out soon enough.

Standing in the doorway, he glanced back at Courtney. Her luscious lips wrapped around the rubber dick in her mouth, working it noisily. He ached to replace that lifeless piece of rubber with his suddenly heavy cock. If she kept getting to him like this, he was going to have blue balls before the week was through. He ran a last lingering glance over her to make sure she was secure, and then shut and locked the door behind him.

The gag and restraints would keep her quiet and out of trouble while he worked, because he sure as hell didn't trust her.

The first thing to do was to see to her fake ID situation. Luckily, he had the best tech in the business on his side. He made his way down the hall to the Slave Bazaar.

He entered the shop to find the newest member of his team, probationary agent Tawny Valentine. Tall, athletic, and charming when she wanted to be.

She was ringing up a customer, one of the other trainers with his student, a short brunette who was pouting as Tawny rang up anal vibrators, beads, and lubricant. Either her trainer or buyer was really into anal. TA didn't give the woman a second glance. Instead, the basket made him think of Courtney's shocked, and then pleasured, reaction when he'd tested her tight little rosebud.

Pushing away the memory, he brought his attention back to the business at hand.

When the trainer and slave left the shop, he walked up to the check-out desk.

Tawny looked around to make sure they were alone, then pushed a button sealing the doors. "About time you stopped by for a situation report instead of gallivanting off to do a favor for a friend. Things have been going off the rails here."

"Don't tell me. You took a new recruit named Laura Evans, who turned out to be a photographer, into protective custody."

Her eyes narrowed with suspicion. "Where the hell do you get your information?"

"Her boss, Courtney Fox, is the favor I did for my old friend."

"So," Tawny said with a shrug. "What's the problem?"

"She's here to get Laura out."

"Son of a bitch." Tawny reached for her sat phone under the counter.

"Don't," he commanded.

Her hand stilled as she cocked a doubtful look at him. "Give me a good reason not to call our Agent in Charge."

He tensed, knowing Tawny's first loyalty lay with Nick Harrison, their AIC, and her presumed lover. At least the two had been sniffing around each other for the last couple of months. "She's my responsibility. Alexander handed her over to me as my first trainee."

Tawny's eyes glittered with speculation.

"Besides, she could be an asset."

"Right," she said scornfully.

"She knows this rat's maze better than the rest of us put together. Law told me her grandmother used to run a dance studio out of the corner building. And the Banner was once run out of the central core. Guess Stringfellow thought it was pretty funny buying up the Fox Block, as it used to be called, the slimy bastard."

Tawny looked him over. "You're serious about this. What happened to Mister Take One For the Team, our only loyalty is to the bureau?"

Yeah, he'd ridden her hard when she'd first joined his team. All part of his job, and he'd meant every word. But now, he needed more. Sheesh, he was losing it.

"That's all true, to a point. But you and I both know that, sometimes, you have to bend the rules for a greater cause." He watched Tawny's jaw drop with what appeared to be shock. Yeah, he could hardly believe the words were coming out of his mouth, either. Still, no matter what it cost him, Courtney would be taken care of. He slid a copy of her bad ID across the counter. "What I need from you is new ID for her."

Tawny wrinkled her nose as she looked at it. "No wonder they didn't buy it. Vick's work is crap. Expensive, but crap. Your woman must have bucks, but very little common sense if she thought this would pass muster with Mario, Alexander's tech."

His woman. As if he'd get to keep her. But for now, yeah, she belonged to him, and he intended to make the most of it. She was intrigued by submission she'd just barely tasted. He had a painful cock swelling sensation when he pictured allowing her to actually taste him. She'd been liquid heat when he'd touched her pussy, her clit being plump, hard, and juicy, and her tight asshole clamping on his finger like a fist. God, it had been pure torture not to take what she'd begged him to take. Masochistic, really, he decided grimly.

"Doesn't matter. I'm stuck with her. I'll tell Nick personally."

She shook her head. "It's your funeral. You know what he's going to tell you. The mission takes precedence, and you don't have time to get hooked on a pair of fabulous tits."

He gave her a hard look, knowing she was right. Didn't matter, he wouldn't back down. He couldn't afford to.

"Alexander's close to going ape shit. Are you going to do this for me or not?"

"Fine, but if things go south—"

"Call for backup as usual," he said with a nod. "I've got to get back to work."

He walked out of the Slave Bazaar. He had to get back to his student. He could still recall her shock when he'd told her to open her mouth for the penis gag. Obviously, she'd bedded less demanding men in the past, ones she could boss around. As her temporary Master, he'd be much more demanding.

He started to make his way up the back staircase. Hearing footsteps in the hall, he went still, slipping into the darkness. As a ghost, he'd had plenty of experience blending into the shadows.

Chapter 4

Kneeling on the floor, body vibrating with outrage, Courtney sucked furiously on the penis gag in her mouth, wishing it was something much more lifelike. Her ass still burned, her sex quivered with arousal, and her nipples were hard as tingling jewels as they touched the carpet. Damn TA, she was going to kill him for leaving her in this needy state. She sucked harder on the dildo and groaned when her pussy clenched, cursing him again.

Oh, rationally, she understood the reason he had bound and gagged her. He didn't trust her. Well, the feeling was mutual. So far, he'd given her no reason to trust him, either.

And what the hell did her editor, Law Clark, have to do with this? The two had seemed pretty cozy at the paper. At least, her instinct not to go to Law with this had proved right. No doubt, he'd have lied to her, too. Damn it, she was tired of people trying to protect and coddle her. She was strong, she was professional, and she could handle anything TA threw at her.

The doorknob rattled, and she melted with relief, squeezing her legs together to stave off her arousal. *Do not let him see how much this turned you on.* She glanced over to see the knob turn with another rattle, and a lowly voiced cursed on the other side.

A chill ran up her spine. *Oh, my God. It wasn't TA. He had a key. Which meant it could be anyone.*

She froze as the lock tried again, and this time, it opened. A smell—stale sweat, coffee, and mints—drifted into the room before a man did.

Simeon Alexander came into the room. Short, paunchy, and mean, he strutted like he had every right to be there. Staring contest, she thought semi-hysterically, when their gazes locked, then his critical gaze raked over her, making her feel unclean. TA's *they're onto you slave girl* echoed through her mind, and there wasn't a damned thing she could do to stop it.

TA would kill him if he touched her, she knew in her heart, but TA wasn't here. All she could do was flash a warning glare Simeon's way. She couldn't object, couldn't say anything with the penis gag in her mouth. Her eyes followed him as he stepped closer, waves of suspicion and disapproval coming from him as he glared back at her. She knew she was supposed to be submissive, but meek just wasn't her style.

"So, he's paddled you."

Her face heated at the indication he was staring at her paddled bottom, and damn if it didn't start to sting more, telling her that the blush had spread. He sounded almost disappointed, like he wanted her and TA to fail. Why? Were they on to TA, too? Was he unaware of that fact? Whatever the truth was, it seemed they were both in more trouble than TA had said.

She shrunk away from him, petrified he'd actually touch her, promising herself that if he dared, she'd get him. Instead, he simply turned with a grumble, and walked out the door.

Sighing, she sagged, her breasts and face pressing against the soft pile carpeting. She seemed to wait an eternity for TA to return.

Tears misted her eyes as she heard the door open again. Was Simeon back?

She turned to see TA walk back into the room, and grinned at him around the gag, relief reviving her spirits. He shut and locked the door behind him, and she melted in gratitude even though it was his fault she was in this predicament. When his hot gaze swept over her, lingering on her hot bottom, her hard nipples, all her fears were temporarily forgotten as her body overheated again. Sucking on the cock gag, all she could think was that she needed TA to soothe her, make her feel powerful. She wanted *his* cock, needed the reassurance of being possessed by him, even if it was temporary.

When he walked up to her, running his hand over her hot ass, she arched it up to meet his touch.

"Have you learned your submission lesson?" he asked.

Irritated by the amusement in his voice, she nodded when she really itched to kick his sexy ass, and then demand that he do her.

He chuckled, "We shall see." He undid the straps and took the gag out of her mouth. "And did you enjoy sucking on your penis pacifier?"

Eyes flashing fire at him, she refused to answer.

At his firm look, she dropped her gaze. "Yes, TA."

He crouched to unlock her bonds, freeing her arms and legs. Then, he attached her leash to her collar and gave it a tug. "Come, it's time for bed. You've got harder lessons to learn tomorrow."

She started to rise, and he pushed her down.

"No, crawl on your hands and knees, to show you've learned your first submission lessons."

She blinked up at him, appalled at the command, but when he gave a little tug on her lead, she did it. Breasts swaying, nipples tingling, pussy hot and wet, she crawled across the soft carpet to the luxurious king-sized bed.

A tug on her lead stopped her cold. She looked up at him, annoyed. *What now?* She was behaving, following his obnoxious commands.

"The bed is for your Master. You may only come on it when he invites you. I've got a nice little nest for you to sleep in, my pet."

She looked at the small trundle bed in the corner, and sighed. Well, at least it looked soft, and she was worn out. Still, he didn't have to be such a jerk about it. She glared up at him, and the corners of his mouth twitched with laughter.

Damn it, he thought this was funny.

"Aren't you going to thank me for my kindness?" he asked, his voice gruff when she scowled at him. "Some slave girls sleep on the floor."

Shocked by the comment and his cocky attitude, she asked, "You expect me to thank you for my cot?"

His mouth kicked up in a reluctant smile. "Ah, defiant to the end. I like that."

His smile would have had her falling at his feet if she weren't already on her knees. It wasn't fair that he should be so sexy, so damned irresistible.

She glared at him, not bothering to hide her annoyance.

He dropped her lead. "To bed now, quick, before I decide to spank you for your insolence."

Shivering, she crawled toward the cot, dragging her leash, the eroticism of the moment making her tingle with anticipation. His hot gaze singed her like a caress, his potent masculinity claiming her. Oh God, if he didn't take her soon, she was going to blow like a volcano. Surely, he'd put her out of her sexual misery soon. She hadn't missed the potent bulge of his swollen cock. So sexy, and tumescent, she couldn't wait to see it, taste it.

Putting a little more sway into her backside than was necessary, she crawled the rest of the way to her cot, drinking in his rueful laugh. Oh yeah, he wanted her. And she was torturing him just as bad. Good! He knew exactly how frustrated she was feeling, so hopefully he'd do something about it.

She climbed into the cot, biting back a whimper when her clit pinched as she moved. She sucked in a breath when her hot bottom hit the cool sheets, her sex and anus on fire, burning for him.

Damn, he'd turned her on there, too, turning her into a slut for him. She glared up at him to tell him off, and the words wouldn't come out when she caught him stripping.

Oh my God, it's like my own private Chippendales show. No, better, she decided, her mouth watering as she took in his potent masculinity. He wasn't even looking at her and he held her captive. Knowing good slaves didn't eyeball their Masters, she still couldn't tear her eyes off him, not worrying about the consequences.

As he shed his leather vest, she decided he looked better without it—tanned skin over powerful muscles, washboard abs, and flat brown nipples. He pulled out a gun he'd apparently had secreted at the small of his back, and set it on the bedside table.

She was instantly chilled, the dangerous situation they were in reinforced, but it didn't stop her from ogling him. He unbuckled his belt, pulling it out of his loops. Doubling it up in one hand, he slapped it against his other open palm and looked directly at her with a smile.

"Tomorrow, I'll use this against your bare ass," he teased.

She shivered, her pussy quivering. It would just get her hotter, she knew.

"Would you like that? Speak."

"Yes, TA."

"Remember that answer when I'm whipping you tomorrow." He unzipped his pants.

Wincing, her bottom burning at the thought of the promised whipping, she still couldn't take her eyes off him as he stripped. His hand went to his zipper, and she stilled, holding her breath as he lowered it. She was dying to see his magnificent cock. It'd felt huge under her belly. He pushed the leather pants down his hips, pulling his cock and balls out of the confining garment, and she let out a gasp. Her eyes widened. He was simply magnificent. Huge, the head like a purple plum, the stalk, heavy ponderous. Her vaginal walls clenched automatically. Could she even take him? It was stirring, at half-mast, seemingly daring her to look at it.

He speared a look at her and smiled, seeing the all-encompassing focus of her gaze.

He walked toward her.

She quivered with anticipation, noting his lack of shame. The man was comfortable with his nudity. In command of his emotions. If only she could say the same. Still, the knowledge he was finally going to take her made her smile at him.

He grabbed her leash to unhook it, bending over her so they were a breath apart.

Their gazes locked.

Her heart skipped a beat.

With a growl, TA tugged her forward, his mouth slanting hungrily over hers.

She moaned, her lips burning under his. When he nipped her bottom lip, she opened her mouth, and his tongue surged inside, mastering her mouth as surely as he was mastering her. She moaned again, her pussy spasmodic, dampening the sheets, her body arching toward him.

And then, he pushed her away, unfastening her leash.

Panting, her body on fire, her nipples hard stinging peaks, it was all she could do not to reach out and grab him.

"Lie down," he ordered gruffly.

She did, shivering with anticipation. What would it be like to be taken by a man like him—hard, demanding, relentless, and *oh-so-hot*? Instead of climbing into bed with her, he turned to walk away with what she thought was a look of regret on his handsome face.

Her eyes widened. "But..." She moved to sit up.

He turned to look at her, frowning. "What part of 'lie down' didn't you understand?"

"I just thought..."

"I wasn't going to do this, but maybe it's just as well. I've been too soft with you."

Soft? That was ludicrous. He'd been nothing but hard, except where she ached for his hardness.

What was he going to do to her? She watched him walk to the armoire and come back with some chains and a dildo. Her eyes widening, her pussy quivered as she stared at the dildo.

"Spread your legs," he ordered.

She did, and gasped when he shoved the dildo into her pussy without a word. To her shame, she was so wet, it slipped right in. Her pussy immediately clamped around it, rippling.

Now, if he'd just move it up and down, she'd be satisfied. Or she'd happily do it, if that was how he got his jollies. She reached for it.

"No." He snagged her right hand and raised it above her head, cuffing it to the headboard. Then he did the same to her left.

She could only gape at him, stunned. When he started to shackle her spread legs to the footboard, she shook her head. "Please don't. I need to—"

"This pussy doesn't belong to you anymore. It will be satisfied when I say so, and not before. Now, be still before I get your cock gag. You wouldn't like sleeping with it."

Her mouth snapped shut. He'd do it.

He spread a comforter over her.

She stared at him, bemused, frustrated, and out of her head with desire. It was like a fever raged through her. As he tucked her in, she couldn't help noticing his cock was hard to bursting. But he wouldn't give it to her, the sadist.

She watched him walk into the bathroom, the shower turning on.

Her pussy rippled helplessly on the dildo, filled but unsatisfied.

She'd hover on the edge of coming all night, and he knew it, the bastard.

Chapter 5

TA stepped into the cold shower, and jacked off under the stinging spray. Damn, what she could do to him with a look, a word. Who was the Master here, him or her? The smell of her needy sex hung in the air, luring him to break the bond of new Master and slave, and take her to his bed.

He never took a new woman right away, but that bridge had already been crossed last night, and Courtney wasn't like any woman he'd ever possessed before. If she didn't ease up, she'd soon learn the folly of the raging beast in him.

But this wasn't a real claiming. It was all a game to her. In six days, the club would implode, and they'd go their separate ways. Why shouldn't he take what she was offering? Because she wouldn't want him under other circumstances, that's why.

Slapping off the shower, he got out, dried off, and stalked out to the bedroom.

Courtney's eyes were wide, tear damp, and fevered. He knew how hungry her pussy was. The dildo he'd inserted in her would tease, tantalize, but not satisfy. It was his job to soften her up, make her bend, keep her from giving the game away to Alexander. Still, he ached to take her. Unable to stop himself, he walked up to her bed. It almost seemed like she was the Master, not him. Her eyes were wide, shining, her voluptuous body writhing in its bonds, beckoning him.

"Do you want me, slave girl?"

She licked her lips. "Yes, sir."

"Show me," he demanded, stepping closer, tugging the quilt off her to reveal her beautiful body. His cock was rock hard again.

She arched her hips off the bed with a whimper. "Please, sir, take me."

Knowing he was a deluded fool, cursing his weakness, he pulled the dildo out of her quivering pussy and slipped a pillow under her writhing hips. He climbed into her bed, making a place between her bound legs. She was spread eagled, open for the taking.

"This is an instructive taking," he said, butting the tip of his throbbing cock against her wet cunt.

"Yes, sir."

"Look at me," he demanded, squeezing her breast. When her fevered gaze locked with his, he growled. "I'm in control. Do you want it this way? Do you want me this way?"

"Oh yes, oh yes, Dragon. Please fuck me."

"Who's your Master?" He bent to take a budding nipple into his mouth, drawing it hard onto the roof of his mouth, nipping at it.

"You, only you, Dragon. Please, I need you."

He gloried in her words even though he knew she didn't mean them. Drunk with the taste of her, he played with her other nipple, sucking it hard, nipping at it, making her moan and arch toward him. Letting it go with a final rough lap of his tongue, he fit his stiff cock to her, and thrust it home. Her hot pussy clamped onto him, making him growl out, "Mine."

"Oh yes," she cried, her hips snapping up to meet him.

He gasped as her cunt rippled against his thrusting cock. Ratcheting up on his arms to deepen the impact, he pounded into her again and again, Courtney's fevered cries driving him on. His pleasure was building, making his cock jerk inside her.

"Come now," he demanded, and she tightened around him like a vise as he spilled inside her.

She was crying, sobbing, coming, moaning his name...and he loved it. He couldn't help kissing her, stroking her, licking the tears off her face. He rolled to the side, and pulled her to him, still bound in her chains. There was enough play so that he could cradle her in his arms.

She sagged limply against his chest. "That was..."

"Intense," he suggested.

"Yeah, intense is a good name for it. You're making me crazy, you know."

"Good, it's mutual."

Courtney smiled against his skin, sated from their fucking. "Someone was here when you were gone."

He looked down at her. "Who?"

She tilted her head to look into his eyes. He was surprised by the information, and tense, she could feel his body tighten as if for battle. "I don't know, but I think it was Simeon. He was an older man with mean eyes. I figured he might be that boss you warned me about."

"Simeon Alexander, yeah. How did he get in?"

"Well, from the way the knob was rattling, I'd say he tried several keys before he found one that worked."

He frowned. "What did he want? Did he say anything?"

"He seemed to want to see if you'd spanked me. And he seemed kind of grumpy, and disappointed, even though you had."

"I should have known he'd have a skeleton key. Did that slime ball touch you?"

"No," she said with a shiver. "He just looked at me, grumbled something about you spanking me, and left. You're not in trouble, are you?"

"No. That's probably just Alexander's way of staying on top of things. Don't worry, I'll keep you safe, and in six days, it'll be all over. I'll set you free."

She lay back, satisfied, and strangely discontent. *He'd set her free. Did she even want to go free? Did she mean that little to him after what they'd just done?* A million questions whirled around in her head. She couldn't even ask who he was working for, CIA, the police, or FBI.

Instead, she decided to focus on the present. "What's going to happen to me during the next six days?"

"Starting tomorrow, in addition to your training with me, you'll be put up for sale, groomed, and instructed to your new Master's needs."

"Up for sale?" She didn't like the sound of that. "Do you mean in a room full of buyers, like a slave auction at a harem?"

"No. A videotape will be made of you, and the sale will take place on the internet or closed circuit television. You'll never actually get to see your buyer until it's all over and you're delivered to him."

"What kind of tape?"

His hand stroked down her back. "Sexual."

She'd been expecting that, recalling the pictures she'd flipped through on the web site. The spread-eagled woman with the dildo came to mind. It kind of reminded her of her position now, in chains in Dragon's arms. If the pictures were made with him, she could do it.

"And after that?"

"You'll be outfitted, trained to your owner's special needs."

"Special needs?"

"Anal sex, oral sex, bondage, the works. Whatever their kink."

Despite her previous sex life, she'd never done those things, considering them too demeaning. Now, a whole new sexual repertoire opened up to her. It was kind of scary and thrilling at the same time. She might not mind trying them with TA, but not with some stranger.

He smoothed a hand down her back.

She cuddled against him. "Tell me about yourself, Dragon, if that's really your name," she teased.

He grinned, and gave her ass a smack. "It's my last name."

"What's your first name?" Agents probably weren't supposed to discuss their backgrounds, their real names.

"Promise you won't laugh."

She nodded, wondering what deep mystery he was about to reveal.

"My full name is Tyrone Power Dragon," he said with a sigh. "Most sane people just call me Dragon."

She grinned. "So, your parents liked old movies. Now I see where the Bogie references come from."

"My mother."

She nestled against him, happy he was opening up a little. There was something else she had to know. "How many women have you trained?"

He chuckled. "I never spank and tell."

She knew she was sounding jealous, and tried to take it back. "Never mind, it doesn't really matter. Like you said, in six days, we'll go our separate ways."

"I will tell you this, I'm a dominant, and I like my partners to be submissive. And yes, I have had other lovers, but no, I've never trained women in a club like this. I prefer my liaisons to be private and personal. I've never been married, and there's no other lover in my life right now."

"Oh," she said, not quite knowing how to respond. It felt better to know she was his one and only, at least temporarily.

"How about you? Ever gone in for the kinky stuff before?"

"No."

He stroked her scar. "Tell me about it."

His touch was enough to transport her back to that day, even though she didn't want to go there. "We were riding home from the Banner's Christmas party. I was half asleep in the backseat. I heard my father swear, my mother scream, and a crunch as our car was hit. Then, everything kind of faded away. The child psychologists said it was temporary amnesia, and that my memory would come back. It hasn't."

"Why do you blame Arthur Stringfellow? After all, your father's crusade targeted several up and coming bad guys."

She froze, bristling at the question she'd been asked a million times. He didn't believe her. It hurt more than she wanted it to.

"Just a feeling I have," she said, brushing off the question. No need to let him in on her proof that had added up to zip.

And her father's words.

Chapter 6

Courtney woke up when her shoulder was jostled. She opened her eyes to find TA standing beside the bed. He was undoing her restraints.

She winced, stretching her limbs. Then, he was there, kneading away the kinks with his big hands.

Catching her gaze on him, he frowned.

"Up," he said, tugging her out of the trundle bed. He took her shoulders and pointed her toward the bathroom. "Go get the shower started for your trainer."

No morning kiss, no *how did you sleep*, or *sorry I handcuffed you to the bed*. Not the happiest morning person, she couldn't help being disgruntled. She thought about balking for a moment, but a swat from his big hand on her bottom made her yelp with surprise. It brought back the pecking order in a hurry. He might have fucked her last night, and shared a few laughs, and listened to her worries, but he was still Master of this domain.

She scurried into the bathroom, and rushed to the large walk-in shower. A glance at her reflection in the mirror told her she looked sleep rumpled and excited. She desperately wanted to shower, but she had TA to think of. He'd probably be pissed if she stole his hot water.

Gazing at her reflection in the mirror, she noticed the collar. Funny, she'd forgotten about it, seemingly gotten used to wearing it. Had he chosen it for her to cover up the scar she was so self-conscious about, or was it all a part of his act? Stepping closer to the mirror, she took a good look.

It seemed like antique silver, beautifully worked, with a star-shaped attachment that hung down at her collarbone. If one didn't know better, they would mistake it for an expensive piece of jewelry. Her hand went to the clasp, and then she glimpsed TA in the mirror behind her. He stood in the doorway, watching her, a speculative gleam in his eye. The man moved as silent as a ghost, just like the spy he was. She couldn't afford to underestimate him.

"You're wearing my collar. It marks you as my property."

"Property?" she repeated with a frown. "How delightfully unenlightened of you, Tyrone," she teased, knowing he'd hate it. "And what are you wearing, if I'm allowed to ask?"

He smiled. "My heart on my sleeve."

She frowned at him, not knowing what to think when he didn't take offense like she'd expected. "And if I believe that, you got a nice piece of swampland in Florida you'd like to sell me."

"Eden Bayou, Louisiana, actually." He stalked forward.

So that's where the slight cajón accent came from. It wasn't fake.

Her eyes widened at his approach. It was as if he was wordlessly staking his claim again. "Really?"

"Yes, really, and believe this, you'd better get my shower started, or you're in for it."

She turned to do his bidding. She switched on the taps, adjusting the heat, and then turned to look for him. She jumped when she found him standing right behind her, a satisfied male expression on his face. How had he snuck up on her so silently?

His heated glance raked her body, and she backed against the tile wall. He smiled as if he knew her reaction before she did, and stalked up to her. Her suddenly nervous gaze swept from his face to his rousing cock. He'd promised her a hard day. Just how hard would it be?

"Come," he ordered, taking her hand, and pulling her into the shower with him. "Wash me."

She stepped under the spray, wetting the sea sponge, lathering it with his sandalwood bodywash. Starting at his broad shoulders, she scrubbed him, her hands slicking washboard abs and thick sturdy thighs, to his even sturdier penis. It jumped, growing under her ministrations. When his hand pressed down on her shoulder, she sunk to her knees before him, the water cascading over her, and gazed up at the intense expression on his handsome face.

"Open your mouth, slave girl."

She obeyed, flicking her tongue to taste the broad tip of his penis, licking away a salty bead of pre-cum. With a sigh of surrender, she opened her mouth, and took the head of his penis inside. Sucking, she took him deeper into her mouth, hearing him groan. Funny, she'd never wanted to do this with any other man, but TA was like no other.

His hands tangled in her hair, holding her steady as he thrust deeper. "That's right, sugar. Show me how hard you can suck me."

She moaned, doing as he said, her cheeks hollowing as she drew on him. His groan was music to her ears as she sucked him hard. She felt awash in his passion, a part of him, as she took him deeper. Her own arousal peaked, her nipples budding hard, her pussy contracting with every thrust between her lips.

His cock jerked inside her mouth, coming in salty spurts. She swallowed his cum, milking it out of him.

"Sweet baby," he murmured.

Her heart contracted with pleasure. He cared for her. She knew he did, even if he hadn't given her the words. Releasing his cock, she looked up at him.

He reached down to tug her to her feet. She stood on wobbly legs, feeling rocked by confused emotions because she cared about him, too.

He let out a little growl as he backed her against the marble shower wall, his hands slicking over her hot, wet body. His mouth slanted across hers, and she sighed, kissing him back. His hand found her stiff clit, and with a firm press against it, he made her come. Her knees buckled until she was just supported by that maddening hand.

And then, he broke the kiss, letting her go. She trembled in the waterfall of spray. She blinked at him, tears of surrender in her eyes, but she couldn't make herself say the words.

Wordlessly, he positioned her under the spray, and started scrubbing her like nothing had happened. He gently shampooed her hair like she was a child, or maybe his prized possession. She stood there, rooted to the spot, enjoying the feel of his hands on her body, in her scalp. He drew away, rinsing her off. She closed her eyes and let the water cascade over her, rinsing away her tears, her cares.

He snapped off the shower and, gripping her hand, drew her out. Without needing to be told, she took the large bath towel and started dying off his back. She was a temporary slave girl, that was her role to play, her job to do, and the fact that she got to run her hands over his hunky body was a bonus, but she kept those thoughts to herself. He turned, and she gave the same treatment to his front. His cock twitched to life, and he let out a groan, pulling away.

"Enough." He stepped back. "Your things are in the medicine cabinet. You've got ten minutes to get ready and report back to the bedroom." He spun on his heel and stalked out of the bathroom, shutting the door behind him.

She stood there for a moment, staring at the closed door. She'd hoped for another tryst, burned for one actually, but he seemed determined to keep his distance. He was already regretting what he'd shared, she realized. It was probably against his code of conduct to tell her the truth about himself. It probably interfered with his mission.

He had his mission, and she had hers. As long as she was here, she'd do her own investigation, gather her own evidence. The FBI would object to her pursuing her story, so she simply wouldn't tell them. A shiver went through her as she contemplated lying to Dragon. It was only then that she realized she was still dripping wet, and reached for the towel. Reining in her imagination, she hurried to brush her teeth and dry her hair, brushing the long red tresses over her shoulders.

She hurried out of the bathroom and skidded to a halt.

TA was dressed. Dark leather pants again and a blue shirt that matched his eyes. Damn, she obviously wasn't getting any action this morning. He was dressed, and she was still naked, vulnerable, and horny.

She crossed her arms, suddenly nervous. A brisk knock on the door made her jump. A quick glance at his determined expression told her he knew how she was feeling, and he still wasn't going to give her any clothes.

"Go fetch breakfast."

She couldn't make her feet move. "But, I'm naked," she wailed.

"Would you rather fetch your paddle?"

Her bottom burned as hot as her face at the amused question. She scowled at him, recalling his mention last night, that this was the order of things. He intended to keep her naked and spanked. There wasn't a thing she could do about it without risking both their necks. Alexander was looking for an excuse to destroy him. She couldn't risk it.

Annoyed, she stalked over to the door. No doubt, it was another sadist sent to torment her. Turning the knob, she tore it open with an irritated scowl. Another woman stood there, bearing a covered tray.

Latina, gorgeous, and frowning, her gaze cut an annoyed swath over Courtney's nude figure.

The woman was wearing a purple gauzy caftan, and her feet were bare. Even though the woman wasn't wearing a collar, Courtney figured she was a slave or else playing one based on her take charge expression as she looked past Courtney to glare at Dragon.

She edged around Courtney. "Breakfast, Tyrone."

"What the blazes are you doing up here Tawny, and cut out that Tyrone crap."

"It's under the plate. And fuck you very much, too." She cocked a doubtful look his way. "I hope you know what the hell you're doing."

Courtney blushed as the other woman thrust the tray into her hands. Tawny seemed to hang onto it a moment more than was needed. Then she gave Courtney a frown before letting it go.

She held it, her stomach grumbling with hunger, trying to ignore the woman's speculative gaze on her. Who the hell was she and why was she so antagonistic? She had to be another agent. One who clearly didn't approve of her, she realized as Tawny walked out of the room.

"Put the tray on the table."

Glad to have something to do, she diverted to the small corner table. She laid down the heavy tray, inhaling the tantalizing aromas of coffee and something savory. She lifted off the cover to reveal one plate of breakfast and one cup of coffee.

"They didn't bring enough."

"Oh, there's enough. You eat when I say you can. Now, slave position number one."

She sank to her knees, blinking back frustrated tears. He could be such a bastard.

She watched him take a seat at the table, not caring she was breaking the rules by glaring at him.

He took a sip of the coffee, letting out a sigh of pleasure. "They make excellent coffee here. Would you like a sip?"

Angry but desperate, she nodded.

He held the cup out, and she lifted a bit taller to accept it, being sure to keep her hands at her sides, and took a little sip. It tasted like ambrosia. She sat back with a moan of satisfaction.

At his stern look, she said, "Thank you, sir."

He buttered a wedge of toast, munched on it, and then held it out for her to take a bite. Her stomach rumbled in anticipation. He ate half a strip of bacon and held the other half out for her to nibble. Bit by bit, he fed her off his plate until it was empty. Then, he wiped her mouth with the cloth napkin when he was done.

She sat back on her haunches, waiting for further instructions.

Leaning back, he looked at her. "Today, we're going to prepare you for your video."

She blinked at him, surprised it was happening so soon. She wasn't quite sure she was ready for this step. "How do we prepare?"

He reached out to smooth back her hair. "We'll go to the slave bazaar for some special items, and then we'll come back here to rehearse."

She liked the sound of that, if 'rehearse' meant another love-making session. And going to some kind of bazaar sounded adventurous, fun. "Slave bazaar. Where is it?"

"You like that, do you?" He smiled. "It's a little shop they've just opened in-house, probably in the basement of your aunt's old dance studio from what you said. Sorry, you won't be leaving the premises for the shopping spree."

The thought of going back to somewhere familiar and comforting had an immediate boost to her spirits. She'd spent some of her happiest moments here as a girl. She didn't mind not leaving, but in-house meant a trip down the hall, maybe in the elevator, heaven forbid, naked. She wasn't sure she was ready to parade the hall in her birthday suit.

"Why do we have to go out? We probably have all we need here."

"What's the problem?"

She looked down. "I don't want to go nude."

"You'll walk through the building bare-ass naked if I order you to, but don't you worry, most of the girls in-house wear caftans, like the one you saw Tawny wearing. They also go barefoot and nude underneath, of course. That's how we can tell them from the members."

"What about collars?" she couldn't resist asking. "I noticed Daisy wasn't sporting one."

"That's a little kink of my own," he said with a twinkle in his eye.

"Really?" She fingered her collar, feeling special even though it was ridiculous.

"After we shop, we'll go down for your second day evaluation meeting with Alexander. Be careful because he's already highly suspicious of you. Follow my orders implicitly and you'll be okay."

She looked at the folder under the plate. What had Tawny brought him, anyway? "Okay."

"If he speaks directly to you, remember, eyes down, and be good."

"Yes, sir," she said, quietly responding to his strict tone. He was almost as tense about this as she was.

"Now, get up." He turned and walked toward the closet. "Come, time for you to get dressed."

She rose and followed him. He pulled a gauzy caftan out of the closet, just as sheer as the lavender one Daisy had worn. It was emerald green, the same color as her eyes. It would cover her, but conceal nothing.

He handed the garment to her. "Put this on."

She clutched it, hesitating.

"Unless you'd rather go nude instead?"

Annoyed, because he'd probably make her do it to prove a point, she put on the caftan. The garment glided over her curves like silk, accenting the eroticism. She gazed down at it—loose, gauzy, and almost transparent in the light. Her nipples instantly stiffened, and she watched it happen, horrified.

She looked at him to protest, but he was already taking her leash off a peg on the wall. Black leather with a silver clasp that matched her slave girl's collar.

She watched him come to her, dismayed when he reached up to fasten it to her collar. Their eyes locked when she found herself efficiently tethered her to him. There was an intense smoky expression in his eyes. This suddenly felt very real, like she really was his possession. A little part of her melted, her nipples hardened, jutting harder against the silky fabric of her caftan. The flash of desire in his eyes told her he noticed her helpless reaction.

With a firm hand on her lead, he pulled her to him, bending to brush a gentle kiss over her tremulous lips. She let out a needy moan, kissing him back.

"You're mine, if only temporarily, so behave. Come," he said, tugging on her lead as he opened the door.

She padded after him, bemused, aroused, and scared. She only hoped they didn't run into anyone.

Her luck didn't hold. Two joking male voices told her they weren't alone. A second later, two black-leather-clad men with hard eyes passed who she assumed to be other trainers. One, younger and good-looking in an oily sort of way, the other brawny and older. She wouldn't want to be in either of their clutches.

The older Dom nodded. "Mr. Dragon."

TA stopped, and she almost blundered into him. "Reynolds." He flashed a dismissive glance at the younger Dom. "Sloan."

She stood frozen as the other Dom's eyes raked over her—the older man's sharp, the younger man's leering. It might have been her imagination, but she thought she felt TA grip her leash tighter.

"Well, I'm out of here," Reynolds said, walking away.

Sloan stayed put, giving Courtney a smarmy smile, and then turned to Dragon. "So, this must be your new trainee. Tell me, how's it going?"

TA smiled, moving a little to block Courtney from view. "As well as can be expected the second day out. How's your new charge? Hillary, isn't it?"

"I took her down to Schoolmaster Hedge's for a caning."

Courtney shivered at the joking mention.

"A little action with the bamboo works wonders for the stubborn ones. I'll have her jumping at my command by the end of the day."

"I'll bet." TA said dryly.

Sloan chuckled. "If you need any help with this pretty one, give me a holler."

"I'll keep that in mind," TA said, leading her away.

She could feel the other man's eyes on her like a prickling down her back. She wanted to pick up her skirt and run, but she knew that wasn't an option. Instead, she padded after Dragon, trying to block out the sights and sounds around her as they passed two other slaves in training, one in a red caftan, the other completely naked, and followed by a big man with a paddle.

The naked woman winked at her.

Courtney couldn't help blushing. This might be the style around here, but it was new to her.

They walked the hall, past the conference room where TA had spanked her. Her face flamed and her bottom warmed as she recalled that stunning turn of events.

Turning right, they went down a new corridor, past other closed doors she could only assume held other training bedrooms. She heard the occasional moan or cry through a closed door. Finally, they came to a large room at the end of the hall with open double doors.

TA led her into the room. Sex toys like the ones she'd seen in the armoire lined the shelves. Other things that looked like electrodes sat there, kinky items that she couldn't identify. Lingerie hung on racks.

Tawny, dressed in a slinky red dress, made her way to them, and Courtney tried not to gasp. As she'd surmised, the woman was more than a slave girl.

"Well, Dragon, I see you've brought your little trainee in for a fitting." She frowned and picked up a big double-pronged vibrator. "See anything you like?"

Appalled, Courtney stared at the device in the woman's hand and fumed. She didn't need a house to drop on her to know she wasn't welcome. Tawny's scowl practically screamed she was screwing up their mission.

She leaned forward to assert, "I can always take the steam tunnels out."

Tawny swore and scowled at Dragon. "Damn it, how could you have told her?"

He shook his head. "She's the one who told *me* about them."

Courtney shrugged and glanced around. "Aunt Gwen's storeroom was down here. Like I said, if you want me out, say the word."

"And you'd walk away?" Tawny scoffed.

"In a heartbeat." Courtney gazed into the other woman's eyes, finding understanding there.

Did Tawny and TA have something going on? It was a stupid, jealous thought under the circumstances. Tawny certainly acted like she had a special claim on him that went beyond duty. She bit back the words she wanted to say.

TA smiled. "I told you she was something."

Courtney glowed with pride.

TA fingered a set of silver Ben WA balls. "These are nice," he said, changing the subject, "but I don't need any toys right now."

Tawny nodded, stepping closer to him. "Oh, that's right, I forgot, you brought your own." She chuckled. "Well, if you ever want to compare wares, I'm your girl."

Courtney kicked the back of Dragon's calf, not hard, but enough to tell him she didn't like this. He turned to cast a repressive frown at her over his broad shoulder. She instantly regretted her hasty action. Thank heavens he wasn't the kind of Dom who'd take her down to Hedges for a caning. He'd take a strap to her backside himself. Her bottom heated at the errant thought.

He'd brought his own sex toys. All those devilishly erotic torture devices in the armoire were his property. Somehow, she wasn't surprised. It proved he'd told the truth, that this wasn't an act for him. He really was a Dom. And she was under his command, his slave girl in training.

She dropped her gaze.

He turned back to Tawny. "We need some lingerie for the video."

Tawny tilted her head and looked over Courtney once more with a jaded eye. "A black leather dominatrix costume should suit her, don't you think?"

He gave Courtney a long considering look, then shook his head. She tingled under his scrutiny. Despite Tawny's intrusive presence, she felt her pulse speed up, her nipples tingle and harden, her pussy melt. All of her reactions on display for both of them.

Dragon's breathing grew faster. "I want the honeymoon night white lace number."

Tawny looked Courtney over doubtfully. "We usually put that on the innocent looking baby blondes. I'm not sure it would work on a brassy redhead. Do you really think she can pull it off?"

Brassy redhead. Courtney stiffened at the insult.

"Trust me, she can pull it off. Besides, you'll make a nice commission off it no matter what she wears. Remember, it's all for the common cause."

Tawny shrugged. "You're the boss." She thrust a shopping bag at Courtney, a tossing bra, panties, a garter belt, stockings, and high heels into it until it was almost overflowing.

Courtney was a bit overwhelmed by the sheer volume and the speed. She wasn't used to being told what to wear, and she didn't take easily to it. A look at TA told her to hold her tongue.

She'd have to pick and choose her battles. She held tight to the bag, heaped full of white lace and ribbons.

"Come on, let's try them on," he said, leading her to a dressing room in back.

Courtney trotted after him, her arms full.

Once in the large dressing room, TA pulled the curtain closed, shutting them off from the offensive brunette, and she felt relieved. The vibes she got from the woman were probing, concerned.

TA took the bag from her and put it on the table, and then he sank into a nearby chair. "Take the caftan off and put the panties on first."

She slipped off the caftan and reached for the white satin panties, getting a little thrill because he was watching her. It wasn't until she pulled up the seemingly prim white panties that she noticed they were crotch-less. She'd been too caught up in his heated reaction to pay much attention. As she smoothed the high cut bikini across her lower abdomen, she noted her pussy was on display.

She looked at him, shocked. "I don't think..."

He raised a brow. "Now the bra."

At his firm tone, she slipped on the matching white lace bra. Maybe it was better to get the shock over with. It was better than going naked in the video, as she'd seen in the website clips. The white satin bra pushed her full breasts up and out, her pink nipples poking out the nipple cutouts. It was downright blatant.

"Very nice." He nodded at the pink and white ribbon hanging out of the bag. "Now, the garter belt, stockings, and shoes."

She did as instructed, then slipped her feet into the impossibly high heels. Her posture changed. Her bottom seemed more outthrust, and her breasts stuck out more. She turned to look at

Dragon. His hungry gaze roved over her, and she was suddenly glad she was wearing them.

"Perfect." He stood, his finger brushing her bare nipple, making it stiff.

Tawny poked her head around the curtain. "Alexander wants to see you in five, Dragon."

"Thanks. So, what do you think of my prodigy?" he asked with a smile.

"I guess she'll do," she answered, cautiously.

TA nodded. "I think we need some baubles to set it off."

Her glance lit with merriment. "What can I show you?"

Dragon's warm gaze raked over Courtney, and she felt like she was glowing in the face of his admiration. Tawny's unwanted presence faded into nothing.

"Nipple clamps, silver to match her collar."

Tawny smiled. "Follow me. I have an excellent selection of costume jewels."

"No. I think I'll spring for the real sterling." At her curious glance, he said, "It's an investment, of course."

She nodded. "I get it, a long term thing."

Courtney got it, too. She might be the first to wear them, but she wouldn't be the last.

He didn't confirm or deny Tawny's insinuation. She was too busy opening the locked jewel case to pick up on it.

TA tugged on Courtney's leash and pulled her closer. She watched him handle several of the nipple clamps, some pairs with chains to link them, some individual. He picked up a single one in the same smoky antique silver as her collar.

"Nice." He casually fanned Courtney's nipple until it budded, and then he clamped the clip on it.

Courtney bit back a moan, her knees almost buckling. It was more sexual than painful. She glanced down at the silver clamp on her swollen nipple, a green stone that looked like a genuine emerald hung from the tip, jiggling when she shuddered. Her eyes met his and she was lost.

"Perfect." He looked into her eyes. "Add them to my account."

"Yes, Mr. Dragon," She eagerly jotted it down.

He took the clamp off Courtney's nipple, and then tugged her back toward the fitting room. "Come. You need to change so we can make it to the meeting."

Courtney quickly changed back into her caftan while TA chatted with Tawny. She couldn't help being jealous that he seemed to enjoy the other woman's company, laughing at something she said. She folded the costume and packed it into the bag Tawny had thrust at her. Mustn't get her costume mussed before her video. The very thought made her knees buckle again.

She stepped out of the fitting room, bag in hand, and leash dragging the ground. It was humiliating. She noticed a different attitude from Tawny now, kinder, a little curious. It made her wonder what they'd been talking about.

"Come." TA took her leash and led her away.

They were heading back to the conference room where she'd been spanked. She'd been dreading this meeting with Alexander since he'd told her about it after breakfast. She didn't relish coming face-to-face with Alexander again. At least this time, she wasn't naked, yet.

"This way," TA said, steering her toward the table. He sat in a chair. "Position number one, and remember what I told you."

Footsteps came their way.

Courtney sank into position number one, hands lying on her thighs, palms up, her head down, grateful that she didn't have to look at him. She saw a pair of wing-tipped shoes stride by. Alexander's, she guessed.

"So, how goes the training, Mr. Dragon?"

"I'm making progress."

"I'll be the judge of that. Bring her forward for my inspection."

"Up," TA ordered.

She stood, trembling deep inside. She'd covered lots of hot spots around the globe, but she'd never felt more vulnerable, and not just for herself. She knew that a wrong word from her would blow Dragon's cover. Stepping forward, she kept her gaze lowered, knowing she was on shaky ground. Suddenly, Dragon's firm hand on her leash seemed like a lifeline.

"Come," he said, drawing her forward with a twitch on her leash.

Biting back a gasp of dismay, she stepped forward. She peeked up to see Alexander sitting at the table, a cup of coffee in his hand, his sour gaze on her.

"Tell me, girl, how do you like Mr. Dragon's training methods?"

She shuddered, murmuring, "F-f-fine, sir.

TA cut in, "She'll be ready for her auction Wednesday."

Alexander's suspicious gaze flicked back to him. "About that, I've moved it up to this evening."

TA scowled. "Tonight? Why?"

"A new bidder just joined the club, and he's looking for something special. A faraway buyer."

Courtney read between the lines. 'Faraway' meaning, she'd be less likely to cause them trouble. Alexander still didn't trust her. Smart man. She never should've bought her fake ID from an unreliable source.

"She'll be ready," TA grumbled.

Alexander leaned forward, a sharp look in his eye. "I'll need to have a look at her. Have the slave girl strip."

Courtney let out a mortified gasp, and Alexander's eyes hardened.

"Remove your caftan, slave girl," TA bit out. "Master Alexander wants to examine you."

She balked, hesitating. Dragon's hands tightened on her leash.

Relenting, her hands trembled as she slipped out of the garment, folding it over her arm. She raised her head to look at the man.

His squinty eyes swept over her, and it was all she could do not to cringe.

"So, tell me, little slave girl, what's your name?"

She cast a furtive glance at Dragon. *Oh no, what name had she used on the fake ID?* She was so shaken, she couldn't remember.

TA nodded, saying, "You may speak."

Good, maybe they'd think her hesitation had to do with her training. Her assumed name on the tip of her tongue, she swallowed.

Alexander's harsh gaze was making her nervous.

"My trainer calls me slave girl," she stammered.

"Delightful," he said, grinning. "And wearing a collar and leash. You must be very naughty, indeed."

She blushed. It reiterated her own thoughts that she hadn't seen anyone else wearing one. "So I've been told."

He burst out laughing. "Excellent. And have you given Mr. Dragon lots of trouble?"

She bit her lip, slanting a tense look at Dragon. He was watching her calmly, seemingly confident of her reply. "Some."

"Good. How about spankings? Has he given you a lot of them?"

Her bottom tensed at the question, and tears misted her eyes. It was too personal. She couldn't. But the commanding look in Dragon's eye told her to comply.

Licking her lips, she said, "Yes."

Master Alexander smiled. "Turn around, let me see."

She balked at that, but Dragon's warning frown made her turn.

"Responsive," Alexander said. The older man's eyes were sharp as they examined her naked body. "First rate breasts. She'll do well at the auction. I approve of your training methods so far, Dragon." Master Alexander stepped away. "Have her ready at eight tonight."

Courtney kept her gaze down, her face heating. She'd passed muster, but to what purpose?

Chapter 7

Courtney followed TA back to their room. Going up for sale so soon, that couldn't be good. She stood still just inside the door as he shut it behind him. A thousand questions were whirling around in her head.

He turned a charged look on her and she forgot all of them.

"We're going to have to accelerate your submission lessons." He stalked up to her.

She trembled with need as he pushed the caftan off her shoulders. It fell, pooling around her feet. She stepped out of it, picking it up to hand to him.

"Yes, Dragon, I'm yours to command."

His eyes darkened. "This isn't a game. You need to be punished for talking back to Alexander. You could have been killed."

She stepped up to him, rubbing her tingling nipples against him. "Then please punish me, sir."

He let out a groan, his arms wrapping around her, his hands exploring her body.

She trembled, needing him so badly.

"Go fetch your paddle," he said letting her go.

Shivering now that she was out of his embrace, she walked to the armoire on shaking legs. Could she really do this, bring him the paddle? A glance over her shoulder told her he was waiting, not overpowering her, and not forcing her. It was an obedience test, she decided, opening the armoire. She picked the paddle up, and clutching it, carried it back to him.

She held it out to him with steady hands. "The paddle, sir."

"Excellent." His hand caressed hers as he took the paddle. "You'll get it bent over the arm of the settee."

She walked to the settee and bent over the high curved arm. It was at the perfect height. Gazing at him, she watched him walk up behind her.

"Today, were going to work on arousal and self-control," he said with a frown, staring at her wet pussy.

He walked to her side, his voice heated, tense.

Her body shook and her pussy quivered. She needed him so bad. "Yes, sir," she said with a sigh, aching for him to touch her, make her come.

Smack! The paddle popped her left cheek.

"Oh." She *oofed* a breath, arching her hips. Her butt burned, and somehow it felt like foreplay.

Smack! He swatted her right cheek.

She whimpered, moaning.

And then, blows rained down, *left, right, left, right,* up from the bottom, making her yelp. Her ass and her thighs were on fire. Her pussy, too. Sometimes, the blows were soft, teasing, as he toyed with her. Each *smack* made her hotter, stinging, arousing, until she was squirming in tears.

"Do you like being paddled?" he asked.

"Yes," she confessed, whimpering as he laid into her harder. "Even though it hurts, it arouses me."

He let out a little sigh as he rubbed the paddle over her hot bottom. "Slave girl, do you have any idea what that kind of response does to a man? Do you know what kind of power that gives me over you?"

"Yes, and I don't care. Do it to me. Do everything to me."

She moaned when he laid the paddle on the settee and ran his hand over her paddled bottom. "Oh, that feels so good."

When his finger probed her anus, she arched toward it, letting out a little moan.

"Please, take me there."

"Quiet," he commanded. "Master is in control. Let's lube that tight little ass."

"Oh yes."

His finger spread lubricant into her tight anus. She bit back a whimper, burning to be taken that way despite the discomfort and slight pain. She moaned, her pussy walls clenching, her anus rippling against his probing digits. But she didn't move, her eyes rolling back in her head. She was so close to coming. She couldn't hold it, couldn't control her orgasm.

The ripples started, and she arched.

He swatted her thigh.

"Oh." She pouted, her orgasm fleeing.

"You can't come yet." He nested the big head of his cock against her anus. "I'm going to take your ass now."

She held her breath as he started to enter. It burned and stung, causing slight nausea, but yet it felt...pleasurable. Filling.

"God, you're tight." He groaned.

When he went deeper, her body trembled, clamping down.

"Mine," he said, thrusting to the hilt.

She gasped, her legs wobbling, and his cock buried deep in her throbbing ass.

He lay still against her, his breathing fast, letting her adjust to the invasion. He reached around her, his big hands cupping her breasts, his fingers pinching and rolling her nipples.

Moaning, arching her hips to take even more of him, she felt besieged, overwhelmed by sensation.

He moved, rocking into her, and she swelled around his big cock. She flexed against it, and regardless of discomfort, started to come.

"No." He pinched her nipple.

"Ow!" The fleeting pain pushed back her orgasm, easing her ripples.

"That's better. No coming until I give you permission. Five more strokes of my cock, and you can come. Any sooner, and you'll be punished."

The threat tamped her orgasm temporarily. Then, he started to ream her. Stroking hard, he pulled halfway out. Her pussy and ass both spasmed.

"That's one," he said. "Now, on the count of five, I want you to come, slave girl."

Five? She couldn't come on command. It was unheard of—barbaric.

She groaned, as he thrust into her.

"One."

On fire, her ass gripping him, he suddenly stroked harder.

"Two."

She gasped as he did it again. Her ripples increased, milking his thrusting.

"Three." He plunged deeper.

"Oh," she cried as his cock vibrated inside her.

"Four," he intoned.

"Five." He thrust hard and pinched her clit.

She exploded, crying as her bottom milked his cock.

He came inside her and sighed, her feeling well-used.

"Perfect," he praised, still atop her, dropping his head to rest against her back.

She sagged, sandwiched between him and the settee. Had she actually begged a man to fuck her ass? No, she'd begged *TA*. There was a big difference. It seemed right somehow.

He pulled out, and she made a little mew of protest. Ignoring it, he grabbed her wrist and led her into the bathroom, turning on the taps. He efficiently scrubbed her, dried her, and led her back out to the bedroom.

"Go lie on the bed, on your back."

She scrambled into bed and watched him go to the armoire. What other torture was he going to devise? He walked back to the bed carrying a red leather pouch-like device.

"This is a butterfly. It provides electrical stimulation to a woman's clit, and can be used to make a slave come for hours," he said, attaching the mouth-like device to her bare pussy, fastening the straps so that it stayed in place.

She gasped as he fit the device close to her already sensitized pussy.

"I'll start you at low and we'll move up."

"Okay." She was curious about the possibilities.

She watched him pick up a remote control box. When he touched the dial, a warm tingling started in her pussy, and her clit seemed to stiffen.

"Oh shit," she breathed.

"No talking." He bumped it up a notch.

She whined at the zing, arching her hips off the bed.

"Down," he said, pushing her tummy.

She had no choice but to feel the fire on her clit and pussy. Her hips rolled uncontrollably as he slowly built up the charge. She whimpered, moaning. It was torture, sweet torture. She gazed deep into his cloudy blue eyes as the pressure built inside her.

"Ready for more?"

She nodded, and he pushed up the intensity.

She shrieked, her orgasm taking her into orbit. Waves after waves rocked her.

When she opened her eyes, he was looking at her hard, his eyes burning with intensity. Was he troubled or turned on? Probably both, she decided.

He unsnapped the butterfly and flattened his hand on her still quivering pussy. He pressed his palm against her mound, and she arched into his touch with a cry, coming again.

"You'll need to thank your Master for his attentions."

She licked her lips. "Thank you, sir."

"Good. We'll practice this later in other positions. I'll need to use it tonight in the video."

She nodded, trembling at the prospect of doing this in front of a camera.

That evening, TA led Courtney down the hall to the video studio.

She shivered, feeling like his firm hand on her leash was a lifeline. Dressed in the crotchless panties, peek-a-boo bra, high heels, garter belt, and stockings, she was glad he had added a matching robe to save her from curious glances.

He stopped outside the door and turned to look at her. "I'll be with you every step of the way. Rely on me for your cues."

"I trust you," she said, seeing the flare of satisfaction in his eyes at her admission. Her trust meant something to him.

He nodded and led her into the studio.

She blinked at the bright lights. She was surprised to see the stage set like a boudoir. It was different than the techno looking set she'd viewed on the website, but the rack was there, the frame she'd once seen a woman tied to.

"About time," Mario said, looking up.

"Perfection takes time." TA led her forward.

Mario looked over his shoulder at another man. "Bob, she's ready."

Courtney looked at the burly frame of the guy she'd seen in the website photos, and shuddered. Not him, the guy who wielded the gigantic dildo.

"I'm doing it." Dragon's hands tightened on the leash before unhooking it.

Mario scowled. "But, Bob—"

TA shot him a determined glance. "She's my trainee, it's my equipment, and I'm doing it."

Bob shrugged. "No skin off my nose. It'll give me time to have a beer before the next one."

TA took Courtney's hand and led her to center stage. "Look at me."

She centered her nervous glance on his solid presence, noticing when he was tense, he lapsed back to creole, and she instantly let go of her fear.

"It's just you and me out there. Ignore those bozos."

She nodded and watched him walk back to stand beside the cameraman.

He nodded, the camera started rolling, and her training came back to her.

She unfastened the robe, slowly taking it off the way TA had told her to, and then her seductive instincts kicked in.

She dropped the robe off one shoulder, shooting a come hither look at Dragon on the other side of the room. His hot gaze made her pussy cream. She turned her back to him and let the robe drop, slowly baring her back and bottom in the cut out undies and garter belt. Letting the robe fall to the floor, she turned to face him, her fingertips running over her body to cup her breasts, holding them out to him, offering them to him. Her fingertips fanned over her nipples, making them hard. And then her hand drifted down over her abdomen to her pussy, tracing the cleft to lightly touch her clit. It was stiff, and she let out a little moan.

TA stepped into the shot then. "I see you got started without me, naughty girl."

"I'm sorry, sir." She still played with herself, getting into the acting.

"You'll have to be punished for that. Come." He led her to the frame, tying her spread-eagle to it.

She couldn't stop gazing at him, lost in his hot eyes, in what she knew was coming. He rolled her nipples, making them harder, and then attached her silver clamps. She whimpered in ecstasy, rolling her hips.

"That should control your naughty nips. Now, to take care of your hungry pussy." He picked up the butterfly and touched it to her pussy, clamping it in place like a hungry little mouth. Then, he grabbed the control box. "I'll start out slow," he said, adding, "And make you come till you scream, my naughty little bride."

She gasped when he pushed the button, a warm tingle focused on her clit. He did it again, and her hips snapped forward as he slowly brought up the intensity.

"Like that, do you?" he asked in a teasing tone.

"Yes, sir," she said, gasping as he zapped her harder.

He did it again, and she came.

Pushing the intensity higher, he made her come with a dizzying scream, passing out.

When she came to, she was in Dragon's arms, on his lap as he sat on the settee. She blinked up at him, at the cameraman, and the video that was still rolling.

The cameraman looked surprised and turned on.

"And what do you say?" TA coaxed.

"Thank you for disciplining me, sir."

He gave a cutting look at Mario, who switched off the camera.

"Damn, that was hot," Mario commented. "I'll bet she makes top dollar in the auction."

"Right," TA said, pulling her robe around her and carrying her down the hall to their room.

He took her into the shower, washed her, and then took her to bed.

She felt safe, protected, and aroused in his arms. She wasn't going to let herself speculate about who might have watched her sexual performance.

He tucked her into bed, and she instantly turned to him, seeking the comfort of his touch.

"There's my girl." He ran a hand over her ass, between her legs.

"Oh please, take me," she moaned, pressing her hot body to him, still on fire.

"No. I don't want you right now. You shouldn't say that. A real Dom wouldn't like you making the moves. When you go back to the real world, forget about all this."

The rejection stung, but she knew it wasn't true. She could feel the evidence of his arousal pressed hot against her leg.

"Why not? You know you want me."

"No."

"I don't believe you. Well, maybe there's another Master who'll take me."

"I should paddle your ass for saying that."

"Why don't you?"

"Don't tempt me, slave girl." He gave her a hard spank on the ass. "You're still under my control for the rest of the week. I can see I'll have to make it harder on you."

Tears of apprehension misted her eyes, but she didn't shrink away. He was so strict, but he was still pushing her away. It made her a little crazy.

"Promises, promises."

His hand came down twice more, smacking her round bottom. "And that's two and three. One for speaking out of turn, and one for questioning me." He pinched her nipple hard. "Never question your Dom."

She sniffed, blinking back tears.

He rolled her over. "Position number two, now. I'm going to take your ass again, slave girl."

She rolled into the position, her breasts pressed against the sheets, her nipples tingling, and her bottom high in the air, waiting for her ass fucking.

Cold lube, and then his cock was touching her, entering, filling her.

She groaned, stimulated and stretched tight, instantly on the verge of orgasm.

"Now we're going to go for a count of seven," he said, resting against her quivering bottom.

She whimpered, nodding.

"Good girl," he praised, sliding slowly in and out of her.

She gasped, overcome by the sensation. She was stretched so tight. Her pussy and ass clenched at his huge cock as he started to piston it in and out of her faster.

"One."

"Two."

"Three," he growled, adding, "And don't you dare come early."

"Oh." She clamped onto him, her pussy pulsing, her ass twitching, pleasure building. She'd never make it to seven strokes. She arched.

"No," he said, reaching between her legs to flick her clit in warning.

She cried out, hurt, sobbing.

"Four." He fucked her harder, deeper.

She gasped, totally focused on the friction, the pressure, the extreme pleasure of having her ass claimed by him. Then he rolled his hips, changing the angle. She let out a surprised gasp.

"Five. Six. Seven."

With a shriek, her body clamped on his thrusting cock, ripples tugging him as she started to come. She felt him shoot deep inside her. When it was over, she knelt panting, his cock still buried inside her. She had a wild wish to fall asleep like that, still connected to him, his cock still buried in her ass.

But then, he was pulling out, and she let out a little cry of protest.

"Stay," he said giving her a playful swat.

She stayed in place, her ass in the air, and watched him go into the bathroom.

He turned on the shower and came back for her, scooping her off the bed and carrying her into the bathroom. She could walk, but it felt right to be taken care of by him. She was his little slave girl, if only temporarily.

He carried her into the shower and set her down, letting her slide down his body, the spray cascading on both of them.

"Oh, sir." She leaned into him.

He washed her like a prized possession, giving her a dark look when she tried to help him. She stood, rinsing off under the spray as he scrubbed himself. As if feeling her eyes on him, he turned and pinned her with a hot gaze. He wanted her, she knew he did, even if he didn't want to admit it or it went against his mission.

He quirked a finger, saying, "Come here, slave girl."

She felt almost shy as she stepped the three paces to stand before him. It was funny, after all they'd shared, all they'd done. She licked her lip, and his gaze flared. His mouth came down on hers as his arms went around her, his hands cupping her ass, tugging her tight against him. She whimpered, rubbing her hard nipples against his hair-roughened chest, and he let out a growl.

He picked her up and impaled her on his cock, thrusting into her.

She convulsed in no time, her pussy tightening. Moaning, she rode him, TA thrusting again and again into her, until they were both spent.

Chapter 8

Ty awoke to soft hands stroking his rousing cock. He opened his eyes to find Courtney kneeling beside him on the bed, and taking his cock into her mouth.

Last night's events seemed to have loosened what remained of her inhibitions. He could see it in her inspired performance, feel it in her fevered response back in the room afterwards. She might not be a traditional sub, but she was turned on by the fantasy. Still, she had to learn that a real Dom would make all the moves, would not put up with an unsolicited morning blowjob. When she'd joked about finding another Dom to take her in hand, he'd almost lost his mind.

Groaning, he thrust his cock into her hot mouth, and pressed her head down to take him deeper, shocking her. He could feel it when she stiffened for a moment, but she just kept sucking, making little noises as she went down on him.

"I'm going to come, and don't you dare spill a drop or you'll be punished." He groaned, tightening as she sucked harder in response to the threat to paddle her ass.

He shot a big load into the back of her throat, hearing her gulp, swallow, and suck. Drops of cum flowed between them, wetting his thighs, and her gorgeous tits.

It was time for his student to get a real picture of submission. He pushed her off of him, and she let out a little squeak as she tumbled back on her ass in the soft bed.

He tried hard to look stern when he really found her charming. "Crawl around to the edge of the bed, position number two for your punishment."

Eyes big as saucers, damp with startled tears, she did as ordered, creeping around so that her curvy ass was up in the air, her tits pillowed against the covers. The blush on her face reached all the way to her tempting bottom.

He walked to the armoire, opening it, and taking out a strap. A few stripes across that luscious butt would reinforce the message that this wasn't something she should try in the real world.

"Time for your whipping." He stepped behind her, seeing her take in a tremulous breath. "Ready?"

"Yes, sir."

He flicked his wrist and gave her a taste of leather.

She let out a yelp, and a red splotch marked her left cheek.

"Now, as I whip you, I want you to repeat, *I'll try harder*. Say it."

"I'll try harder," she said.

He swung the strap, lashing her from the bottom of her butt.

"I'll try harder." Her hips writhing, she arched her back.

"Good," he said, watching the red stain spread across her gorgeous ass. Her whole body seemed to glow, and she appeared to be taking it as foreplay. "Bottom higher, please."

She raised higher at his command.

He gave her another swipe. A smack caught the bottom of her other cheek.

"I'll try harder," she cried.

"You bet you will," he muttered, more turned on than he wanted to admit. He swung the strap.

Smack! It hit her right in the middle.

She jumped, squealing, "I'll try harder."

He bit back a groan, his cock twitching. "No jumping. Stick your bottom out as far as it will go."

Trembling, she obeyed, arching her back, stretching her bottom toward him. She grew still—holding her breath—waiting for it.

"Now, spread your legs," he said with a growl.

Whimpering, she moved them a few inches apart.

"More." He nudged her knees apart. "I want to spank that bad pussy." He could smell her arousal, see her wet pussy, her stiff little pink clit. It would hurt like hell, and it would be the dose of cold water she might need to snap her out of her slave girl mentality. He rubbed the warm strap against her sexy mound. "Ready?"

"Yes, sir," she said with a whimper.

He drew the strap away, giving her a final flick to the mound.

She screamed, her pussy twitching. "I'll try harder, sir."

Her cunt rippled on the verge of orgasm. God, to be in that tight little pussy, to feel it squeezing his cock as she surrendered her body to him. He couldn't stand it.

She rolled her hips. "Please take me, Dragon. I need you inside me."

His cock stiff, bobbing behind her, he gave in to his base desires, dropping the strap. Fitting his cock to her pulsing cunt, he thrust home.

She moaned, her walls clamping around his dick. He wanted to moan, too, because she felt so good.

Gripping her hips, he pulled almost out of her and then surged back in. She whimpered, her whole body trembling, wetting the head of his cock, enhancing the friction as he slowly and thoroughly fucked her. He changed his angle, rubbing tight to her G-Spot, and she let out a mewling noise, turning him on more.

And then, she came, tremors that milked his cock, making him thrust deep and holding her as he spurted his tribute.

"Oh my," she murmured when it was over.

He leaned against her hot bottom, catching his breath. This wasn't going as planned. Instead of driving her away from the thought of becoming some other Dom's slave, she was making him crazy with lust.

Telling himself that the time to start distancing himself was now, he pulled out of the warm harbor of her cunt and gave her a brisk swat to the bottom. "Up."

She rolled out of bed, blushing, and he wanted nothing more than to tumble with her again.

But it didn't work that way. He had a job to do, and a mission to run. He didn't have the time to get lost in Courtney's arms. Besides, he didn't do long term relationships, and if by some miracle they found each other when this was over, she was definitely the kind of sub who would require a relationship.

Except, she wasn't really a submissive, just playing a role. It wasn't her fault that she got seduced by the power of Dominance. He'd have to do the thinking for both of them.

Deciding to get his head back in the game, he stalked to the dresser, pulled out a silver caftan, and tossed it at her.

She caught it with a hurt look in her green eyes.

Chapter 9

Courtney followed TA to the conference room, feeling hurt and abandoned. He'd been so cold as she'd dressed this morning—polite, distant—she didn't like it one bit.

Added to the misery of feeling cut adrift by her trainer, she had to face Alexander again. She wasn't looking forward to it. It was time to find out who'd bought her.

Just thinking about the sale brought back memories of her strip tease and what came after. She was embarrassed by her shameless performance last night, but the way TA had loved her afterwards had almost made the whole thing worth it. He was the only reason she'd made it through unscathed. She certainly couldn't have done it with Bob, but with Dragon, it was like she'd forgotten about the cameras.

This time, when he led her to the conference room, Alexander was already there, seated at the table, waiting for them. He smiled and motioned them forward. "Bring the little slave girl here, Dragon."

When he steered her to one of the chairs, she was startled, but gratefully slipped into it. She felt too shaky to kneel on the floor.

"There's my little star." Alexander was suddenly all smiles. "You were a big hit, slave girl."

Courtney's face flamed and she shot a troubled glance from Alexander's greed-filled gaze to Dragon's troubled one. She took small consolation in the fact that he obviously didn't like sharing his woman with the world. "Oh."

Alexander smiled at Dragon. "And you, Dragon, may have a future as a porn star. There were a few ladies who made inquiries."

"Not for sale," he muttered, scowling at Alexander.

Alexander shrugged. "That's what I figured." He turned to look at Courtney again. "It's time for you to see your new Master." He flipped open a folder containing an eight by ten black and white photograph.

She blinked, gazing at the cold image of the club member who'd purchased her. He was older, and there was a cruel set to his mouth.

"He wants you to call him Sir when you meet him on Saturday."

Courtney shivered, but then immediately calmed. What Alexander didn't know was that TA would have saved them both by then. He'd promised to get her out of here, and she believed him. On top of that, she wasn't going to call anyone but TA 'sir.'

Still, she saw Alexander was waiting for a response, and nodded.

He seemed satisfied with her silent acceptance because he turned to look at Dragon. "The buyer wants to know which brand butterfly you used and how many volts."

He scowled. "Right. I'll tell Tawny everything she needs to get ready for him."

"Excellent, that little slave bazaar of hers has turned out to be a gold mine." He smiled and closed the folder. "Then everybody's happy."

Courtney started to rise, but a cutting glance from TA made her settle back down. What now? She wanted to get away from this odious mob boss.

"Any special requests?" TA asked.

Alexander nodded. "The usual bondage, corporal punishment, and lots of anal."

She shivered, chilled by the mention she'd do those intimate acts with anyone but Dragon, yet she knew better than to show her shock. Folding her hands in her lap, she tried to look blasé about the whole thing, giving Alexander a little half-smile when he looked at her.

"Right," TA said gruffly.

Keeping his focus on Courtney, Alexander said, "I trust she's been opened by you."

"I have," she cut in before TA could answer.

She saw his strict glare from the corner of her eye, and bit her tongue. A proper submissive wouldn't be talking back to the mob boss. If he took it the wrong way, they were both in trouble.

Alexander only chuckled, and she let out a sigh of relief, but glancing at the stern look on Dragon's face, she knew she was in trouble with him.

TA let go of her leash. "Get down on the floor, training position one, in the corner, now."

She trembled, standing. She rushed to the corner of the room with a troubled glance back. Alexander's watchful gaze stayed on her. TA however, was instead paying vigilant attention to the mob boss's every move. She sank on her knees, hoping she hadn't given them away as frauds.

Alexander's eyes narrowed. "Dragon, I can see you've got your work cut out with this one. I trust you'll have her sharp tongue in check before we hand her over to Charles."

Courtney tried to tune Alexander out, keeping her eyes focused on Dragon's strong presence. He met her gaze with a steady one of his own, and she felt like she was able to breathe again.

"Don't worry, I've got her well in hand," he said, rising.

Alexander leaned back in his chair, taking a sip of his coffee. "Dragon, one more thing. Her client likes to be milked. You and Tawny will instruct her."

Courtney tried not to shudder as she knelt, waiting for Dragon's command to rise.

Instead, he stalked over and took hold of her leash giving it a twitch.

She stood, her eyes only on him. She could do this if she kept focused on him.

He nodded, and led her out into the hall.

What did Alexander mean by *he likes to be milked?*

Chapter 10

Courtney followed TA directly from the conference room to the slave market. Apparently, she wasn't going to be given time to prepare for the job. TA seemed hyper-focused, looking over his shoulder at her as they moved. His mind was no doubt on his mission, while she was agonizing about spending time under Tawny's thumb.

Her only comfort was that the halls were relatively empty today. No leering poaching slave trainers lurked about. She didn't even see any club members, girls, or semi-naked giggling women, nor coolly assessing Doms. It was pure paradise, except that she was being led to Tawny. She was nervous, wondering what the woman would teach her, do to her.

TA hustled her into the Slave Bazaar. "Now, be good for Mistress Tawny," he said, unhooking her leash.

Courtney blinked back tears. She didn't want to be anything for Mistress Tawny, didn't want to fall into Mistress Tawny's clutches one little bit. Didn't he know how much Tawny disliked her, or were men oblivious to such things?

Funny, but she almost felt naked without her leash.

"You're late." Tawny breezed in from one of the fitting rooms, the one where Courtney had done her striptease for Dragon, bringing back memories.

This probably wouldn't be sweet. She turned to look at Tawny, today decked out in black leather, the picture of a dominatrix.

TA walked over to say something to Tawny, and Courtney couldn't take her eyes off the two of them as they talked in hushed tones. They both exuded power. From their glances back at her, she could tell that the conversation was about her. She strained to hear, but couldn't.

Tawny turned to look at her.

Busted, she faced straight ahead.

TA walked back to her. "I'll leave you in Tawny's capable hands, slave girl. See you in an hour."

A whole hour alone with this woman? She didn't know if she could bear it. She watched him walk away and tried not to cry. She looked back at Tawny and saw a speculative expression on the other woman's face. Tawny seemed to have guessed how Courtney felt about him.

She was falling hopelessly in love with her trainer.

"I've got a rack of garments set up in the dressing room for you. Try them on, and then we'll get down to business."

Courtney rushed into the fitting room, eager to get this over with. She took off her caftan and slipped into the first garment, little more than a crisscrossed web of red leather that left most of her bare. It was embarrassing. She didn't want to show it to Tawny, and hopefully, she wouldn't have to model it.

"The first one fits," she called from the fitting room.

"Come out here. I must inspect each one."

Courtney sucked in a deep breath. She'd been afraid of that. She stepped out to notice several customers in the shop now. One of them, Stringfellow.

She froze in her tracks. She'd been dreading this since she'd come. Based on his glare, he still remembered her snooty attitude and didn't like it. But there was no other recognition in his cold eyes.

She let out a relieved breath as his grip tightened on the riding crop. She tried to ignore him as she walked toward Tawny.

"Not bad," Tawny said, looking her over. "They fit you well."

"Thank you." Courtney bit her lip, feeling proud but self-conscious.

Her neck prickled a warning a second before the riding crop slapped against the counter, inches from where she was standing. Stringfellow stepped in front of her, raking a hot gaze over her body in the revealing lingerie. Blushing, she stood her ground, glaring back at him.

Tawny leaned over the counter. "The bazaar is about to close, sir. Are you buying that riding crop, or are you just looking, Mr. Stringfellow?"

"Buying," he said, pulling out a gold card and sliding it across the counter to her, all the while never taking his focus off Courtney. "When does she go up for sale?"

Courtney felt dirty from his ogling glance. She balled her fists at her side, standing tall, refusing to let him intimidate her. That's what his action with the riding crop was probably intended to do.

"You're too late."

"Quiet slave," Tawny reprimanded as she handed the credit card back to Stringfellow. "But she's right, sir, I'm sorry. You're too late if you were thinking of buying her contract. She's already spoken for."

Courtney stared into his icy gray eyes, suddenly grateful for the woman's strong vibes.

He kept his gaze locked on Courtney. "When?"

"She went on the board last night, and was purchased within half an hour. Apparently, the bids were coming in fast and furious."

"Damn, I knew I should have blown off that business dinner." He scowled. "Is it a firm offer?"

"Rock solid."

Courtney felt his gaze rove over her again, as if he couldn't look away.

"Slave girl," he said, inching closer. "How about I buy you out of your contract, and you come up to my private quarters for some fun?"

Trying not to show him how vulnerable she felt, Courtney simply shook her head. She wasn't going anywhere with him.

Tawny cleared her throat. "The store is closing, sir. Please take your purchase and go. You know the girls don't have any say in who they go to."

"Back off, woman." He reached for Courtney's arm. "I'm a charter member. I'll go when I'm good and ready."

Courtney shrunk back, barely eluding his grasp, snatching the riding crop off the counter. She held it in front of her, backing away, when Tawny suddenly came around the counter.

Tawny grabbed him, bending his arm behind his back, and force-marched him toward the door.

"Hey, bitch, I'll get you fired. You can't treat me this way."

Tawny jerked his arm up higher, making him squeal. "The Slave Bazaar is its own separate entity, sir, and I make my own rules. If you don't like it, don't shop here. Now, out you go." She gave him a shove, his momentum making him crash against the far wall.

Stringfellow straightened and turned. Glaring, he took a step toward the bazaar. A glance at Tawny standing in the doorway and Courtney brandishing the riding crop behind her seemed to make him reconsider.

"I'm going to report this to Alexander, bitches."

"Be my guest," Tawny shut the door in his face and locked it.

"Thank you," Courtney said.

Tawny turned an amused glance at the crop in Courtney's hand. "You're welcome. We're on the same side here. Come." She turned to walk into a side room.

Courtney put down the riding crop and followed her, warmed by the mention of being on the same side. She'd known Tawny didn't trust her and thought she was bad for Dragon.

"TA told me he's already taught you training positions one and two. I'm going to demonstrate some more advanced moves, requested positions from your buyer." Tawny sank to the floor on her knees. "In position number three, I want you to kneel and open your mouth. When your Master inserts his penis into your open mouth, you will milk him orally. Now, you try."

"But we don't really have to...I mean, it's all fake and..."

Tawny's grudging approval faded, and Courtney sighed. She got down on her knees, hands at her sides. She opened her mouth wide, her cheeks flaming.

Tawny approached her with a funny looking slim dildo.

"This is a training unit of my design. I'm going to insert it into your mouth in a moment, and I want you to draw on it. First you suck, next you rub the penis with your mouth, and then you repeat. The sensors on the unit will tell me if you're doing it right."

Courtney didn't pull away as the vinyl dildo was inserted into her mouth. It was lifelike with a bulbous head. She sucked on it, and then drew her mouth softly but firmly along it.

"Excellent," Tawny praised. "You need to keep doing it until your Master is drained. But for now, I'll set the timer for five minutes."

Sucking, her jaw aching, Courtney struggled to master the technique. The bell went off twice when she fell out of rhythm.

Tawny came back the second time. "Just pretend its Dragon's cock, honey. It should help."

Courtney blushed, then closed her eyes, picturing Dragon's cock slipping through her lips, her mouth drawing hard on his tip.

What seemed like seconds later, there was a tap on her shoulder. She opened her eyes to find Tawny's indulgent smile.

"Your five minutes are up. You did well. Now, watch me as I demonstrate position number four. Tawny got down on the floor, and lay on her back. She spread her legs up and out, her inner thighs and pussy exposed. "Your new Master will expect you to flow into this position gracefully. He'll take you this way, and whip you this way, too."

Courtney nodded, still holding onto the wet dildo. She gazed at Tawny's wide-open position and the other woman's comfort with it.

Tawny rolled out of it and stood. "Take off your garment and lie down, taking your training dildo with you. You're going to practice milking him vaginally."

Courtney reluctantly stripped, folding the lingerie and placing it on a table. Gripping the dildo, she sunk down onto the floor, and opened up into the position, not quite as gracefully as Tawny had. Her face heated because she was naked, on display, but the other woman looked at her with an understanding smile.

"Tell me about you and Dragon," she asked curiously.

Courtney blinked up at her with a blush. "There's not much to tell. He must be a friend of my editor's. He showed up at the paper and conned me."

"Yeah, he's good at that."

She rolled her eyes. "So I noticed. Anyhow, I was all set to go off on his wild goose chase when I found out Laura was here."

"And you gave up on your obsession, just like that."

She glared at Tawny. "Does the whole FBI think I'm obsessed?"

"Yeah," she said with a grin. "But don't take it too hard. We're all a little twisted."

"You and Dragon."

"Good God, no. He's like the annoying big brother I never had."

"I can see that," she said. "It hasn't been an easy adjustment for me, but he's been patient."

With a sigh, Tawny turned away. "I agree, he needs someone like you. But I've got to warn you, don't get too attached to him. You know this is only temporary."

That was the problem. She'd fallen for him, and the other woman obviously knew.

Lying there, waiting for the command to get up, she watched her face. Tawny's body language was tense, like they'd crossed some invisible line.

"Insert your training dildo into your vagina, please."

Courtney complied with a wince, the wet dildo easily slipping into her pussy.

"It's essentially the same technique, but you only get to use your vaginal muscles. I want you to squeeze your muscles, then let go, and repeat, milking him vaginally until he comes."

Courtney squeezed.

Tawny nodded. "That's it. Keep going. You're going to have to learn to do this for an extended period. Gentlemen from his area of the world love this technique.

Mortified, Courtney kept at it, milking the dildo, arousing herself helplessly. She closed her eyes, pretending it was Dragon.

Chapter 11

Ty took a walk outside, slipped around a corner, and jumped into the passenger seat of the panel van idling at the curb. He slammed the door shut and turned to look at Nick Harrison. The agent in charge looked a little worse for wear. The way this mission was going, he couldn't blame him.

"What's up? Why the sudden summons?"

"Ned Barnes is dead. Shot execution style outside the safe house last night."

"Crap. I just saw Alexander. I didn't see any signs he was in on to the operation. It could be just an unrelated case that caught up with Barnes."

"Yeah, we both know he was on a lot of people's hit lists, but I don't like it."

"Me, neither. I want to pull Courtney out ASAP."

"Right. I suppose that can be arranged."

"I left her with Tawny, who's teaching her some new techniques."

At Nick's sharp glance Ty took pity on him and said, "Tawny's fine, in her element, selling stuff. You know she can handle herself. Man, when are you going to make your move with her?"

Nick closed his eyes, saying under his breath, "None of your damned business, swamp thing."

Ty smiled, knowing exactly how the other man felt. His days with Courtney were coming to an end, and his gut ached at the thought. "Don't fret, the mission will be over in a few days, and you'll have her back."

"I'll cook up a good excuse to spring your girl a day early. An urgent summons from her buyer, accompanied by an extra fee should grease the wheels."

Ty looked down the sidewalk to make sure the coast was clear, and then got out of the van. "Later."

Courtney bit back a little moan, milking the dildo with the trembling walls of her vagina. Good grief, this was making her horny. Where was TA when she needed him?

Tawny was busy restocking shelves, paying her no mind, but every time she stopped squeezing, an alarm went off on the base of the dildo.

There was a tap on the door, and Tawny unlocked it to let TA in.

Courtney's heart leapt at the sight of him. The dildo beeped because she relaxed. Her face flamed with embarrassment.

TA looked at her and smiled. Stepping closer, his eyes darkened as he gazed at her.

Tawny turned to him. "Your protégé has quite a future before her."

"She's doing well, is she?"

"Too well." Tawny pulled him into the corner to talk.

Courtney picked up scraps of conversation, something about Barnes and Stringfellow. She didn't know who Barnes was, but at the mention of Stringfellow's name, TA turned a possessive glance her way that made her gasp. Something was very wrong, she could feel it.

He walked over where she was still doing her sex exercises. He knelt beside her. "Want to try that with the real thing?"

"Yes," she confessed, her pussy tremulous when he looked at her that way.

His hand went to her abdomen, softly. "That's enough, relax."

She sighed, feeling everything release inside her.

He smiled and eased the dildo out of her twitching pussy. "Come on," he said, helping her up.

He took the caftan Tawny handed him and slipped it over Courtney's head, dressing her. She wanted to protest, but she was just too worn out.

He was there to steady her, holding onto her until she got her bearings. Then, he set her free and attached the leash to her collar. "Come."

Chapter 12

Courtney followed TA back to their room.

The instant the door closed, he was tugging off her caftan, his hands roaming over her.

She moaned, arching toward his magic touch, needing him to make her come.

He pushed her back. "You may undress me, slave girl."

Her hands flew to his shirt, unbuttoning it, tugging it out of his pants. Then, she unbuckled his belt, unsnapping and unzipping his pants. She started to pull them down and then realized his shoes were in the way. Crouching, she untied his shoes, tugging them off, almost toppling him in her hurry.

"Easy, we've got all day."

Hearing the amusement in his voice, her cheeks flamed, but she kept stripping him, slipping off his other shoe, pulling down his pants and briefs.

"Show me what you've learned, slave girl. Position number three, now."

She knelt, opening her mouth.

He slipped his cock between her lips, and she sucked hard on the head, then rubbed her mouth up and down the shaft, only to suck the head again, milking him with her mouth. It was even better than she'd imagined.

"Very good," he said with a groan as he pulled out of her mouth. "Now, flow into position number four, quickly."

She stretched out on her back, her legs flowering out, wide open, her pussy on display. He liked what he saw. She could tell when his eyes dilated.

"Stay like that," he said, going to the armoire.

She held the pose, watching him pick up something that looked like a crop with a small leather flap on the end. She trembled, heating at the thought of what he was going to do to her. He walked back and gave her a flick to the inner thigh.

She gasped at the sting. It didn't really hurt all that much, but it made her hot.

"This is your flogger," he said, snapping it at her other thigh.

She moaned, trying to hold them open.

He snapped the flap against her pussy, and she let out a shriek as heat flooded.

"Hush," he said, playing it up her left inner thigh and down her right.

She was trembling, burning with each blow, beads of perspiration damping her body as she arched toward the flogger's blows. "Please, please."

He flicked her pussy, making her squeak. "What do you want, slave girl?"

"You, please, sir."

He knelt on the floor with her, sliding between her wide-open legs, and slipped his cock into her wet pussy. He held his upper body up on stiff arms so that their only point of contact was his cock buried in her pussy.

"Milk me."

She clenched her pussy around his hard cock. The pulsing shaft rubbed against the sensitive walls of her vagina as she milked him. His eyes were dark and he was sweating, the muscular arms holding him up trembling. She felt the same way. Her body was rippling along with her rhythmic vaginal contractions.

She whimpered, starting to come, the ripples intensifying, and he bit out what sounded like an endearment, his cock jerking, spurting inside her. She cried out, coming again.

When it was over, he pulled out and rolled onto his back, taking her with him. He held her, his hand stroking her back, soothing her.

She lay there, listening to his thundering heartbeat slow, thinking about the first time they'd made love. She'd been in chains then, and even so, it had been an earthshaking event.

Her training would be over in two days, and she'd be sent away for safety. She didn't want to go. All of his protestations that she forget about this kind of life, go back to her tame world, were wrong. She'd been made for this, for him.

What he didn't seem to realize was that he'd awakened something in her she wanted to explore, but only with him.

She was waiting for him to ask her to stay, but he still hadn't said anything. Instead, he was trying to break her of the notion of seeking a new Master when this was over. His possessive feeling might be the edge she needed to establish some kind of relationship.

That evening, she cleared away their dinner tray. TA had hand fed her again from his plate, and she was getting used to the cosseting, the small humiliation. It made her feel closer to him.

She was naked, as usual when they were in their room, but he had gone down to the conference room for a trainer's meeting.

There was a tap on the door. He unlocked it, coming in.

She looked up, surprised he was back so soon. "Is there a problem?"

He shook his head. "Alexander's having a party tonight, and we're invited. We have to make an appearance."

"We?"

"Stand," he said, tightly. "I'm going to prepare you."

She got to her feet.

He still seemed on edge, quick to anger. Was he even going to miss her when she left?

She watched him go to the dresser and bring out the white lace costume she'd worn for the video. She glowed with the memory. She quickly slipped it on and then turned to him.

He leaned against the dresser, watching her, an appreciative glint in his eye.

She glanced down, saw the nipple clamps cradled in his big hand, and boldly walked up to him.

"You're beautiful," he said, toying with her nipples. Tugging them, tweaking them, lengthening and hardening them, he added, "And very sexy."

"Thank you, sir." She moaned at the pleasure of his touch.

He put on the first clamp, and she felt the pinch all the way down to her toes. She trembled, her knees buckling at the erotic sensation. Whimpering at the pinch, she tried to stand still for him to attach the right one, his hand cupping her tender breast.

Her breasts felt bigger, more exquisitely tender because of his attention. Stilling, she held her breath as he clamped the matching one to her tingling right nipple. The emerald at the tip refracted the light. She stared at it and Dragon's big hands working her aroused nipple, unable to look away. He moved his hands, the jewel dangled, and she felt the pull more fully.

Cupping his hand under her chin, he made her look into his eyes. "This could be a tricky situation tonight, so behave yourself."

"I will." She'd felt his tension, and had put it off as his reluctance to part with her. His careful words made her wonder if there was something else wrong?

Instead of elaborating, he walked over to pick up her leash.

He turned, leash in hand. "Come, it's time to go."

She walked over to him, her high heels sinking into the thick carpet. She stood obediently as he attached her leash. Their eyes met, and she caught the dark flare in his.

They were both thinking about her leaving, she just knew it, yet he said nothing. Tomorrow, she'd have it out with him. She had nothing left to lose.

He dropped a quick kiss on her lips, gave a twitch of her leash, and opened the door.

She followed him, silently wondering who would be at the party. He led her down the hall and to the elevator. He pushed the button for the third floor. She was intrigued. The reporter in her had wondered what was up there. Now, she'd get to find out. When the doors opened, he led her out into a huge room that took up most of the third floor.

It was set up like the jazz club in the lobby, only on a grander scale. A large teak bar occupied one wall, with cozy booths and tables scattered around the room. Sultry jazz played from a hidden sound system, setting the mood. Couples danced—members in business suits and naked slaves.

She was suddenly glad TA had dressed her.

She followed him off the elevator. Her gaze swept the room. Most of the trainers were easy to spot, going in for black leather with whips tucked into their belts. She was so relieved that TA had more subtlety than that. If he wanted to chastise her, he'd take her to their room and do it in private. Up on a dais, a nude woman was tied to a frame on erotic display like a living statue.

TA drew her to a halt by the edge of the bar. She kept her eyes down, trying not to look like a snoopy reporter. He unhooked her lead.

"Go help serve drinks, slave girl," he said softly.

She lifted her head up, hearing something tender, maybe regretful in his tone for a moment. He knew she was nervous, embarrassed, scared, and he was trying to protect her.

She nodded and turned to do as she was bid, walking up to the bar, snagging the bartender's instant attention for some reason. Then she noticed that none of the other slave girls were bellying up to the bar.

"I'm here to help…"

"So, you finally made it." He winked at her and handed her a tray laden with champagne glasses. "There you are, me girl. Serve the bubbly and be quick about it."

She hefted the silver tray full of champagne flutes, and turned to face the milling throng of men. Wading through that mob wasn't going to be easy. Balancing the tray as best she could, she edged into the crowd. Stepping up to the first cluster, she held out the tray. "Drinks, gentlemen?"

An older, austere looking man in a pinstriped gray suit looked her up and down. Taking a glass from the tray, he flicked the gem dangling from her nipple and smiled. "Nice touch."

Courtney resisted the urge to kick him as the jewel jiggled. Her nipples were hard, so tender. She felt all eyes on her, the object of avid curiosity. She did stand out, being one of the only clothed slave girls. Nudity might have given her more anonymity. Casting a glance where she'd left Dragon, he stood talking to Tawny and Mario, the video photographer, his back to her.

She scurried away to the next cluster of men before TA could notice and come to her aid. His probable possessive reaction could blow both their covers. A man sitting at the next divan ran a hand up her leg as he reached for his drink. She shivered, keeping silent as she moved away.

And then she saw him. Stringfellow, the cold man who'd come on to her in the Slave Bazaar. Even worse, he was standing and chatting with Alexander. She knew the moment he spotted her because he cut an icy glare her way and said something heated to Alexander, who gave her a speculative look.

Spanks and a woman's muffled cry filled the room. A woman who'd been on display was turned around, her backside to the crowd, and she was being publicly caned. A man holding a long reed was whipping it through the air. It whistled and landed with a snap across the brunette's ass.

This had to be the Schoolmaster.

She flinched, but stared, fascinated. The Dom laid into the brunette, making her beg for her caning. The woman's bottom was crisscrossed with red stripes, and she was sobbing. When he stopped and undid her restraints, she followed him to a dark corner of the room. All around her, Doms and members were laughing and joking.

"Well, there you are, my dear."

Hearing his gravelly voice, Courtney turned to see that Alexander had sidled up to her side. She shuddered as his speculative gaze roved over her in the lingerie.

"Quite a show, wasn't it?"

She bit her lip, casting a panicked look at Dragon. He was still chatting with Mario, his back to her.

Alexander took the tray of drinks out of her hand, regaining her attention. He thrust it at a naked blonde, and waved her away, all the while keeping his focus on Courtney. "I see Mr. TA has given you some jewels."

"Yes." She bit her lip, embarrassed when his mean eyes stayed focused on her aching nipples.

"They suit you, green like your eyes. How would you like to make a bonus? One of the members would pay handsomely for a night with you."

Stringfellow, her stomach clenched at the suggestion. "I'm not trained."

Alexander smirked, looked over her shoulder at Stringfellow, and nodded. "You're trained enough for what he's got in mind, honey."

TA turned away from Tawny to set his beer down on the bar, and noticed Alexander chatting up Courtney. His blood chilled as he watched the mobster give the nod to Stringfellow, who walked their way.

Tawny had told him how they'd had to fend off the wealthy member. The CEO could buy anything he wanted, and money talked with Alexander.

"We got trouble," he said under his breath.

Tawny grabbed his arm. "Hold it, Ty, and don't do anything you might regret."

"It's a bit late for that warning." He shrugged off his compatriot's hand.

Tawny frowned. "You'll ruin the mission."

"Screw the mission."

"I can get her away."

"Do it then, or I swear, I'll deck the guy and let the agency take the consequences. You can tell that to Harrison if he's listening."

She rolled her eyes. "Damn, you've got it bad. Be patient for a few minutes more, and Harrison will arrange a call from her alleged buyer. There's no way Alexander can ignore that. I'll go set it up," she said, rushing to a secluded corner.

TA watched her make a call, then headed for Courtney.

Time for the cavalry to stage a rescue. If the scheme didn't work, there was always the concealed weapon he wore under his shirt.

Scowling at Stringfellow's leering face, he decided he'd rather take the asshole out with his hands. He knew a few moves that would take him out permanently.

Alexander glanced up at his approach and scowled. Stringfellow gave him a dismissive glance and went back to staring at Courtney, who looked at TA like he was her knight in shining armor, and he lost another piece of his heart.

He closed the distance between them, insinuating his body between Courtney and the other men. "Alexander, there's a phone call for my student."

Alexander scowled. "Phone call?"

"From her new Master." TA attached her leash.

"Wait a minute. I'm not done here," Stringfellow interjected.

Alexander nodded. "Dragon, bring her back after the call. Mr. Stringfellow will need her services for the night."

Stringfellow smiled.

Courtney scowled at the man. "No!"

"What did you say?" Alexander turned to bark at her.

"No." Fists balled at her sides, Courtney rounded on the mobster. "Not unless you want me to report this to my buyer. I'm sure he wouldn't take it too kindly you're renting out his property."

Alexander shot a disgruntled glance from her to Dragon. "Do something with your student. She's out of control."

TA tugged Courtney behind him, and she let out a startled yelp, then he shifted to block Alexander and Stringfellow's path. They'd have to go through him to get to her. Alexander's step back told him he got the message, but Stringfellow wasn't such an easy sell.

"Hey, he can't do that," Stringfellow complained.

TA stared him down. "The slave girl is right. A deal's a deal. However, rest assured, I will chastise her for talking out of turn."

Stringfellow scowled at Alexander. "Do something about this!"

Alexander snapped his fingers, and a smiling busty blonde was hustled over by her trainer. "Let me present slave girl, Stephanie. She'll be happy to serve you all night long."

Stringfellow raked a jaded look over Stephanie. "She's not who I had in mind."

"She'll be on the house for the inconvenience."

"Okay, I guess she'll do, for now." Stringfellow stalked away, Stephanie in tow.

Alexander turned back to Dragon. "Get to that phone call. You can take it in my office. Oh, and Dragon, any more crap from you, and I'll fire your ass."

TA nodded. "Let's go, naughty slave." He tugged her behind him. He just had to stay the next two days.

"You'd better toe the line if you want to stay in my employ," Alexander called after him.

TA rushed Courtney into the elevator and pushed the button, closing the door, knowing they'd just dodged a bullet. Alexander was now more wary than ever, and this last minute party spelled trouble. It might mean more than just a desire to make a few extra bucks whoring the girls. It was time to get Courtney out.

He led her back to Alexander's office.

Courtney hurried after him, silent. She was probably stunned from the party and her near escape. She wasn't used to being on display in her underwear, a purely sexual object in nipple clamps and high heels. It was a part of her journey into sexual submission, but he was going to have to cut short her training.

He was honest enough with himself to acknowledge that he wasn't training her for some faraway buyer, but for himself, yet it couldn't ever be real. She'd walk away, go back to her old life, probably write one hell of a story about the collapse of this sex ring, and he'd move on to the next assignment. The sooner he got that through his head, the better off they'd all be.

He shut the door. Stacks of papers littered the mobster's desktop, videotapes of the girls lined the shelves. He pushed Courtney into the desk chair and handed her the phone.

"Take your call, line five. They'll be watching the switchboard to make sure you do."

She took the receiver. "Is it really him?"

He shook his head. "The agency set up the call to keep Alexander from selling you to Stringfellow for the night."

"Thank you."

Courtney watched TA go through Alexander's tape library, and punched in number five on the multi-line phone with a shaking finger.

It was chilling knowing how close they'd come to disaster. Tawny had helped stage her escape. Now that she realized it, it wasn't that surprising Tawny was an agent. It fit with her curiosity about their relationship, the way she'd handled Stringfellow, and the warning not to get hooked on him. She knew better than anyone that this was temporary.

"Yes?"

"Hello, slave girl," came the low bass voice on the other line.

She couldn't help wondering who it was. "Hello, sir."

He chuckled. "Good girl, you remembered how I wanted to be addressed. Tell me, how is your training coming along?"

"Fine, sir." She blushed, glancing at her scanty lingerie, her nipple clamps.

"Tell me about your trainer. What's his name?"

"Dragon." This was met with uproarious laughter on the other line.

"Oh my, that's priceless. For tits and ass, no doubt."

Courtney blushed harder, realizing he was probably right. She hadn't made the connection before. She looked at Dragon. He was watching her, probably because of the mention of his name.

"Is he strict with you?"

She licked her lips. "Very."

"Good. I like my slave girls well disciplined, as I'm sure he does."

"No doubt," she commented, warming to the subject.

He laughed. "A sassy one. I'm sure he loves that."

"I wonder sometimes."

"And Tawny? Tell me, how is she?"

"Fine." She caught the tension in his voice. The woman was more than just a subordinate to him. "She's a strong one. She's okay."

"Good. I'm glad to hear it. Listen to Dragon, and don't worry, this will soon be over."

"I know." She gripped the phone tighter, feeling stupidly depressed by the thought. Foolish as it was, she didn't want to part from Dragon.

"Let me talk to him," he said.

She held the phone out. "He wants to talk to you."

TA walked up and took the receiver.

She only heard one side of the terse conversation, but she could tell things were escalating. Dragon's posture became tense, the look he shot her watchful. When he hung up the phone, she stood.

"Trouble?"

"One of our operatives is missing. We're not sure if there's a leak in the pipeline. That's why it's imperative you don't leave my side."

She nodded. That sounded like heaven to her. She followed him back to their room. He picked up the pace, making her hurry behind him, her body shaking. When she stepped into the bedroom, he let go of her leash and shut the door behind them, locking it.

She stood there, waiting, her leash dragging on the floor in front of her. The very air she breathed seemed sexually charged.

He turned back to her, gazing at her like he wanted to devour her. Her pussy flooded with moisture, her clit stood at attention, her nipples throbbed behind the clamps. She trembled, aching for his possession.

"Hold still," he ordered, stalking up to her, unfastening her leash.

His hand slid down to cup her breast, the nipple clamp's jewel jiggled, creating a pull deep inside. Her swollen nipples were stiff, on fire, tortured, begging for his touch, for release. The tug inside her seemed to reach right down to her hungry pussy. He cupped the other breast as if weighing them both in his palms.

"You're beautiful like this, slave girl. Tamed, and turned on, and obedient for your trainer."

She could only moan, pushing her breasts into his hands.

He bent to flick his tongue at one, wetting it. His rough tongue laved her tortured nipple and the clamp perched atop its swollen peak. She moaned, her knees buckling. He pushed her back against the wall, his thigh between her legs. He pressed his jeans-clad knee against her tremulous wet pussy, holding her up as he lapped at first one aching nipple, and then the next. She whimpered, pressing tight against his leg, feeling aroused from all angles, her heat expanding.

He released one clamp, and she gasped at the rush of pain that surged through her. Then his mouth was on the tender peak, sucking on it hard. When he drew it onto the roof of his mouth, she screamed, grinding against his leg, coming in an explosive flash. He kept sucking, gentling now, laving away the pain. she hung limp in his arms.

Then, with a final little kiss to the nipple's red tip, he moved on to the next.

"Oh no," she moaned. It was too much. She couldn't take it, the pain, and the explosive orgasm.

Hiss eyes darkened as his mouth closed over hers, shutting off her protest, taking her out of her fear. When he pulled away, she lay back against the wall, calm but aroused. Looking deep into his stormy blue eyes, she nodded.

He undid the left nipple clamp, she gasped at the renewed surge of pain. Then, his mouth was on her, sucking, laving, nipping as the pressure built inside her body. She couldn't help rubbing her aching pussy against his muscular leg, waves of orgasm sweeping through her again.

Just when she thought it was over, the sound of his pants being unzipped broke through her stupor. Kissing her, gripping her ass with his strong hands, he picked her up, and lowered her onto his cock. She whimpered as she settled onto him. His shaft pushed deep inside of her, filling her, and her pussy rippled on his thrusting cock.

She wrapped her arms around his neck, her legs around his waist, holding on as he took her standing up. His big hands easily raised and lowered her repeatedly onto his cock.

Their eyes locked, and she couldn't look away as her body convulsed around him. He pushed into her once more, pulling her down so that his head was tight against her cervix, and he exploded. With a groan, he came.

She panted, her pussy tightening.

Come what may, he was her lover, her Master, and his saying it wasn't true wouldn't change that.

Chapter 13

Courtney awoke in the morning, rolled over, and winced. Her butt was still tender.

TA had ridden her hard once they'd made it into bed last night. He'd been insatiable, taking her every way she'd imagined, and a few that were new to her. The bed felt empty, and she knew without looking he was gone.

Where was he? Maybe down for another trainer's meeting. Alexander was probably livid at being denied her services in Stringfellow's bed last night.

She frowned, deciding not to think about the odious man. It was her last day, and she planned to make the most of it. If all went as planned, she'd coax a promise from him to meet in real life. This wasn't a good start. It was disappointing not to wake up in his arms.

She didn't care. She was his submissive, even if he wouldn't say the words.

The door opened, and she looked over to smile at Dragon.

He didn't stand there. Tawny did, looking at her with something akin to worry in her eyes.

Courtney sat up with a little gasp. "What's wrong?"

Tawny walked toward her. "Get up. It's time for you to go."

"What?" She stared at the other woman in disbelief. She couldn't leave like this, with things unfinished between her and Dragon. "I still have another day. Where's Dragon?"

"He's working." Tawny offered a sympathetic smile. "I know this can't be easy for you, but you'll have to go along with the plan for all our sakes. It's been decided to get you out early to keep you out of danger."

Courtney sat on the edge of the bed and gave her a curious glance. "Did TA ask for me to leave?"

Tawny handed her a caftan and Courtney slipped it on over her nakedness. "Yes, and it was seconded by Nick, the agent in charge."

The soft way Tawny said Nick's name told Courtney she was correct in guessing there was something personal between them. "The man I talked to last night?"

"Yes."

"You and he...?"

"You're wasting time. Move it."

Courtney reluctantly slipped out of bed. Wasn't she even going to be allowed to say goodbye? It wasn't fair. "And Dragon? Will I see him before I go?"

Tawny frowned. "I warned you not to get attached. This lifestyle can be seductive, but if it's not for you, you'll find out when you get back to your old routine." At Courtney's pained glance, she added, "Don't worry, if you're meant to be together, Cupid will find a way. Hurry up, now. Shower and change, just like you're going to your new owner."

Courtney went through the motions, feeling like she was cut adrift, slipping back into the freshly laundered street clothes she'd worn in here. Putting on her pink lace underwear, she recalled TA calling them sexy, pulling them down to spank her, tucking them in his pocket, and she blinked back tears. She couldn't help worrying about his safety, but a little part of her wondered if it was something she did that made him send her away early. Her heart broke a little. She put on her suit and white silk blouse, and slipped on her heels. They pinched. She'd grown used to being barefoot.

It was time to go back to the real world. She unbuckled her slave collar, taking it off. Laying the collar on the bed, she let out a heartsick sigh, then turned and walked away.

Tawny was waiting for her by the door. "Come on, we've got to get through the exit interview with Alexander, then you're home free."

Keeping her tears at bay, Courtney followed Tawny down the hall to Alexander's office. When Tawny tapped on his door, Courtney hung back, not wanting to face him. Her distress probably showed, and she didn't want to give TA away by clinging to him.

"We're ready to head out now, Mr. Alexander," Tawny said.

"Send the slave girl in here, then," he bit out in an impatient tone.

Courtney stepped into his line of vision, but didn't venture into his office. Keeping her distance seemed like a good idea.

Alexander shuffled a sheaf of papers on his desk and looked up with a scowl. He was angry at being done out of his pandering fee last night, she figured.

He crumpled his Styrofoam cup and tossed it on top of the pile littering his trashcan. "Your buyer is so eager, he couldn't wait another day. It's most unusual."

Tawny smiled. "She's an unusual kind of slave girl."

Alexander turned his sour gaze Tawny's way. "Tell me again why you're doing this. Where is Mr. Dragon?"

"Indoctrinating a new student."

Courtney's heart sank at the casual remark. Was it true? Had he already moved on to someone new? She didn't dare ask or let her distress show. Alexander seemed ultra-suspicious of them. Was he onto them?

"Out with the old in with the new, eh?" He chuckled. "I hadn't heard of anyone new coming in."

"She's a retrain, held over from the last group."

Courtney burned with the possibility that it might be true.

Alexander shrugged. "It doesn't matter anymore." He picked up an envelope from his desk and handed it to Tawny. "These are her travel documents. Get her to the airport, pronto."

She pocketed the tickets. "Will do, chief."

He turned to Courtney. "Your new owner sent you a gift." He handed her a small wrapped box. "You're not to open it until you're airborne."

Courtney stepped deeper into the room and took it, trying not to act nervous. She clutched it, hoping that it was a parting gift. Of course, TA would do that, ever the plotter, ever the Dom. Even after he sent her away. She slipped the package into her pocket.

He smiled. "I trust your training here has been satisfactory."

Her startled gaze flashed back to him. Was he talking about her spanking, her submission? The twinkle in his eye said yes.

"It's been instructive," she muttered.

She turned and headed out before he could comment, barely keeping her tears at bay. She followed Tawny to the elevator. They got in, and the doors were whisking closed when she thought she caught a glimpse of TA going into the conference room. She blinked, and he was gone.

Obviously wishful thinking. They went down to the receptionist who had her bag.

Courtney took it, blinking back tears. She had to get out before she broke down and cried, making a total fool of herself.

Just as she was turning to go, an explosion rocked the room, coming from somewhere above. A gunshot ricocheted overhead.

She cast a panicked look at Tawny.

"Move!" Tawny pushed her toward the door.

Courtney dug in her heels. "But Dragon! We can't just leave him."

"He's a big boy, he can take care of himself," Tawny shouted, propelling her forward. "Go!"

Courtney stumbled toward the door, Tawny at her heels. She didn't want to leave. Tawny practically forced her out the door, and then Stringfellow suddenly materialized on the sidewalk, blocking their way.

"Going somewhere, bitches?"

Tawny pushed Courtney aside and lashed out at him with a karate kick. A glancing blow from his meaty fist sent Tawny reeling.

Courtney picked up one of the vases flanking the entryway and brought it down on the back of his head as he bent over Tawny.

Stringfellow sank like a stone.

Tawny rolled to her feet with a groan. She grabbed Courtney's hand, yelling, "Come on," and pulled her toward a van idling at the curb. They dove in, and the driver took off.

"You two okay?" the driver asked.

"I'm still in one piece, thanks to Ty's slave girl."

That gravelly voice was familiar. Nick, the agent in charge. Courtney gazed up at the big blond guy behind the wheel. He reminded her of an aging surfer.

"It was nothing, really. We've got to go back and rescue TA," she complained.

"No need. He and delta team have already taken Alexander into custody. Right now, he's leading the squad who are rounding up the few stragglers."

"So soon," Courtney said with a gasp.

"He's good."

She nodded. She believed it. "Are you sure he's okay? What about the explosion, the gunfire?"

"The explosion was a concussion grenade, harmless, but scary as hell. The gunfire was from Alexander. He didn't want to go down. Don't worry, the guy couldn't hit the broad side of a barn. TA took him out, and the rest are falling like a house of cards."

Courtney sat back, satisfied. Things couldn't be over just like that. She hadn't had the chance to gather the evidence she needed. And then there were the other girls to think about. She couldn't let them pull her out and leave the others in jeopardy.

"What about the slave girls?"

"They'll be screened by EMS, and we'll bring in agency counselors to help them adjust. Speaking of that, do you want to talk to a counselor?"

"I'm fine. The only one I need to speak to is TA."

Nick and Tawny exchanged a pitying glance in the front seat, and her heart sank. She didn't have to be told. TA didn't want to see her.

"Sorry," Nick said.

She didn't ask again. She sat, twisting her hands in her lap, and then she remembered the gift box in her pocket. She pulled it out and quietly unwrapped it. It was a small package about the size of a ring box, but she knew he wouldn't be giving her a ring. She lifted the lid to find her nipple clamps. Sunlight refracted off the emeralds, filling the van's backseat with rainbows.

Why had he given them to her? To remind her? It gave her a small glimmer of hope. She pocketed the jewel box, wanting to keep it private.

Nick pulled up to a sprawling ranch house in the suburbs. He parked and turned to look at her. "We're here. I'm afraid we'll need to take your deposition before we can let you go."

"Fine," she said, getting out of the van.

She fell into step beside Tawny. She couldn't help noticing how Nick and Tawny brushed arms when walking. They were so into each other, it shut the rest of the world out. She and TA had been that way. Her heart panged at the thought.

She sat in the safe house's den, giving an edited version of her misadventures without incriminating Dragon.

Nick clicked off the tape recorder, stood, and stretched. "Thanks, Courtney. This should put the final nail in Alexander's coffin."

"You're welcome." She rose with a yawn. It seemed like they'd been at it for hours.

There was a tap on the door, and Tawny poked her head in. "You two ready for me?"

"Absolutely," Nick said in an intimate tone.

Tawny turned to Courtney. "I've got someone who'd like to see you."

She opened the door to let Laura in.

Courtney's eyes widened as she saw her bubbly blonde protégé breeze into the room. She hadn't expected her, and relief she was alive swept through her. "Cara, what are you doing here? Are you okay?"

"I'm fine." She smiled. "But between you and me, I went through some kinky things. We'll have to trade war stories. They told me you went in to rescue me."

From her sassy tone, she knew Laura was going to be okay. "And needed rescuing myself," she added dryly.

"Somehow, I doubt that. You always did have balls, my mentor. Come on," she said with a wave of her arm. "I'll settle you into our room."

"Our room?" Courtney looked at Tawny for clarification.

"You'll need to stay here overnight and go through processing."

Courtney didn't object. The longer she lingered, the more likely she'd be to run into Dragon. Hopefully, he'd check in here after the mop up mission.

She followed Laura down the hallway to what looked like a dormitory—a large room with six twin beds.

Laura sat on a rumpled bed and pointed to a crisply made bunk across from hers. "That bunk's yours. I chose it so we could talk. The other girls have already been processed and sent home. I stuck around because I thought you might need me."

Courtney smiled, appreciating the gesture. She set down her suitcase, plopped on the edge of her bed, and gazed into Cara's wide brown eyes, looking for any sign of distress. "Are you really okay?"

Laura bit her lip and looked down, tears pooling in her eyes. "I am now that I know you're safe." She blinked away tears, her composure resurfacing. "I'm sorry I got you into this. I was a fool."

"That's okay, it's what mentors with brass balls are for." Courtney smiled, trying to alleviate the heavy cloud of guilt that seemed to close in around Cara. "I'm fine, honestly, it's you I've been worried about. Do you feel up to talking about it?"

Laura nodded. "It was exciting at first, and you know how much I like sex."

"I remember." She recalled very well her protégé's frank talk about sex during their tenure together.

"After a few hot days and nights at the club, I made my video." Her cheeks flamed. "I was nude, my trainer worked me over with a vibrator, and well, you know the drill. Anyhow, I was auctioned off, and by then, I was scared because I realized I was in over my head. Imagine my relief when I wound up here instead of some brothel in Arabia."

Glad that her protégé had bounced back so well, Courtney nodded. "My experience wasn't as bad."

The next day, as Courtney was following Laura out of the building, Tawny walked up to her.

"Are you here to see me off?"

Tawny pulled her to the side and handed her a card. "Go home, go back to your life. If you still feel the same way in three weeks, call me at this number, and I'll tell you how to get in touch with him."

Courtney's gaze searched Tawny's furtive expression. "Did TA tell you to do this?"

"Hell no. He'd be pissed if he knew. Frankly, so would Nick. But it just tears me up to see you and Ty so miserable."

Courtney's eyes widened. He was miserable, too? "You've seen him?"

Tawny licked her lower lip, looking around. "Last night."

"How is he?" Courtney grabbed her hand.

She shrugged. "Grouchy, but very stubborn."

Courtney slipped the card into her pocket. It nestled next to the jewel box with her nipple clamps. "Thanks. I needed this. I'll be calling."

Chapter 14

Two weeks later, Courtney dressed with care for her return to work. She'd gone with Laura to an exclusive hotel after leaving the FBI control, using up what remained of her vacation. While she composed her exposé with the laptop and files Nick had provided, Laura had indulged herself with seaweed wraps and facials. It'd taken Courtney three days to work things out cathartically with the best weapon she had: the written word.

Alexander and his backer Stringfellow were going down, big time.

Walking out of her townhouse, she knew she looked put together, but she didn't feel whole, wouldn't be until she saw TA again. The idea of being with any other Dom was laughable. The story had gone national last week, garnering her rave reviews, while she'd laid low. Now, nothing was left but to start the rest of her life.

Last night, unable to take it anymore, she'd broken down and called Tawny one week early. To her relief, the woman had taken pity on her and given her an indirect way to contact Dragon.

All she had to do was figure out how to seduce a Dom.

Considering the possible ways to go about it, she walked into the renovated art deco building where her paper was housed.

Laura waved at her from the fax machine. "Hey, mentor. No fair being late on your first day back."

Courtney smiled. "How are you enjoying being back at work?"

She followed Courtney toward her office. "It's been fun. Your messages are on your desk."

She laid her purse down on the file cabinet and looked over at Laura. She was lingering, a troubled look on her face.

"He hasn't called?"

"No, but I called Tawny and found out a way to contact him." She handed Laura the website address she'd written down.

"Well, let's fire this baby up."

Laura walked around to click a key on Courtney's computer, bringing up the internet. Dragon's picture came on the screen. Direct, brooding, he stared right at the camera.

"Oh, I can see why you're hooked."

Courtney plopped in her desk chair, her knees growing weak as she stared at his handsome face. She read the copy.

"Experienced Dom for hire."

She clicked on the email highlight, and it was live. "Oh, my God, Tawny wasn't sure if the website was still live. The agency set it up to fool Alexander."

"What are you going to do?"

"I'm going to sign up for a Master. When he sees it, he'll know he has a choice—keep me or lose me."

"I just hope he picks the right one."

"Me, too," she said, starting to type.

Dear Master,

I'm a hot and partly trained submissive who's looking for a new Master. Meet me and teach me to serve you. I'll help you forget your troubles. I'll bow for you.

Please be mine.

"I'm attaching a photo so he'll know it's me."

Laura looked at the photo of Courtney wearing only the nipple clamps and a smile, and let out a whistle. "Hot stuff. It's an inspired plan."

Chapter 15

Courtney sat in the bar, watching the other couples dance. She was wearing the same clothes she'd worn the first night at the club, with one difference—she was wearing his nipple clamps under her pink lace bra. Would Dragon appreciate the gesture? Would he even show up?

Her ad had received a flurry of answers, mostly dark and obscene. But one, clipped and direct, ordering her to be at the bar this evening, was pure Dragon. He was furious at her.

Stirring her straw in her slushy drink, she decided with a smile that he'd just have to spank her for her impertinence.

She watched a couple walk by, arm-in-arm, and couldn't help feeling depressed. She ached to see him. The way he'd distanced himself made her insecure about his reaction. Had he moved on?

As more people started to arrive at the neighborhood bar, she hoped that it was why he'd picked this busy bar. He probably figured she'd behave herself and not cry if she was in a public place when he rejected her. That errant thought was demoralizing.

She felt a few admiring male glances thrust her way, but ignored them. They couldn't hold a candle to Dragon. And then, she saw a dark head, taller than the crowd. Her breath caught in her throat. Was it him?

No! Salt and pepper hair, older, and one of the sports editors from the paper.

"Hello, Courtney," he said, sidling up to her. "I haven't seen you here before."

"It's my first time."

"Can I buy you a drink?"

She blushed. "I...um, I don't... No thanks, I'm waiting for a date."

"I'll keep you company."

"Beat it," TA grumbled from behind him.

Courtney spun around on her bar stool so fast, it made her head swim. Her heart skipped a beat.

He was really was here, standing inches from her, and he looked frustrated, angry. His eyes wore a determined glint, which she knew meant trouble.

The older man shrugged and dropped his hand. "Sorry, I didn't mean to poach."

She couldn't take her hungry eyes off Dragon, even at the risk of being impertinent. She took a deep breath of his sandalwood cologne, as he stepped into her space, his crotch brushing her hip.

"You came."

He frowned. "Of course, I came, Miss 'Be Mine.' You shouldn't be doing this, shouldn't be here, Courtney."

The rejection was so impersonal, it made her angry. "I'd say that's for me to say. You don't own me, anymore." she bit out, trying to goad him.

"Don't put words in my mouth, naughty girl. I ought to take you over my knee for that remark."

"I wish you would." She saw the startled humor in his eyes, and her heart leapt in response, her nipple clamps rubbing against her bra. She saw him eyeing them, and licked her lips.

"Come." He grabbed her hand, towing her away, past the crowd, out into the night.

"Where are we going?"

"Hush," he said walking her to his car.

She slipped into the passenger seat.

They drove to a high-rise apartment building only a few blocks from her townhouse. He slipped into his parking space and turned off the engine.

He turned to look at her, and she gazed back at him, refusing to back down.

"Do you have any idea what you're playing at?"

"I think I do."

He pulled out his keys, got out, and walked around to open her car door.

"Come on."

Courtney let him guide her, thrilled that he was taking her inside. They went into the elevator at the end of the parking structure, and he punched in the number for the second floor. She shivered, anticipation building inside her. A sidelong glance at him told her he was excited, too. She recognized the fevered look in his eyes, but there was an edge of caution there, too. He didn't like being pushed into this situation, but pissing him off was a chance she was willing to take.

The elevator doors dinged open, and he pulled her out of the elevator, marching her down the hall to the third door on the left, apartment 215. She stood there, quietly pressing her nervous body against him as he unlocked the door.

Once he had it open, he turned to look at her, his hot gaze raking over her body. "You'll enter my home naked. Strip."

Her nipples hardened, and her middle melted at the order. His appreciative gaze made her cream her panties.

Without question, her hand went to the button of her blazer. She slipped out of it and its matching skirt, then quickly took off her blouse. She unhooked her bra, and pulled down her panties in an instant.

Just then, the elevator doors dinged open. She just stood there, unashamedly naked for her Master.

His eyes darkened as he scooped her up in his arms and carried her inside. Depositing her on the floor, he picked up her clothing from the hallway floor and slammed the door, shooting home the lock.

When he turned back to her, her heart fluttered. She stood naked and vulnerable while he ran a hot look over her. She was at his command, but she could see he still fought the idea.

She whimpered, arching wordlessly toward him, closing her eyes, wishing he would close the distance between them and touch her.

And then he was there, tracing his fingertips over her breasts, playing with her nipple clamps. She moaned, pressing against his fingers. She needed. She wanted. Rubbing against him, she felt the bulge in his pants. He wanted her even if he was fighting the idea. She couldn't resist stroking against it, she needed it so bad—needed him.

When he stopped, she bit back a sob. She blinked her eyes open to look at him. He was watching her, studying her, with an intense look on his face.

"You shouldn't be here, Courtney."

"It's where I want to be."

"You don't know what you're saying."

"Yes, I do. I want you, and I'm willing to fight for us, even if you're not."

He held out a small silver key in his hand, palm up. "Leave your shoes on. I like the spiked heels. Very erotic, like you. Take this key, and go unlock my top desk drawer."

She picked it up with trembling fingers, recognizing that tone—hot, determined. Her pussy aching, she tottered over to the big mahogany desk in the corner of his neat, but sparsely decorated living room. A woman's touch would soon set that right. Feeling wanton in nothing but heels, even more aware of her nudity, she couldn't help blushing.

She unlocked the drawer and tugged it open, letting out a little cry of delight. Her collar was nestled there, wrapped in pink tissue paper. She turned to look at him as he watched her closely.

"Bring me your collar if you want to be mine."

If? She was aching to be his.

Tears misted her eyes as she picked up the collar. She was touched that he'd saved it, treasured it, if the tissue paper was anything to go by. Holding it gently, she rushed back toward him where he'd remained by the door.

She noticed the glimmer of relief in his eyes, and her heart leapt as she held it out to him palms up. "My collar, sir."

His eyes twinkled. "Very good, and are you going to be a good slave girl?" he asked, teasing.

She smiled. "On occasion. I'll probably push all your buttons."

He chuckled and put the collar around her neck. "There's my sassy slave girl. I wouldn't want you any other way. Who do you belong to, Courtney?"

She pressed against him, shivering. "You, sir, only you." She'd known it all along. It was essentially giving him ownership over her, but she didn't care. "And who do you belong to, my Master?"

"Do you even have to ask?" His arms tightened around her.

"I'm afraid I do."

"You, my sassy slave." He gave her a swat on the bare butt, and she let out a little yelp. "Never question my desire for you."

She hugged him as his big hand rubbed the spank's sting away. She wanted to be loved by him, ached for him to make love to her. She even burned for his spankings.

She felt his sensual mouth curve into a smile as he kissed her shoulder.

"I will punish you as I see fit." His hand slid up her side to lightly toy with a clamped nipple. "You will be naked when we're alone, submissive. I will dominate in the bedroom. Do you understand this?"

"I understand." She moaned as he tugged on her nipple.

"Good." He let go of her breast, and she let out a little whimper of complaint. He pulled a jeweler's case from his pocket and handed it to her. "Open it."

She opened the box to a beautiful ring, antique silver with an emerald to match the ones in her nipple clamps, surrounded by diamonds.

She gazed at him with tears of joy as he dropped down on one knee. "Please, Courtney, be my submissive. Be mine."

"Yes," she said, falling into his arms with a cry of pleasure.

He slipped the ring on her finger, and then pulled her down to the floor with him, his mouth slanting over hers. She moaned as his hot body pressed her onto the floor, feeling loved, dominated, cherished.

It was just how she wanted it.

Taste of Honey
Book 3
Once
in
Love
JULIE CASTLE

Chapter 1

"It is a big decision, is it not?" Madame Imogene said. "You are wise to read it over so carefully."

Read it over. Laura Brooks looked up at the elegant Parisian Courtesan Service owner, bemused as the lady's cultured French accent washed over her. Imogene was chic, dressed to kill in a designer suit, while Laura knew she looked like a ragamuffin by comparison in her peasant blouse and denim skirt. She also knew she was lucky she had even that after being robbed.

Shell-shocked by the trio of disasters she'd been through, she could hardly focus, much less read the detailed courtesan's contract in front of her. In the last week, she'd been dumped by her mentor, artist Pierre Gallo, abandoned in Paris, and mugged. Now, all she had to her name were her passport, twenty dollars, and the stuff in her backpack.

Why the auction recruiter thought she had what it took to be a seductress, she didn't know, but she was ready to jump at the chance. For three months' work, she'd receive comfortable lodgings, a new wardrobe, and enough money to go back to the States in style. It would also enable her to set up her own studio in Wisconsin once she got home.

The exchange sounded more than fair, even though she knew she'd have to fake it in bed. She'd never had an orgasm before, and doubted the situation would change because of the job. Although she had to admit, she was sexually curious. It probably all came from reading erotica, like the book lying innocently in her backpack.

Her gaze dropped to the sexual stipulations, and she gulped as she scanned the list of demands. Heck, she'd never even tried most of them, and probably wouldn't be any good at them, truth be told. The most she'd been able to accomplish with her vibrator was a sneeze.

"I'm not sure. I mean, I haven't done a lot of these."

"Just check off the ones you're willing to do, and there is also a space to write in a few stipulations of your own choosing."

Laura nodded and blithely checked off the lot, all but kissing. Somehow, it seemed too intimate. She slid the signed document over to Imogene and watched the lady smile.

"You do not wish to risk your heart, I see," Imogene murmured.

That wasn't her reason, was it? No, she just wanted to keep this impersonal. "I don't think there's any danger of that," she said dryly.

"I understand. You're very wise." Imogene smiled again and stood. "Come. We must prepare you quickly. You're going to be last as it is."

Last sounded good to her. At least she wouldn't have to compete with the others—model-thin beauties she'd seen in the outer room.

She stood on wobbly legs and followed Imogene into a dressing room to find a pink bra and matching panties laid out on a table. She let out a sigh of relief. She wouldn't be nude like a few of her competitors.

She quickly changed, and when she glanced at herself in the mirror, she was shocked with how provocative she looked, even though she was too curvy, with a crooked smile and wild red hair. Her blue eyes were bright with excitement, and she was blushing, a little excited.

A formerly suppressed part of her was getting off on this big time, she had to admit, chagrinned. Maybe faking it wouldn't be necessary, after all. The outline of her budding nipples was just barely visible, her plump mound and cleft clearly delineated by the satin panties.

"If I may make a suggestion." Imogene stepped up to her. She undid the topknot Laura had put her hair in, and her tresses tumbled to cascade around her shoulders. "Lovely. Now, we must go."

Nick Renault took a sip of his sparkling water and glanced at his diver's watch, counting the minutes until he could get out of this meat market. He'd only come to appease his concerned sister-in-law, Simone. He'd stay long enough for Immy to report back to Simone that he'd cooperated, and then he had to head out for a business meeting. Simone had claimed he was turning into a cynical workaholic since his divorce six years ago.

He frowned as her words replayed in his mind. *You've spent enough time moping over that stupid woman, Nicky. It's time you learned to relax, let go, have a little fun.*

A lot she knew. Work was fun for him, and building his empire in spite of the fact he'd been born on the wrong side of the blanket had driven him to the top. He'd rescued his aristocratic father's family despite their displeasure, and it only made it sweeter. There was a big difference between moping and being busy.

He went still when a bewitching redhead stepped out onto the catwalk, forgetting all about business. Her hair, a fiery blend of copper, gold, and auburn, tumbled around her shoulders, reminding him of a fire goddess he'd seen once in a painting. Pink frilly underwear enhanced her full figure, shapely breasts, and the womanly flare of her hips. From where he sat, he could make out the shape of her stiff little nipples—perfect pink strawberries just waiting for his attention.

Well hell, this was a distraction he didn't need. Still, his mouth all but watered as he looked at her, and he picked up the excitement in her blue eyes.

Her sexy little mouth formed a perfect O as they locked gazes, and his damned cock twitched in response. She was a trifle scared and a lot turned on. What he wouldn't give to have those pouty lips wrapped around his randy cock.

He didn't want a relationship, but his throbbing dick wasn't listening. She was new to the game. He could tell the gorgeous little lady was getting off on the experience. He was also sure she didn't have a clue about the true rules of the game.

His thoughts darkened as he glanced at some of the other sharks trolling these particular waters. Growing up the hard way, he knew bad blood when he saw it, even if it was tied up in a slick package. He shuddered to think of this impertinent redhead being under anyone else's dominion. He knew that a few of the Doms in the audience had bad reputations. Could he really risk her being sold to that sort?

Shit, he was finding himself irritatingly close to signing his life away for the next three months—a summer of lust.

Laura locked eyes with the compelling hunk in the front row like he was a lifeline. Concentrating on him was the only way she could get through this. He had dark hair and eyes, a sultry mouth that screamed sex appeal, and an aura of strength that set him apart from the other dilatants. Whoever the sultry hunk was, he might actually be able to make her come. The others faded into oblivion as she stared at the forceful stranger, her whole body coming to attention. The air conditioning kicked in, fluttering against her breasts, making her nipples tingle and harden while her pulse raced.

The PA system came on. "This is Laura. A college graduate with a degree in art history. She's a novice, but quite charming as you can see. From her contract, she is open to most fetishes and is eager to try a few."

Laura blushed, hearing herself auctioned off and her lack of experience explained. It was all happening too fast.

And then the forceful hunk she'd been staring at got up to leave, making her gasp. For a moment, he caught her gaze, and her knees grew weak, but then he turned and walked away. Her hopes, not to mention her excitement, fizzled.

Shit, why had she let herself hope that he'd want her? She rushed offstage, sure that she'd blown it. Why else had the only truly desirable man in the audience left right in the middle of her pathetic performance? The next step would be to call home, beg George, her old boss at The Tribune, for her job back at the paper and an advance, then crawl home on her knees.

Madame Imogene grabbed her wrist as she came offstage. "Come with me, my dear, to sign your papers."

"Papers?" she said with a gasp and looked at Imogene's twinkling eyes. "You don't mean someone bought me?"

A dizzying fifteen minutes later, Laura found herself alone in the back of a black limousine as it sped out of Paris and into the countryside. She'd been told her buyer's name and that she was going to his summer home, but little else. Who the hell had bought her and why hadn't he picked her up personally? She was dying to know because she wasn't sure if she could actually go through with this.

The weirdest part of this adventure so far was the detailed past history Imogene made her fill out, right down to the erotica she liked to read. The lady ought to be a spy rather than a Madam. She supposed her would-be Master wanted to make sure she was trustworthy and wouldn't steal the silver. Not to mention, she would be willing to service his needs.

Why had she been so upfront about her wicked fantasies? Just because she favored kink in her mind didn't mean she'd enjoy it when it really happened. What if the man was a sadist? Does Madame Imogene have a way of weeding out the bad guys? At least she knew he'd passed a blood test. It was the one thing they had in common.

When the limo pulled into the long manicured driveway of a gorgeous French château, she was stunned. This wasn't some little summer place, it was a mansion. Her Master was obviously no pauper. She noticed the driver punching in a code to open the gate. Once it opened, the car smoothly pulled up to the house, and she knew it was time to jump ship or do what she came here for.

"Well, you waiting for an engraved invitation or what?" the driver snapped through the speaker.

Laura jumped in reaction. His thick Chicago accent both surprised and comforted her. Another American! She was going to smile when he turned to scowl at her. After she recovered, she scowled right back at him as she appraised him. He wasn't wearing a chauffeur's uniform, and with his salt and pepper hair and heavy physique, he reminded her of an aging prizefighter. What was a fellow expatriate doing driving for Imogene? Maybe he'd been stranded here, too. But his fierce glare told her he didn't want to talk to her. She could take a hint.

Without a word, she opened the limo's door and got out. The longer she put off meeting her buyer, the more her apprehension grew. It was better to get it over with. With that thought in mind, she walked up to the door and knocked. She stepped back when a butler opened the door and peered down his long nose at her.

He flicked a sour glance at the leaving limo, then looked back at her. "Go away."

She frowned back at him, irritated. Her would-be owner was one hard man to get to, but this forbidding gatekeeper wouldn't run her off. "No. I'm here for Mr. Renault."

"He's not here," the butler said, starting to close the door.

Laura stuck her foot in the door, refusing to be brushed off. She needed this job. "I'll wait."

***

Nick parked his motorcycle in the carriage house and made his way to the front of the château. The tableau playing out on his doorstep made his mouth twitch with laughter. Laura, his feisty American courtesan, was standing on his doorstep and staring down Bridges, her chin tightened in defiance. She had a lot of attitude. He had to give her that, because anyone who could hold her own with his ill-tempered butler had spunk.

He'd rushed through his meeting with the Lax Consortium, much to Mike Labroid's surprise, and his eagerness to get to her was irritating. True, he was about to start out on his annual vacation, but that didn't mean he had to get totally absorbed in her. He stepped up behind her. She was so engrossed in her standoff with Bridges that she didn't even notice him.

"I'm telling you that I'm expected," she said, heatedly. "Imogene sent me."

Nick smiled at her sass and let his appreciative gaze linger on her full curves. She was dressed in a peasant blouse and denim skirt, both of which clung to her luscious body in all the right places. And she was flushed, her tone and body language militant. She was excited, but cautious. At least she was smart enough to realize she was in over her head. She was lucky he was a good Master. His blood heated as he silently tracked her, confirming his impulsive decision to buy her services.

Hell, he never acted on impulse. Knee-jerk emotions were bad for business. But the moment he'd laid eyes on Laura, he'd known he had to have her. Now that she was here, he'd have to make the best of things. Maybe Simone was right. He needed to blow off steam and decompress, and the fire goddess would be a challenge.

Her scent when he drew nearer intrigued him—strawberries and sweet woman. She was completely natural. He breathed in deeply.

"It's all right, Bridges. I'll take it from here. I'm expecting the lady."

He waited while Laura turned to gape at him. Her expression went from troubled to hopeful in a heartbeat, hitting him where he lived. He told himself not to take it personally. He was just a means to an end for her and he couldn't afford to forget it.

Chapter 2

Laura stared at the commanding hunk from the auction, her mind whirling. She didn't quite know how to feel, but he was the owner she'd hoped for. Her backpack dropped out of her slack hand, and she let out an embarrassed sound when it crashed onto his marble stoop.

Up close and personal, he was even more devastating to her senses, giving new meaning to the phrase *tall, dark, and handsome*. As he invaded her personal space, she noticed his dark hair had a few sprinkles of gray at the temples, and pegged him to be in his late thirties. What a hunk!

His chocolate-brown eyes appraised her with unvarnished male interest that made all her formerly suppressed female hormones sizzle. And then her gaze dropped to his sultry mouth, the one she'd vowed not to kiss. Damn, but she wanted a taste. Her pulse raced as her body heated in a crazy response, and he wasn't even touching her. As his scent—a spicy mixture of leather and him—wrapped around her, she blurted, "I'd hoped it would be you."

"Did you now, Laura?"

"Yes." His French accent was enough to make her melt where she stood. It was completely seductive, and he probably knew it, based on his half-smile.

One of his raven brows arched. "Unfortunately, you've already forgotten one of my rules. No speaking unless I give you permission, my sassy little courtesan. Just so you know, Laura, I'm not the kind of Master to discipline you by docking your salary. I'll take you over my knee when you need correction."

Well, that left her in no doubt he'd meant it when he'd put down BDSM. She quivered, both appalled and excited at the mention of him taking her over his knee. Wow, it was just like the erotica she'd read, and she only hoped she was ready for it. She stared him down, knowing he was just earthy enough to carry out the sensual threat.

"Are we clear?" he demanded.

"Crystal," she bit back, knowing if she didn't like it, she could quit. Somehow, when she looked at him, she didn't think that was going to happen.

"Good," he said with satisfaction.

"After all, if we don't suit each other, I can always go back and get another assignment," she said, and watched his smile vanish. It was an empty threat, but apparently, he didn't know that.

Shit, she needed this job, and she was blowing it yet again. "Besides, I thought it was a typo."

"It wasn't," he said.

When his determined stare bored into hers, it gave her strange tingles throughout her body. "Fine," she shot back at him, breaking the silence rule again. "Just so you remember my limits."

He nodded, picked up her backpack, turned and walked away. "Ah, yes. No kissing. That shouldn't be a problem, Laura."

She raced after him as he headed into the house with the last of her possessions. "Come back here."

"I'm merely showing you to your room," he said over his shoulder.

The amusement in his voice pissed her off as she followed him up the staircase. She barely had time to look around at her magnificent surroundings, taking in gleaming marble floors and antique furnishings. She hurried to catch up with him, noting that Nick Renault moved like a predator on the prowl, not like a rich playboy who bought courtesans. It seemed there was more to him than met the eye. He certainly wouldn't have needed to pay for sex, so why had he?

When he walked into a room at the end of the corridor, she entered behind him. It was beautifully decorated, but completely impersonal. A guestroom. She frowned, recalling his stipulation that she sleep alone. He obviously wanted to keep this arrangement impersonal, too, and she'd do well to get on the same track. This was business, pure and simple. So, why did her heart beat faster when he stepped up behind her? As if a hot, confident man like him would ever want more than sex from a plain, inexperienced woman like her.

She waited breathlessly for him to make the first move, say something. Instead, he gently grasped her shoulders, and her foolish heart skipped a beat. *Keep it impersonal*. She knew she couldn't. She wasn't made that way. When he gently turned her around to face him, a heat wave shot up her body, and the secret spot between her legs grew heavy and dewy. She was shocked by her primitive reaction. Heck, she didn't even get a response like this from her vibrator.

Oh, hell. She was nothing like the cool, world-weary courtesan Nick Renault thought he'd bought, and he'd find that out any minute now. Still, she couldn't help getting lost in his warm chocolate-brown eyes as he gazed at her. Instinctively, she leaned forward, knowing she had to kiss him or die.

He smiled, and pulled her into his arms while he turned his head to nuzzle her nape, making her burn where he touched her.

"I haven't forgotten your prohibition on kissing, Laura, and I'll abide by your wishes."

His whisper and his hot breath stirring the tendrils escaping from her topknot made her shudder as she pressed against him. Damn it all, he made her want to break all her own self-protective rules, and now her needy reaction had shown him he could play her. She'd have to be on her guard. His hand stroked down her body making her melt as she leaned into his strength. When he cupped her bottom and squeezed, she whimpered with pleasure.

"Good. As we've come to an agreement, let me see what I've bought."

Her heart raced at the sultry demand so soon after their meeting. He wasn't wasting any time claiming his rights. The fact that she secretly wanted to get naked with him was just as shameful. She knew then and there that she'd have to work to hide her attraction to him. If he was going to be so cool and businesslike, she would respond in kind.

But when he started to unbutton her blouse, she couldn't help the blush that flamed through her, or the needy motions of her body. He gently tugged the peasant blouse off her, tossing it on the bed. She looked down as his hot gaze lingered on her breasts, encased in the pink lace bra she'd worn on the catwalk. She hadn't thought he'd cared then, but she could feel his gaze like a caress now, making her nipples harden, tingling as if they felt his touch.

"You look just as scrumptious now as you did on the cat-walk." He bent to lick at one of her nipples through her bra. "Like perfect pink strawberries."

She cried out as his hot wet tongue touched her sensitive bud. "I didn't think you noticed. You were leaving." It thrilled her to know that he'd stopped to admire her then as he did now.

"I'll have many pretty things for you to wear."

What kind of things? She pictured leather and peek-a-boo lingerie. Just what kind of kink does he go in for? The question made her tremble a little, even as it intrigued her. She tried to remember all the things she'd checked off. Then he unzipped her skirt, bringing her musing to a quick halt as it fell to pool on the soft carpet at her feet. Heat surged up her body and she sizzled as his seductive, hot gaze roved over her. The irritating part was that he was still dressed, his tailored suit enhancing what she guessed was a lethally toned body, and he was also still in control.

"Kick your shoes off," he demanded.

She stood there mutinously for a moment, wanting to insist that he get naked, too. But his determined gaze weakened her defenses. With a frown, she did as he asked, kicking off her shoes, her toes curling into the soft carpet when he just looked at her. She couldn't help feeling like a provocateur as she did so, even though she'd never thought of herself as sexy. She glanced at him, trying to read his hooded expression.

Did he like her? Was he sorry he'd bought her?

He frowned. "Keep your eyes down, Laura. The first lesson a submissive courtesan needs to learn is not to frown at her Master."

He was her boss, not her Master, but even so, she looked down, knowing she'd been doing just that. She wasn't very good at being submissive, and he was wasting no time proving it. His threat to take her over his knee still lingered in her mind. She'd probably have the reddest bottom in France. The errant thought popped in her head, and she blushed, her bottom heating as she pictured it in her mind. She had to stop reading erotica. They were warping her brain.

"What are you thinking, Laura?"

There was no way she could tell him, so she shook her head. He had too much power over her as it was.

He reached out to stroke her cheek, brushing a tendril of hair off her heated face. She quivered, her resolve weakening as she leaned into his hot, hard masculine body.

"You may speak," he said firmly.

"I'm thinking you're a control freak and I must have been really desperate to try this," she said honestly.

His hand fell away from her face, and she almost crumbled at the loss. Her skin still tingled where his hand had touched her, and she wanted it back, even if it was spanking her.

"Very well," he said formally. "You may go if you wish."

She missed the masterful lover from moments before as she looked at his suddenly reticent expression. She wasn't running. She needed this job. And deep down, she craved the adventure he could give her.

"No. I'm not going."

He smiled, and she wondered for a moment if she'd just imagined the relief in his eyes.

He reached out to undo her hair clip, letting her strands fall. Then, he fingered her tresses. "Your hair is lovely, Laura. You'll wear it down for me when we're alone."

Yes, Master, she wanted to moan, tingling at his intimate words, her sex growing wet and creamy. She had to fight herself not to squeeze her thighs together, guessing it would be a dead giveaway for him. Her body wasn't listening to her lecture to behave and throbbed as she vacillated between excitement and panic. Maybe her pure ineptitude for the job would save her from falling for him. Once Nick found out she was a dud in bed, he'd sever her contract. The idea made her sad, but she knew it was only a matter of time.

He broke her out of her brooding when he unhooked her bra. She let out a startled gasp, embarrassed he'd caught her unaware. His probing glance seemed to catalog her every reaction as he slipped the bra off her, making her tremble. His talented hands covered her breasts, warm and rough. She stopped thinking and instead thrust her sensitive tits into his touch. He smiled with satisfaction as his fingers teased her nipples, pulling and lengthening them, making her blush harder. She bit back a moan, past caring she was falling under his sexy spell.

"You have beautiful breasts, Cherie," he murmured. "And they are so responsive for me."

She blushed harder at the sultry compliment, because it was true. His touch made her crazy and she whimpered helplessly when he toyed with her tingling nipples, shocked at what he could make her feel. He pinched her nipples harder, and a jolt of pleasure and pain went through her, tightening her pussy.

"Oh," she gasped, shocked. "What are you doing to me, Nick?"

"No talking," he warned. "That's one demerit."

She glared at him through her fog of arousal, and watched him smile in response. She didn't care if he punished her. Before she could even react, he tugged down her panties, stripping her bare. She instinctively moved her hands to cover her mound and he gave her bottom a sharp spank, making her yelp.

"No." He spanked her bottom again for emphasis. "I want complete openness from you."

Heat flooded her sex and his handprint throbbed on her bottom. Her traitorous body was taking the spank as foreplay, and she guessed her butt was about as red as her blushing face. It wasn't fair he wanted complete openness from her, yet he got to remain a mystery. But that was the gig she'd signed up for, and those were the rules. Relenting, she obediently took her hands away from her mound, not wanting to risk another spank. The two he gave her had really gotten to her.

"Better," he said softly, and rubbed her bottom.

She tried not to sigh with pleasure as he stroked, but couldn't seem to stop herself from arching to his touch.

"Good, now go lay down on the bed." The honey-voiced command had her quivering inside.

Shimmering with excitement, she did as he commanded, walking across the room to lie on the bed. The satin bedspread was cool on her overheated body. She couldn't help but notice he watched her every move, and couldn't resist adding a little extra sway to her movements. At least she wasn't the only one overcome by the sexual heat in the room. A glance at the masculine bulge in his pants told her he was just as involved.

"Excellent," he said, his eyes eating her up. "Now, move to the center of the bed, and reach for the headboard."

She did as he commanded, sliding over and reaching up for the spindles of the headboard. It stretched her out, shoving her breasts out for him, exposing her for his smoldering gaze.

He was an advertisement for hot sex as he stood watching her. He was going to make love to her, maybe spank her. Her breathing shuddered as she considered the erotic possibilities. Even if she didn't have what it took to be the sexual wanton he thought she was, she wanted a taste of paradise.

"Open your legs, Cherie. I want to see your charms."

Her legs slowly slid open at his command, even though she was shocked by his demand. Her open sex rippled as his hot gaze lingered on her. She'd never felt so exposed or vulnerable.

"I'm not so sure—"

"Shh," he said softly and started to undo his tie. "You've nothing to fear from me, love."

Strangely, she believed him, and that made this even more surreal. She lay there breathless and throbbing for him as she watched him strip for her, holding her breath. Her fascinated gaze locked on him as he shrugged out of his suit jacket and then unbuttoned his shirt, popping a few of his buttons in his haste. Her eyes widened at the sign he was just as hot for her. He unzipped his pants, his impressive cock in view. He was huge, and even semi-hard, it hung halfway down his thigh.

"Wow."

"No speaking." He opened a dresser drawer to pull out a padded blindfold.

Her body flamed as he fingered the blindfold, her mind racing as she considered all the kinky stuff he might have on hand. He wasn't kidding about this bondage stuff. As he stood, looking down at her, she lay there spellbound as excitement and apprehension warred inside her. She'd only read about these kinky things and never tried them.

When he lifted and slid the blindfold in place, tears misted her eyes. It was frightening to be blinded like this, but also unbelievably erotic. Being sightless seemed to sharpen all her senses. She could actually hear her heart racing, feel her skin tingling. She waited for him to touch her. Why wasn't he taking her?

Then the bed sagged as he lay down next to her, and she quivered inside. His fingertips lightly stroked her wide-open pussy, and she almost shimmied off the bed, her sex rippling in reaction, her clit tingling. She was so shocked, she could hardly breathe.

"You're charming, Laura," he said softly. "Your pussy is so creamy and ready for me to claim it."

He was right. She was embarrassingly wet. She blushed behind the blindfold, hoping he wouldn't see it as he stroked her again. She arched against his blunt-tipped finger, craving more.

"What do you want, Cherie?" he asked. "You may speak."

She heard his amusement and trembled, even though she couldn't bring herself to answer. He was what she wanted, what she craved. He kept circling her sex, playing with her, driving her mad.

Why didn't he take her?

"Answer me!" he demanded, pinching her clit.

It sent heat flooding through her body and made her sex spasm.

"Oh," she gasped, throbbing as he rolled her stiff nub between his thumb and forefinger. "I want you. Inside me, please."

"Was that so hard to say?"

"Yes." Her pussy convulsed as cream coated her thighs.

His seeming delight in her discomfiture embarrassed her even more. He thrust one finger inside her, and she cried out as her walls clamped around his teasing finger.

"And are you going to be an obedient courtesan for me?"

"Probably not," she snapped back, angry he was toying with her.

"Wrong answer." He stopped his delightful torture.

"Please don't stop." She twisted toward him, on the brink of ecstasy.

"Then ask me nicely to fuck you," he demanded, thrusting another finger into her. "Speak."

A big part of her rebelled at the very idea, but she wanted him. And when he moved his fingers inside her, she shuddered with pleasure.

"I desperately need you to fuck me, Nick," she admitted with a needy sob.

He pinched her clit, making her moan as heat flooded her mound.

"I don't think you're being honest with me."

His words reminded her that, once he tried her, he'd know she was cold, and he'd dismiss her. She needed a taste of him now. "Fuck me, please, Nick, please. I need you and I'll try to be obedient."

"And do you want me to spank you when you're bad?" He pulled his fingers out of her to give her mound a light smack.

Her stiff clit burst into flames at the teasing blow. "Yes, please," she said with a pleasured gasp, even though it stung. Her pussy clenched, aching for him.

A moment later, he slipped between her splayed legs, and she whimpered with ecstasy. The blunt tip of his hot cock pressed against her, and she felt it throb. Instead of taking her, he bent to suck and nibble on her nipples.

She arched up, rubbing against his cock.

"Shh," he said softly. "No sound."

"Please, Nick," she sobbed, rubbing against him.

"Be quiet. You've got to learn patience," he chastised as he leisurely moved on to suck the other nipple.

Burning as he drew it into his hot mouth, she groaned, completely on fire now. The foreplay was just making her hotter, more desperate for him, and he knew it.

She writhed under him. "Please, Nick, fuck me," she wailed.

"Shh," he said as he started to enter her.

She felt a burst of fire blaze through her as her body clamped around him. He thrust deeper, completely filling her, shocking her with his sheer size. He was huge, relentless, perfect, and she quivered, her mind leaving her.

"Seven demerits," he bit out.

Not giving a darn how many demerits she chalked up, she absorbed the feel of his fullness inside of her, their joining. Her hands still clutched the headboard, her legs still splayed wide. His cock throbbed, buried to the hilt inside her. Her sex rippled around him, dazzling her as she tightened, sending jolts of pleasure through her. When he pulled halfway out and surged back into her, he made her see stars under the blindfold. Her body constricted around him, her pussy milking him. Their mingled rapid breathing and the feel of his cock mastering her were the only real things in her world right now. He rose up on his forearms, changing the angle of his possession, deepening it. She tightened again on the precipice of shattering.

"Don't you dare come until I give you permission."

Shocked by his ragged tone and the order, she sighed. "I don't have org—"

"I mean it," he grumbled, surging into her anew.

So, he didn't want to hear she wasn't orgasmic. She groaned, meeting his thrusts with pleasured ones of her own.

He thrust deeper, his cock throbbing madly, wildly, inside her. "Come now," he ordered in a harsh, raspy voice.

She gasped as he pulsed inside her, and shook as her body seized around his pulsing cock.

And then, she exploded, screaming his name uncontrollably, her body out of control. "Nick," she cried out over and over, as waves rippled through her pussy and her world went black.

When she came to, he was lying beside her, pulling off her blindfold.

"Are you okay?" he asked.

His worried gaze pleased her, and she smiled dreamily up at him. "I'm fine, never better, as a matter of fact." She snuggled against him. She got warm and tingly as she sank into the soft mattress, yawning. "I guess I'm a little tired," she said apologetically.

Moments later, she fell asleep in his warm arms.

Chapter 3

Nick lay there, bewitched, as his feisty courtesan slept beside him. He gazed down at the smile on her pretty face and the glow on her seductive curves. He couldn't help giving her an indulgent smile in return, even though the disobedient minx deserved a spanking for just scaring him half to death when she passed out in his arms. But she'd woken a moment later, sated, with a surprised smile on her face. It was as if she'd never come before. She touched his heart in ways he sure as hell didn't need. This was a business arrangement, a summer fling, and nothing more. He had to remind himself of that. He knew the danger that mixing business and pleasure could bring.

He ought to know after Yvette had damned near ruined him. Growing up as the bastard son of a French aristocrat and a free-spirited American mother, he'd learned early on that he had to fight to get and hold what he wanted. He'd thought he had Yvette until he found out she was only after him for his money. When he'd caught her in bed with his royally born cousin, Francois, he'd learned a bitter truth—women weren't to be trusted.

Still, Laura would be a charming summer diversion. And they'd both get what they needed out of the association. She needed discipline, excitement, and his protection. He needed the challenge of taming her and teaching her how sexy she could be. Shocked to find her a near virgin in his arms, he knew she needed schooling in the ways of love. As a man with plenty of experience, he'd be happy to take on the task.

He stroked a hand down her luscious curves, smiling when she murmured pleasurably in her sleep and turned toward him. She'd be an apt pupil, but he was disturbed by his own tendency to fall for her charms. He had to keep this on a strictly Dom/sub basis so he could keep his distance.

He rolled out of bed and stalked into the bathroom to clean up. When he dressed and walked into the kitchen a few minutes later, his chef, chauffer, and sometime bodyguard, Al Franks, gave him a frown. Al, an ex-con distant relative through his mother's side, was like the older brother he'd never had.

"Well?" Al asked.

"I'm keeping her," he said and stifled a grin when Al gave him a disapproving look. He smiled back. It had been far too long since he'd rankled his reprobate of a third cousin that much. Maybe having Laura around was a good thing.

"Hell," Al muttered.

"Isn't it, though?" Nick chuckled.

"I hope you know what you're doing."

"I do."

Al nodded. "How'd negotiations with the Lax Consortium go?"

Nick tensed, reminded of his reason for walking out on Laura's catwalk. He'd made a deal with Imogene, doubling any other offer Laura would receive, to make sure he got his fire goddess. The stiff bill Imogene had given him told him she'd, no doubt, padded it, but he could care less. In exchange, he'd insisted that Immy have Laura fill out a full personal history. He needed to know what made her tick.

He became aware Al was looking at him wryly, and got his head back on business. "About like I anticipated. They're playing hardball."

"Want me to have my associates lean on them?" Al offered.

Nick knew he was only half kidding. Al had a murky past.

"No, I don't think we need to involve the mob."

"Hey, that was never proved."

"Did a fax come in for me?"

Al looked toward the staircase. "Yeah, it's in your office. And the bio Imogene gave me is on your desk."

Nick heard the soft way Al said Immy's name and cast him a thoughtful gaze. He wasn't the only one with a crush. "Why don't you just get it over with and ask the woman out?"

Al shot him a rude sneer. "Who says I want to ask Imogene out?"

It'd been obvious that the Madam and Al had the eye for each other after the two had met at Simone and Carlton's wedding last year. But he wasn't going to play matchmaker.

"My mistake," he said, turning to go toward his office.

"Does she know you had a gumshoe check her out?" Al asked dryly.

Nick slanted Al an implacable look. "You know how I am about taking care of details," he said, evading the question.

"Yeah, I know," Al said gruffly.

Nick hesitated at Al's rueful tone. It'd taken determination and a first class PI to get Al cleared of the bogus charges that'd thrown him in prison back in the States. "I couldn't get along without you and you know it," he said, smiling, and Al lightened up.

"Yeah, you'd starve to death," Al said, going to the stove.

"Not to mention there's nobody else I'd trust to watch my back in a dark alley."

"Good to know I'm being appreciated," he said with a grin. "How about a raise?"

"I'll take it under advisement." He turned to go before his cousin could give him any advice on women. "We'll have supper in her room tonight," he said, heading to his office.

***

Laura woke up when a door closed. She didn't have to reach out to know that Nick wasn't in the bed with her. How embarrassing. She'd actually fallen asleep on him. It was something no professional courtesan would do.

Nick dressed in casual clothing. When he started peeling off his clothes, she ogled him.

"Happy to see me, Cherie?" he asked, tentatively.

She nodded, unable to find the words and wondering what he was hinting at. Did he think maybe she'd change her mind about him? She knew deep down that wasn't going to happen. A big part of her welcomed his dominance. It allowed her to release, let go of her cares.

He smiled and walked over to her, holding out his hand. "Come."

Trembling, she took his hand and let him tug her out of bed. Her knees buckled a little as she stood, and he caught her. She blushed up at him. She'd never been so well fucked in all her life. Heck, she'd never really come before.

He gave her an amused smile and whisked her into a well-appointed bathroom.

She looked around, impressed. The double shower was the height of luxury. When he turned on the taps, she smiled. A shower with him would be heavenly. Instead, he abruptly sat down on a bench and pulled her over his knee, making her shriek with surprise. Talk about dominance. His sexy chuckle sent a heat wave through her.

"Quiet, unless you'd like the staff to hear you getting it."

The playful yet stern reprimand made her bite her lip. He seemed on edge for some reason. Hell, she was bare-assed naked, her bottom raised in the air as she awaited his punishment.

Nick's big hand slapped her ass, and she moaned, heated by the sting. Her sex quivered in response.

"Hush now, Cherie, or I'll have to gag you."

He probably had a gag in that naughty drawer of his. She melted. She was damned if she'd give him the satisfaction of crying out.

"Fuck you," she muttered under her breath.

"I think you just did," he said before a laugh.

She moaned as his hand came down on her bottom again. *Smack.* Her clit brushed against his leg, sending jolts of pleasure through her. Damn it all, he was a master manipulator, and she wouldn't come for the brute this way. She choked back a groan as he drew back his hand and caught her on the bottom of her ass. *Slap!* She bit her lip as her clit bumped him again, swelling. Mewling at the spark of pleasure, she arched for his spanks, no longer wanting to fight him.

"Better," he praised, rubbing her ass. "You'll take four more, Cherie, and you'll count them for me."

She grumbled at the demand, tensing even as her sex grew wetter. "No."

"You signed away the right to say no, remember?"

Swat! His hand slapped the bottom of her ass, making her jump forward. "Two."

"No, you start at one," he insisted, giving her another spank.

She shuddered as he landed a blow that sent heat rushing through her bottom. "One," she moaned.

"Good." He drew back his hand.

She gasped as she waited for it, then wailed when he landed a spank on her left cheek. "T-two," she stammered as her clit bumped his leg again. "Three."

"Excellent," he said.

Damn it all, he knew she was close to coming and he was playing with her, enjoying it. And her pussy was getting wetter, her sex tightening. Her legs inched apart as she waited for the last spank.

He drew back his hand and smacked her mound, sending shots of tingles throughout her entire body, clear to her ass.

"F-f-four," she said, with her breath coming hard. Sagged over his knee in the steamy bathroom, after-spasms rocking through her, she was shocked by the change in her and more turned on than ever before. When Nick gently rubbed her bottom, his caress now tender, it completely undid her. Tears misted her eyes, and she began to cry.

"I knew you'd cry, Cherie," he said softly as he pulled her up and onto his lap. "Was it a good spanking for you, Laura?"

Her world spun around, and she clung to his broad shoulders. The man had some fast moves. She gazed into his dark eyes, seeing satisfaction there. He wanted to be her Master and she'd allow it. She wondered what he thought of her. She must look a sight sitting there, naked, spanked, and flushing from the pleasure of being fucked.

"I don't have anything to compare it to," she said honestly.

"Then, I was your first," he said, smiling.

"Uh huh."

"Tell me, Cherie, what brings you to France?"

The question brought her up short. There was no way she wanted to share her foolish mistake with a man she was growing to…like.

"A temporary position."

"Just a little diversion?" he asked.

His serious tone made her wonder if he knew about her being fired and nearly arrested, but that was impossible. She certainly hadn't put it down on the questionnaire Madame Imogene had her fill out. She just wanted to forget it and try to move on.

"That's right," she said, watching him frown.

Then, he stood with her in his arms, making her gasp and wrap her arms around his neck. She looked at him questioningly. What the heck? Was he thinking of firing her, too?

"It's time for your shower." He carried her into the stall.

Relieved, she let out a pleasured giggle when he stepped them both under the pulsing spray, feeling so content in his strong arms. She sighed when the water cascaded over her, and she clung to him with longing. His dark gaze on hers made her body quicken again, her sex pulse anew. What was he thinking?

He bent to kiss her, and damn, she wanted to, but couldn't. She turned her head away at the last minute, and he muttered a dark curse as his hands tightened on her. Her heart contracted because she wanted to kiss him, too, but this would mean too much to her. Already, she felt too much for the man. Well, at least she wasn't the only one involved, but it would be foolhardy of her to give him an emotional tie to her. Even if he liked her, he'd get rid of her as soon as the contract expired, and she couldn't risk her heart.

Putting unpleasant thoughts aside, she nibbled his ear, him groaning in response. Then, she moved on to kiss his throat, sucking on him hungrily, trying to memorize his essence. When this was over, she didn't want to forget an inch of him after going back to her humdrum life. She knew she'd never meet another man like him. His hands tightened on her ass for a moment before he let her go to slide sensuously down his slick body.

She quivered, the erotic sensation curling her toes, hell, even her toenails. She stood on trembling legs, leaning into his hard strength, absorbing him. There was no way she could settle for less than passion after this. The thought made her smile mistily. At least Nick had taught her that she wasn't frigid. Far from it with the right man. Or maybe just with this man. She gazed up at him through a steamy orgasmic cloud, seeing the banked fire in his dark eyes. He was absolutely perfect. She wanted him again, and she'd have him.

"I want you," she said, rubbing her nipples across his chest.

He spread his feet shoulder-length apart, and pulled her wet curves against his body.

"Behave," he said, reaching behind her to give her a sharp spank.

She whimpered with pleasure, pressed her mound against his cock, and gazed up at him.

"Yes, sir," she said, unrepentantly.

His sensual mouth was set in firm lines, and she ached to take a taste of him. She was in trouble deep, and she knew it, but she was past caring.

As if he read her intentions, he let her go, stepped back, and picked up a sea sponge. When he passed over the large bottle of sandalwood body wash to reach for a small one of jasmine scent, she couldn't help wondering what other female had shared his shower. The jealousy was stupid, she knew that, but couldn't help it.

When he started to wash her, swirling the sponge over her sensitized body, she thought she'd died and gone to heaven, it was so good. She bit back a moan when he paid special attention to her breasts, teasing the nipples until she was trembling with need, her breath shaky. Her knees wobbled and she murmured nonsense as she leaned into him. Staring up at him, she watched his whiskey-brown irises contract.

"I'm your Master," he said, shaking his head. "Do you want me to stop?" he asked, stilling the sweet torture.

She let out a panicked gasp. "No. Please don't stop."

"I won't for now," he said gently, and turned her around, spreading her feet apart. "Let's scrub that saucy bottom of yours."

She sighed, as he swirled the sponge over her raw bottom and then moaned when his fingertip toyed with her anus.

"Have you ever had anal sex, Cherie?"

She quivered when his little finger teased her puckering orifice, shocked at the pleasure that rocked through her. "No. That's dirty."

"Nice and dirty," he agreed, tickling her. "Would you like me to take you there?"

"Yes, please," she gasped, stunned by the way it aroused her and embarrassed when she heard his chuckle. She blushed and arched against that teasing finger, completely under his spell.

"When the time it right, that too will be mine," he said, teasing her tight portal with a soapy finger.

She went both hot and cold, her body clenching him. Her legs wobbled as he teased her, setting off spasms in her vagina. *When*, she wanted to ask him, but kept silent, hoping to show him she was submissive.

"Very good," he praised. "Convince me that you want me to possess you there."

The husky demand made her ripples start anew. She arched back, riding his finger, her tight passage pulling at him, and whimpered at the dirty/good feeling. She moaned, giving him better access. Then he reached out to adjust the spray, driving her crazy as he aimed it at her stiff clit.

"Come for me, Cherie," he husked.

She tightened around him and cried out as she came. When her legs gave out, he caught her and held her tight as she drifted back to Earth. His sexy chuckle made her quiver again.

Nick Renault was a truly sinfully wicked man, and she loved it.

She turned in his arms, loving the slippery feel of his body against hers. She'd wondered about anal sex, and this only made her want it more.

"That was..."

"Sexy," he filled in.

"Earth-shattering." She lapped at his nipples, drinking a droplet of water off his skin. His cock pressed hot into her, and twitched against her, making her crazy.

"No. Now it's my turn," he said, handing her the sponge. "Wash me, my sexy little courtesan."

She blushed at the title and took the sponge from him, seeing his lips twitch with amusement. Did he really think of her that way? As his bright-eyed glance swept over her, she decided that maybe he did. The scent of her hung heavy in the air and she knew he liked it when his nostrils flared. When his wicked cock bobbed before her, throbbing, she felt a sense of feminine power. The fact he'd given her pleasure without taking any for himself made her feel cherished.

She stepped forward and started to wash him, lathering his chest with the soapy sponge.

"Tell me about yourself, Laura," he insisted. "You may speak."

The question startled her, and she wasn't sure how to answer.

"What do you want to know?" she asked, watching his mouth firm at her evasive tactic.

What could she tell him? That she came from a poor but happy family, lived in a small Wisconsin town he'd no doubt never heard of, and she was a suspected jewel thief? Oh yeah, that'd get her canned, for sure.

"How about other relationships, for starters."

A sense of relief went through her. Past relationships, or the lack thereof, she could discuss. "That's easy. I'm not in one and don't have time for one."

"You're not interested in marriage?" he asked, his brow quirking.

She met his doubtful gaze with a steady one of her own. It was clear he didn't believe her and she wondered why. Women had tried to trap him for his wealth, she supposed. He needn't worry about her, this was strictly business, and she wasn't interested in marriage. She wanted to pursue her budding career as an artist, although the debacle she'd just been through might have put an end to that.

"I know for men in your culture it's probably a shock, but I'm not interested in getting married, Nick."

His eyes narrowed. "Is that so?"

"Yes." The stiffening of his body told her he didn't like her crack about his culture. She was careful to hide her smile. Well, at least she figured out one way to silence him—piss him off.

"Really," he said tightly.

Avoiding his steaming gaze, she swirled the sponge over his abs and then moved on to his impressive manhood. She sank to her knees on the shower's stone floor, driven by the undeniable need to taste him. That she'd never even considered doing this before didn't matter. He was different. The burning look in his eyes made her quiver.

"I'm learning that the domineering part can be fun, at times."

She knew her smile was tremulous as she gazed at him. She watched a nerve in his tight jaw pulse.

"Sit back on your heels, Laura, legs open, and hands palm up on your knees," he ordered darkly.

She flowed into the vulnerable position, quivering. Why was he being so gruff?

"Excellent," he said, gazing down at her. "This is submissive position number one. On my command, you'll flow into it as gracefully as you can."

She warmed at his husky tone.

"Now, lean forward and open your mouth for your Master," he commanded, harsher than usual, maybe due to her comment about Gallic men being domineering.

She'd never given oral sex in her life, but gazing at his cock, she was tempted to taste him. And she knew there'd be no denying her Master.

She leaned forward to experimentally flick her tongue out to taste him, making a yummy sound. Nick was salty, sweet, and all man. Hers, at least, for three months. He was even better than she'd imagined.

He shuddered, his hands tangling in her hair.

She lapped a glistening drop of pre-cum off his slit and thrilled when he growled in response. Emboldened, she swirled her tongue around his hot velvety head, then opened her mouth to take him in. His groan excited her, made her suck on him hard, trying to take more of him in. He tasted unique, manly, wonderful, all hers.

"Good girl," he said, thrusting between her lips. "The first moment I laid eyes on you, I had an image of you servicing me this way."

His naughty words excited her, and her pussy pulsed as he fucked her mouth. She tried to take him deeper, gagging a little, then trying again.

"Sweet Cherie," he said, throbbing inside her mouth. "When I come, swallow it all, or I'll paddle your sexy ass."

She thrilled at the sensual threat and sucked harder, milking him, feeling him jerk inside her mouth. He came with a roar, spurting inside of her, and she greedily took his salty cum as the excess flowed down her breasts. She left him with a lick and a promise, and when she leaned back on her haunches to look up at him, he was smiling.

His finger traced a trail of cum down her left breast. He lifted up a drop and held it to her lips. She obediently licked it off his fingertip, watching his eyes flare.

"You spilled," he said tenderly. "I'll paddle you later."

She couldn't wait. Gazing up at him, her body raged with desire.

"Good," she said with a smile. "I think I might like it."

***

Nick stared down at his feisty fire goddess, totally bemused. Teaching her to be silent was going to be a challenge, but she was the picture of sweet submission as she knelt before him with desire in her eyes. Her lips were reddened and a little puffy from giving him head, and her nipples were hard as rubies. He didn't need to touch her to know that her pussy was wet and ready for him.

He was still troubled by the private investigator's report he'd just read, and even more bothered by the fact that she was trying to hide what had happened. And he really wanted to put a hurt on Pierre Gallo, her shady former mentor. Just the fact that the police hadn't charged her with a crime was telling.

"Up," he said, tugging her to her feet.

She stood and promptly tumbled against him as her legs wobbled. He smiled and held her tight, supporting her, savoring the feel of her lush curves against his rapidly hardening body. Would he ever get his fill of her? He rubbed his aching cock against the fiery curls covering her mound and she lifted her head off his shoulder to look at him, her eyes filled with longing.

"Again?" she asked, breathlessly.

"How many spankings will it take to teach you to keep silent?" he asked, amused when she glared at him.

Still, it didn't stop her from rubbing against him, inflaming him.

"Tell me, Cherie. Where did you learn to give head like that?"

Her blush confirmed his thoughts that she was a gifted amateur.

"My personal library," she said, her stare wavering a little, her cheeks flushing beautifully. "You're the first chance I've have to put it into practice."

"And I'd better be the only." The possessive feeling that went through him was strong, but he wasn't fooling himself that he could keep her forever. A summer fling was all he could have, and he'd make the most of it. "I won't share you with anyone, Laura, so don't get any ideas of trying it on another man. You're mine," he insisted. "Until I let you go, you're mine."

"I'm yours," she agreed with a pleasured sigh, rubbing her nipples against him.

His hands cupped her ass and squeezed. "And this ass is mine to spank," he said.

"Yes, I belong to you."

He felt like the one owned as she rocked against him, inflaming his desire. His aching cock pulsed against her. He picked her up, his hands clutching her lush ass as he commanded gruffly, "Wrap your legs around your Master's waist, Cherie."

She moaned, her long legs wrapping around his waist as she trembled against him.

He thrust into her creamy heat, biting back a groan as her honey walls tightened around him. God, she was going to milk another one out of him, but he wanted to control the pace.

Gripping her ass tighter, he pulled back to surge into her, making her cry out with pleasure. He basked in her cries as he took her, backing her against the marble tiles as he fucked her harder. She was like a drug, and he couldn't get enough. And then, she came, little mewling noises escaping her throat. He drove into her one more time as she wrung his orgasm out of him and came.

"Laura," he groaned, knowing he'd never get his fill of her.

Chapter 4

Laura blushed when they came back to the room. To her dismay, she found supper laid out for them. The table was set with roses and candles, making for a beautiful, intimate scene. It meant someone had been in here when they'd been making love in the shower. Her cheeks flamed with heat. The intruder might have even heard her getting spanked.

It was then that she noticed her clothes were gone. "Where are my things?" she demanded.

"Put away until I let you go. You'll wear what I choose for you from now on," Nick said, going to the wardrobe. "I'm afraid I was only able to pick up a few items."

She watched him pull open the wardrobe and stared at what looked like lingerie in the almost empty closet. It irritated her once again. Just how many courtesans had he bought over the years?

"Blue to match your eyes," he said, pulling out a silk peignoir set in cornflower blue.

She reveled at the vintage nightgown and robe's beauty, seeing their exquisite workmanship. Having worked as her mother's seamstress shop assistant, she recognized the fine handiwork.

"They're beautiful," she said grudgingly, still pissed that he was giving her another woman's clothing.

"I'll tell my sister-in-law," he said with a half-smile.

"Your sister-in-law?"

"Yes. She's the designer and left these here from her last collection. I'm sure Simone won't mind."

He stood quivering as he dressed her in the exquisite lingerie, intrigued by the little bit he'd revealed about himself.

"So, your sister-in-law's a designer?"

The firm look he gave her told her he regretted he'd told her.

"Sit at the table." He indicated the small table that had been laid out for dinner.

She hurried to comply. At least he couldn't question her with his mouth full.

She watched him walk over to her unashamedly nude. He was magnificent, she had to admit. She'd love to paint him that way.

He served her dinner. She watched him lift the lid, and her stomach growled when the savory aroma hit her. She blushed and hoped he hadn't noticed.

"You really were starved."

Lord, she hoped he didn't know how true that was. There was no way she wanted him feeling sorry for her. "I've been too busy to eat."

He frowned. "You won't be missing any meals from now on."

Her panicked gaze flashed to his determined one.

"It's not good for you, and you'll be of no use to me if you starve yourself."

She felt a little better. He hardly sounded as if he found her pathetic.

"Try the *coq au vin*. Al's recipe is an old family one."

She inhaled the heavenly aroma of the chicken in wine sauce, and then took a bite. It melted in her mouth, it was so good.

She smiled at Nick, realizing he was waiting for her comment. "It's delicious. My compliments to the chef."

"I'll tell him, but the old reprobate might get a swelled head."

"He can't be that bad," she protested.

"You tell me. You met him."

"I did?" she said, thinking of the gruff butler.

"Sure, he drove you here."

"You mean the surly driver?"

Nick grinned. "That's him."

"I didn't mean any insult."

"Don't worry about it," he said, stoking her cheek. "Being surly has saved his ass plenty of times."

She smiled at the description. Maybe Al had been a prize-fighter like she'd imagined. She took a sip of her wine, savoring it and the moment. "Okay."

"So, tell me about your private library," he said suggestively.

She choked on her wine and coughed as her face flamed. The delight on his face told her he'd enjoyed shocking her.

"Um, I..."

"Yes?"

"I've been reading erotica," she admitted.

"Have you now?"

"My latest read is in my backpack."

"And it taught you how to give head like a pro."

"Did I really?"

He smiled. "You did, but I think you can get better. I'll have to see if I can enlarge your naughty reading list. I have suggestions."

He pulled her onto his lap. The book he pulled out of her backpack made her blush. *Enemy Mine*, a really hot erotica. The book practically fell open to a bookmarked page.

He removed the bookmark and smiled. "Read it to me, Cherie. A little bedtime tale before I paddle you."

Blushing at the reminder that he'd promised to paddle her, she clutched the book, a little embarrassed. *Enemy Mine* was a sizzling novel about a captive woman, and was heavily into BDSM. No wonder she was taking to this like a fish to water. But there would be no denying her Master, that she knew.

She licked her lips, and felt Nick's hand slide down her back, gentling her frayed nerves. Her gaze fell to the passage she'd reread six times, and she began to read.

"...Diablo stepped back and watched Cyn with hooded eyes. "Go to the trees for the ceremony. Show the others you're willing to warm my bed, be my naughty little sex kitten.'

Cyn walked to the two trees with ropes tied to them, knowing what was coming. Still, she couldn't help but be apprehensive. Her plaintive gaze went to Diablo. He stepped up to her, and touched her arm. She gained strength from his touch and held out her right hand for Diablo to tie to the tree. She stood trembling a little when he tied the other wrist to the opposite tree, and fastened her ankles. When he had her bound, spread-eagle, Diablo ran a hand up her leg. She couldn't help the needy shudder that shook her.

"It's just you and me, Angel," he said, standing.

His smile, his hands cupping her breasts, his rough fingertips rolling her nipples, all combined to seduce her. She whimpered in ecstasy, arching her back for him. The restraints just made her hotter and frustrated because she couldn't move. She glared at him when he pulled away, making him smile.

"First your nipple clamps." He picked the beaten gold clamps from his shirt pocket. "Nice" he said, absentmindedly fanning Cyn's nipple until it budded, then clamping the clip on it.

Cyn gasped when he put them on her, feeling the pull right to her toes. She whimpered in ecstasy. Her knees would have buckled if she hadn't been bound. It was way more sexual than painful, and caught her by surprise. She glanced down at the gold clamp on her swollen nipple, the sapphire jiggling as she gasped. She stood there shuddering, even though she thought she was prepared, and gazed into his eyes, looking for a safety line. The reality of the situation set in as he gazed resolutely back at her. This wasn't a love game. She was his love slave, at least until she got the goods on Carver and made her escape.

"Good girl," Diablo said, stroking her hair.

She leaned into his touch, warmed by his heated tone, her pussy quivering and getting wet as her heart raced. She, a Delta Star washout, was now thrown into the deep end of the pool, and it was time to sink or swim.

"Are you ready to wear my collar?" Diablo said in a clear tone that carried across the campground.

She nodded, then held her breath when he pulled the matching antique gold collar out of his pocket. It was beautiful, like a fine piece of jewelry, and intricately worked. He slipped it around her neck, the star-shaped pendant dangling, making it look like a choker. Something inside her softened even though she knew it was playacting. He didn't really mean to claim her, if she could trust what he'd said.

"I'm your Master now, Angel," he said, inches from kissing her. "Your loyalty is mine, and mine alone. Say it," he demanded.

"My loyalty is yours and yours alone," she repeated, adding silently—and not Proclaim's.

He nodded. "Excellent. You agree that it's my duty to bend you to my will, to lash your sweet ass with my paddle and belt, and open you with my cock."

"Yes, Master," she said, a secret part of her glorying in it. She'd fantasized about masterful men for years. It was a shameful secret she'd never shared. Her eyes widened when she watched Diablo unfurl the leather strap from his belt loop. If a hand spanking had made her come, what might a whipping do to her? She wasn't sure, but wanted to know.

"Time for your whipping." He stepped behind her.

She took in a tremulous breath, glancing at the leering crowd. "Yes, sir."

"Ready?"

She nodded.

He flicked his wrist and gave her a taste of leather. She let out a little yelp as the strap wrapped around her left cheek. Her sex got creamier as her body quickened.

"Now, as I whip you, I want you to repeat, I'll be loyal. Say it."

The strap caught her again and she whimpered. "I'll be loyal."

"Excellent." He swung the strap, lashing her.

Cyn gasped, her hips writhing. "I'll be loyal."

"Good."

She could only moan as her whole body caught fire, taking the whipping as foreplay. A smack caught the bottom of her other cheek.

"I'll be loyal," she cried.

"You bet you will," he muttered, his voice husky.

He was turned on, she could hear it in his voice, and it made her hotter. When he swung the strap, catching her on the bottom of her ass, she shuddered, her pussy rippling.

"I'll be loyal."

"No jumping."

Trembling, Cyn tried to obey, even as her sex pulsed. She didn't want to come in front of the others, she couldn't. The tip of the strap hit her mound, and she screamed, convulsing.

"I'll be loyal, sir."

The men sitting around the fire cheered.

Diablo stepped up to her and released her, catching her when she would have crumpled to the ground.

"You're mine," he said huskily.

"Yes," she moaned, wrapping her arms around him as she shuddered with after-spasms.

Diablo set her back on her feet and clipped the strap to her collar like a leash.

She was shocked, but didn't move."

Nick took the book from her hands, stopping her.

She glanced at him, apprehensive, and guessing what he wanted.

"Have you wished for a Master for very long?" he asked, gazing at her.

She blushed because she knew it was true. "It's just a fantasy."

"Not anymore," he said with a smile.

"Will you collar me?" she asked, blushing, thinking of the passage she'd just read.

The possessive light in his eyes made her breath catch and her nipples bud. As if he noticed, he reached up to stroke her nipples through her gown, making her squirm on his lap with arousal. Her pussy was wet and already tightening for him.

He stood them up, taking her hand. "I haven't decided yet," he said, gazing at her. "Right now, it's time for your paddling."

"I thought maybe you forgot."

"Not a chance," he said, smiling as he led her to a corner of the room.

She followed him, her body quivering. How hard would it be to be paddled? Would it be worse than the spanking? Would it make her come, too?

When he pulled off her gown, she stood there, shaking. Her nipples tugged, and she shivered.

He walked over to the funny exercise equipment—the frame with pulleys.

"Reach up and grab the bar," he commanded.

She did.

He bound her wrists to the upper corners of the bar. It was just like the book. How did he know? She whimpered at the tug to her rock-hard nipples, as both her breasts lifted. She was stretched, taut, apprehensive, and more turned on than ever.

Then he crouched to bind her ankles, effectively spread-eagling her. Her pussy was creamy, aching, and she knew there was no going back.

Was he going to take her like this? It was an exciting possibility. But he'd promised to punish her. She watched him walk to the dresser and pick up a black paddle. Her bottom clenched as she stared at it, looming large and hot in his hand. He caught her looking and smiled, a wicked heartbreaker's smile that told her he knew how turned on she was.

Oh, no! He stepped up beside her and kissed her shoulder, making her shudder.

"It's time for your paddling, Cherie," he said softly.

A shot of heat bolted through her, and she felt a little breathless as he rubbed the padded leather against her vulnerable ass. He had all the control.

He licked her nape murmuring, "Ready?"

"I'm not sure," she said, being truthful.

His sexy chuckle just made her cream more.

"You're more than ready," he said, drawing back the paddle.

She sucked in her breath in anticipation, and then shrieked when the paddle landed with a. Heat spread through her bottom.

"No sound," Nick lectured, "or I'll gag you."

Would he? She bit back a cry as he landed another *smack*, and moaned as her pussy clenched in reaction.

"Better," he praised, paddling her again.

She wasn't able to hold back her cries.

He growled and covered her mouth with his hand, muffling her. She gasped against his palm as he heated her bottom again and again.

He paddled her once more, and tears filled her eyes.

"No! Ouch," she cried, turning her head from his hand. As she sobbed quietly, she heard him drop the paddle. What other sexy tortures does he have in mind?

He brushed a teardrop off her cheek. "Sweet tears of sweet submission, Cherie."

That's exactly what they were, and she trembled in response, mopping the tears with her lashes. When he held out his finger, she obediently licked the teardrop off. He went behind her, kissing her neck, sucking on it, biting. She shuddered, getting aroused. His hot lips ran down her spine, making her shiver as he knelt behind her. She felt his lips on her paddled bottom, kissing, licking, soothing the fire. He nipped her, and she shuddered and moaned, pure ecstasy.

His hands spread her ass cheeks, and he stroked her anus.

She gasped, quivering.

"You're too tight," he said, rubbing lube.

She froze at the unexpected touch, her bottom milking at him while her pussy pulsed. Who knew anal sex would be this good?

"More," she whimpered.

He chuckled. "Not until I decide the time is right," he said and left her with a spank.

She pouted when he withdrew to walk to the dresser. He came back, carrying what looked like a short, stubby, thin dildo. Her eyes widened. She'd read about butt plugs, but she wanted him, not a substitute.

"This is your butt plug, my feisty courtesan."

"I'd rather have the real thing," she said with a grumble.

He smiled, holding it up to her lips, and she kissed it, reluctantly. It warmed under her mouth, reminding her of his very hot cock. She'd much rather be sucking on that.

"Very good," he praised with a smile. He walked behind her.

She tensed, feeling him part her cheeks. The plug touched her, and she let out a gasp.

"Relax, Cherie," he said. "I'm opening your ass, but I'll take you nice and slow."

She forced her flaming body to still, and then she felt it entering, spreading her as he wedged it firmly inside her.

He backed away. The plug stayed in place, holding her open, feeling too big—naughty.

She cried quietly as he stood, then walked around to face her. She stood, captive and stretched, her bottom plugged, and she peeked at him. He was smiling, satisfied, because he'd done this to her. She couldn't stop the shot of heat through her body. He stepped closer, nearer. Was he going to kiss her? She wanted him to, despite her stipulation that she wouldn't kiss.

He leaned closer and she sighed with pleasure, closing her eyes, getting ready to throw the contract to the wind, and good riddance. But instead of kissing her lips, he brushed tiny kisses on her eyelids, her cheeks, everywhere but where she wanted. She groaned with frustration and then sighed when he touched her breasts, pinching the nipples. Her aroused body flooded at the pleasure/pain that zinged through them, making her pussy contract, her anus ripple on her butt plug, and her eyes pop open.

The sultry look on his face had her breathless, and then he bent to suck one tortured nipple into his hot mouth, making her squirm in her bonds. He kept drawing on it, bathing it with his rough tongue, making her cry out with pleasure. It was almost enough to make her come. He moved to suck on her right nipple, drawing hard on it while he pinched the left one and her knees wobbled. She was putty in his hands, and he knew it.

His talented mouth left and she missed his touch, heated where he had been. He knelt, spearing his tongue into her pussy, flicking his tongue at her clit teasingly, sucking on the lips of her labia. She was writhing, groaning, when he stabbed his tongue into her cunt again, then sucked her clit into his mouth. He gently bit down on her while reaching behind her to swirl the plug in her anus.

She came, shuddering, hanging limply afterward.

"And do you pledge your loyalty to me?" he asked.

She remembered the passage from the book and blushed, nodding.

He gripped her chin. "I want the words, Cherie."

All he'd wanted from her before was silence, but she sensed that this meant something to him. "I pledge my loyalty to you, Nick. I'm yours."

For three months, then pushed that thought away. But his sober look told her he had his doubts. What woman had hurt him? She really didn't want to know. This was just a job. But deep inside, she knew the walls were crumbling.

He carried her to the bed and got in beside her, snuggling with her. "Go to sleep, my fiery concubine. You've got more obedience lessons to learn in the morning."

She felt him tuck his semi-erect cock between her cheeks. He could have her any way he wanted her, and she loved it, she admitted. He'd known her deepest fantasies, even before she had.

Before she fell asleep, her last thought was how much trouble she was in, that she could never consider this only a business arrangement.

He placed a large hand on her breast, cupping it firmly as she drifted away into slumber.

Chapter 5

A tap on the door woke Laura the next morning. Opening her eyes, she was amazed she had slept so well in a strange bed. Nick had just plain worn her out. But where was he? He must have left in the middle of the night, keeping his sleeping solo rule, even though her self-protective rules were crumbling.

Whoever was tapping on her bedroom door wasn't him. Nick wouldn't bother to knock, he would just come in and take her by command. The thought both troubled and thrilled her as she sat up in bed, pulling the covers up to her chin.

"Come in," she said nervously, not used to being a courtesan.

The door was thrown open and the surly chauffer from yesterday shouldered his way inside, carrying a silver tray. He was wearing an apron over his jeans and polo shirt.

"Breakfast," he said gruffly, giving her a curious onceover.

"Um, thanks," she said, feeling awkward as he laid the tray on her lap. "Where's Nick?"

"Downstairs, in his office." He frowned. "You're to follow the instructions he left you after you eat."

She gulped, hearing the gruff disapproval in his voice. Surely unmarried people sleeping together wouldn't shock a man of the world, but she sensed it was more.

"Fine," she said shortly, frowning back at him. She wasn't going to let him intimidate her. Then the aroma of the omelet on her plate made her stomach growl, reminding her how hungry she was, and she forgot to be mad at him. "You made the *coq au vin* last night?"

"What of it?" he asked in a snarly voice.

He had a suspicious nature, but she could sense his kindness. She smiled at him, thinking he wasn't as tough as he let on.

"It was heavenly, and this smells just as good."

He tried, but couldn't hold back a smile.

Coughing, embarrassed, he said, "It was nothing."

"No. I appreciate the trouble you went to. I don't mind telling you I was starving." The questioning look he gave her made her wonder. Still, it was good to feel like she might have an ally on the staff.

"Don't keep him waiting."

"I won't," she said, eager to see Nick again.

As Al walked to the door, he turned to say, "See that you don't hurt him."

She was so shocked by his words all she could do was stare at him as he firmly closed the door behind him. Why did he think she had that power or that she would want to hurt Nick? Maybe one of her predecessors had. For all she knew, Nick made a habit of employing some wild courtesans. She'd suspected as much several times. The thought brought her spirits down and she sagged against the plump pillows.

This was a hell of a mess, being jealous over her temporary Master. She'd be wise to keep her distance. With that thought firmly in mind, she quickly finished her delicious breakfast.

Then, she got out of bed to get the sealed envelope Nick had left for her.

Shower and be ready for me at nine, but don't dress.

She shivered with delight at the command and rushed to the bathroom to shower. Just stepping into the stall and smelling Nick's sandalwood body wash brought her back to their steamy shower session last night. She felt like a changed woman today, and he was responsible.

She waited for Nick, her body trembling, more intrigued than ever. Why all the mystery?

Then she heard his familiar footsteps coming down the hall. Odd and exciting that she could already recognize his tread. As the door opened, she flowed into the submissive position he'd taught her and bowed her head, sneaking a fast peek up at him.

He stopped in the doorway and smiled at her. She could feel the satisfaction he radiated as he walked into the room and shut the door behind him.

His gaze roamed over her. "Very nicely done, Cherie."

"Thank you, sir."

At his frown, she remembered too late his no speaking rule. Would he paddle her for it? She spotted a bondage bar in the corner, and her ass heated along with her face.

"We'll get to that eventually, Cherie," he said, walking up to stroke her cheek. "I trust that you slept well."

She nodded. "You wore me out," she replied, even though he hadn't said she could speak.

He gave her a minute shake of his head as he dropped his hand from her cheek.

"Your new wardrobe will be delivered later today. I got your sizes from Immy."

So, that was the purpose of that part of the detailed history she'd filled out for Imogene. She couldn't help noticing he was on such a casual basis with the Madam.

"If you were truthful, the clothes I bought you should fit." He walked to a closet. "Come here."

Of course, she'd been truthful. She wasn't vain enough to lie about what size she wore, but she refrained from saying so. There was no need to court demerits, not that she minded the spankings. Still, she knew he was trying to set things up his way, he the Master, she the submissive little courtesan, but something inside her rebelled at the thought. She considered getting to her feet, but instead crawled over to him on all fours. When she sat back on her haunches before him, she could see the reluctant humor on his face.

"Will I ever be able to tame you?" he mused aloud.

She knew he already had, but wasn't about to tell him that. Instead, she bowed her head, but peered up at him through her lashes.

"Just be glad that I'm not annoyed enough to keep you naked all day in retribution," he said.

She shivered, a burst of excitement going through her at his gruff threat. He was just sinful enough to do it. She could only push him so far. She watched as he pulled a red bustier out of the drawer. She never wore red, thinking it would clash with her hair and accentuate her full curves. Besides, only bad girls wore red, but that was what she'd become. It would cover her from the bottom of her breasts to the flare of her ass, leaving all the erogenous parts exposed.

She stood and reached for the garment, only to have him frown.

"That's my pleasure," he said, lacing her into the scandalous garment.

She couldn't help blushing as he smoothed it over her hips.

"You call this dressing?" she teased, and then gasped when he cupped her breasts, teasing them. She moaned in reaction, going boneless.

"Bend over." He pushed her over his arm and reached for a tube of lubricant.

A thrill went through her. He was just full of surprises this morning.

"You're finally going to take me," she said.

"Hush. You're not ready until I say so. I'm opening you with your butt plug. I want you to keep yourself lubed and use it every day."

She shivered when he stroked the globes of her ass, caressing her already creamy sex, his lubed finger tickling her puckered anus. She cried out when he slipped his finger into her heat, her body rippling on him. Instead of staying there, however, he pressed the accursed butt plug in place. He ignored her when she protested his finger's withdrawal.

"Up now," he said, helping her to stand.

The plug moved a little inside her, causing a tidal wave of arousal in its wake. She focused on Nick with a pleading glance. The sultry knowing look he gave her in return just made her creamier.

"I've got some jewels for you to wear," he said, opening a case.

Her eyes widened when she glimpsed at what looked like sapphire earrings. She'd never owned anything so fine.

"They're beautiful."

The smile he gave her made her wonder.

"They're nipple clamps, Cherie, and they perfectly match your eyes." He cupped her breasts.

She went weak inside as he played with her, tugging on her nipples and teasing her.

She was fascinated by the idea of nipple clamps, something she'd read about in her erotica. She found her sex dampening.

How would they feel? She held her breath, watching him pick one up and open it. Then he fastened it onto her turgid peak, and she whimpered, feeling a delightful pull down to her toes.

"Lovely," he said, fanning her other nipple until it budded harder, then clamping the clip on it.

She bit back a moan, her knees almost buckling at the sexy feeling. She glanced down at the gold clamps on her swollen nipples, sapphires dangling from the tips. They jiggled when she shuddered.

Nick turned and looked deep into Laura's gaze of sensual surrender. She was finding out just how seductive being submissive could be. His gaze slowly traveled over the alluring picture she made as his cock twitched in his pants. The bustier set off all her lush curves, making her look like a sexy angel, as her breasts pillowed over the top and her hips flared. He was tempted to take her downstairs that way, but he didn't want to risk losing her to another. Instead, he pulled a sundress out of the closet.

"It's time for you to dress," he said, a little rougher than he'd intended. He had to set the pace and tone of this summer fling, or she'd ride roughshod over him.

"Yes, Nick," she said softly.

He slipped the rayon floral sundress over her, its built-in bra hiding the fact that he had her in nipple clamps. Her delicious, womanly figure was enough to divert him from his goal, and he needed to keep it in his pants for now.

He watched her glance pointedly down at his raging hard-on. She hadn't lied about her sizes as he imagined most women would. He'd had Simone express just about everything in her summer collection.

"Every morning, I want you dressed and ready to service me precisely at eight in the morning. I'll come to you for our morning sessions."

The sour look she gave him made him smile.

"Not an early riser?"

She shook her head.

"You will be," he said. "You'll be at my beck and call for the rest of the day, except for a rest break of your choosing. Then, you'll attend to me in my chamber before coming back here to sleep." He walked up to her and stroked her arm, watching a flush spread. "Are we clear, Cherie?"

"Yes," she said.

The sultry look she gave him told him that, despite her fears, she was looking forward to it. It made him feel like her Master and protector all at the same time. He cupped her breast again, feathering the stiff nipple with his fingertip, drinking in her gasp.

"Let's start with my morning session," he said, and she immediately went to her knees, looking up at him hungrily.

"Don't spill a drop now," he warned playfully.

"Yes, sir." She unzipped him.

He bit back a groan when his stiff cock popped out and she flicked her hot little tongue at it. She was a natural. She drew him into her mouth, forcing him to brace his legs to keep upright, and he was gone. She sucked on him hard while her hand fisted the base of his cock. When her other eager hand squeezed his balls, he came with a groan, shooting a huge load into the back of her ravenous mouth. She sucked, draining him, and pulled away, leaving him with a lick.

"Good girl," he praised, losing part of his heart.

***

Laura gazed up at Nick, bemused, her body tingling as her pussy creamed. Who knew giving head would turn her on so much? It was a revelation to her.

He zipped his pants and she blushed, making him smile. It seemed her lack of experience was pleasing to him for some reason. Boys never did like to share their toys.

"Up now," he said, reaching for her hand.

She let him effortlessly pull her to her feet, realizing just how strong his was. Wow! Their bodies collided and she pressed against him, needful. If he would just touch her, she'd come.

He set her back on her feet, his expression firm. "You can't come yet. You'll hold it for me," he said.

She looked at him, shocked. He couldn't demand that she not come, it was barbaric. She'd just have to get herself off in private.

"And you can't touch yourself, either."

She glared at him, annoyed that he'd read her thoughts.

He smiled. "Disobey me on this, and I'll add a chastity belt to your outfits."

Was he kidding? His smile was impossible to interpret in her fevered state.

"Bastard," she muttered under her breath.

"That's one demerit," he said, going toward the door. "Come with me and I'll give you the grand tour."

Well, hell, she was dying to see the place. She hurried to catch up with him, following him out into the hall.

He led her to a turret, and into what was obviously the master bedroom. She gazed around in awe at the antique furniture and the room, all done in cool masculine tones. She gazed at the king-sized bed. Would he ever take her there?

He stepped up behind her to stroke a hand down her arm and then cup a breast. "In the evenings, you'll attend to me here, and then go back to your room to sleep."

She bit back a moan as he plucked at her nipple, and she pressed her ass against him, despite his words. Why didn't he want to sleep with her? The question plagued her.

"Attend to you, huh?" she said playfully. "Just what does that entail?"

"Whatever I decree." He stepped back to give her bottom a smack.

She let out a quick, surprised breath as it made her pussy ripple.

***

Nick knew she wanted him to take her, and make her come, but he also knew he couldn't allow her to call the shots. She'd lied to him last night when he'd questioned her, and it bothered him. Why, he wasn't sure, but he figured it had to do with her dismissal from her post and her near arrest.

Diamonds were stolen from a client Pierre Gallo had been painting, and she'd gotten blamed. He didn't buy it. Nick could tell it was a set up, she'd been the victim in more ways than one, and he was going to prove it. Still, it bothered him she didn't trust him enough to tell the truth.

The little fool thought she could keep silent about it and he'd be none the wiser, but she was wrong. He'd take steps to help her, whether she asked for it or not, and he was certain who the culprit was. His private investigator, following leads, would soon get to the bottom of the situation. The next step was hers to take. He wanted her to open up to him, trust him with the truth.

He stepped away from her tempting curves and took her hand, leading her back out into the hall. "Come with me."

He led her toward the grand staircase, ignoring the other bedchambers that weren't currently in use. Al lived in his own apartment above the carriage house, and Bridges, the butler, lived in the servant's quarters at the rear of the house. The housekeeper came in three days a week to tidy up. Usually, it was just the three men rattling around in this empty house, and they rarely bumped into each other.

Still, he loved to come here for his vacations because of its solitude and family associations, not that he was a legitimate heir. He'd bought the estate from receivership after the last owner, his uncle, Maurice, had squandered his wealth away.

Laura's hand was warm in his, and he gazed at her, realizing the house seemed more alive now that she was here. He frowned, knowing it was a perilous thought, one that he shouldn't be feeling.

He deliberately thrust his thoughts back to his semi-aristocratic paternal ancestors. In his great-grandfather's day, the estate had been host to some wild orgies. Great-grandfather Joe would, no doubt, approve of him hiring a courtesan.

Nick held Laura's hand a little tighter. Maybe he was proving that blood did tell, after all, but he didn't regret taking her on, no matter how complicated things got. However, he, unlike his ancestors, preferred to confine himself to one woman at a time, and Laura heated his blood like no other woman ever had, including Yvette.

He watched his animated courtesan as she gazed wide-eyed and awed at the estate. He wondered what he'd ever seen in his plastic ex-wife. Simple, she'd been chic and sophisticated, and had all the right connections. It'd been more a business arrangement than a marriage, he realized. She'd actually done him a favor by screwing around and leaving him.

He steered Laura through the formal front parlor with its chintz covered settees and Oriental rug, and into the paneled dining room. The long gleaming oak table topped with silver candlesticks and a huge floral centerpiece could seat a huge dinner party.

"This is where we'll have most of our meals."

"We'll have to peek at each other over the centerpiece," she said with a grin.

He looped an arm around her waist and pulled her to him, wanting to groan when her soft curves pressed against him. "I think I'd rather pull you onto my lap to feed you or have you kneel at my feet." He nibbled her ear. "How does that sound to you?"

"Good," she said, biting her lower lip. "Why didn't we dine here last night?"

"I thought you might be tired," he said, remembering when she'd literally passed out on him, and her hunger later. She'd been though a lot because of that crooked artist, and he was going to see that the rat paid.

"I was," she said.

"And I figured you might be a little shy about getting spanked in public," he added, smiling when her blush turned crimson. How would she have handled it if he'd taken her over the arm of the settee? It was a provocative thought.

"I might have," she agreed.

"I'll have to introduce you to it slowly," he said, smiling at her sudden intake of breath and the intrigued look in her eye. Just as he suspected, she'd gotten off on the little bit of exhibitionism on the catwalk, and wouldn't mind trying it again. He took her arm and breezed her by the kitchen, where Al was rolling out pastry.

Al, a flour coated-apron over his solid middle, glanced up to give them a distracted look. "I'm kind of busy now, Nicky."

"I'm just giving Laura the grand tour." He turned to Laura. "This is Al's domain. Tread cautiously here."

"Bridges doesn't do any of the cooking?" she asked.

Al stopped spooning strawberry filling into the tarts to frown. "He's not allowed in my kitchen. The snooty bloke is an amateur."

Nick chuckled. "They duked it out over the chore and Al won."

"It smells fabulous," Laura said.

"Right back at ya," Al said, turning to get a batch of strawberry tarts out of the commercial-style oven.

Nick smiled when she gave him a quizzical look. "He's in the zone right now and he won't make any sense."

He led her out of the kitchen and toward the sunlit back terrace. She slowed down when they passed his book-lined study, his gleaming computer the only touch of modernity in the room.

"Your office?"

"And library," he said, noting her interest in the books. "My grandfather had a collection of vintage erotica if you'd care to look at it some time."

"I'd love to." She beamed.

He was warmed by her forty-watt smile. "Later." He steered her toward the French doors that led to the courtyard.

She issued pleasured sigh when they walked outside into the bright summer sunshine. "This is beautiful," she said in awe.

His gaze lingered on her in the sunlight. Backlit, her rayon sundress was almost transparent. He focused on her budded nipples and the heat between her legs.

"Very beautiful," he said, thinking about her. "Come with me." He took her arm and led her into the knot garden.

Laura trembled when Nick touched her arm and escorted her toward a bit of wild beauty away from the house. They were soon surrounded by a riot of summer blooms, and screened behind shrubs. She could only guess why he was waltzing her off to this secluded glen, and her body trembled in anticipation. He was like a fever in her blood now and she knew she'd never get enough of him. She gazed at the flower bedecked secret garden, bemused. There was even a swing hanging from the large branch of a tree.

He came to a stop, and she looked at him, finding heat in his eyes.

"Strip for me, Cherie. I want to see you naked in my garden."

She trembled at his words, but hurried to comply, unzipping her dress and letting it fall onto the soft grass.

His hot gaze on her in the red bustier, the nipple clamps dangling from her quivering breasts, make her feel as beautiful as he thought her. Her ass clenched around the butt plug as she stepped toward him, needy and shaking.

He un-clipped her hair, letting it fall, and she leaned toward him like a flower toward the sun. He smiled, stroking her cheek and running a hand down her front to cup her breast, flicking the nipple clamp, making her feel the pull deep inside.

She moaned, leaning into him, silently begging for more.

He growled, bending to lap at her clamped nipple. "Mine."

She whimpered in agreement as he toyed with her, making her melt as she felt herself tightening. She tipped back her head, and mewling kitten sounds poured from her throat. She pressed against him as he played her body like a fine violin.

He kissed his way to the other breast, murmuring, "Hungry for me, Cherie?"

"Starved," she said, sucking in a breath as he tongued her other nipple, the jewel shuddering.

He plopped her onto the swing. Her bottom hit the seat, making the butt plug move inside her, her sex and ass rippling. She let out a needy laugh and hung onto the swing's ropes as the seat wobbled. Wow, she'd never expected him to take her there, but she was intrigued. He was smiling at her shocked but excited reaction, and it turned her on even more.

"Spread them for me, Cherie," he commanded.

She spread her legs as far as the wide seat would allow, blushing when his hungry gaze lingered on her exposed pussy for a hot moment. Her body pulsed in response as her sex got wetter.

He unzipped his pants in a rush, the teeth hissing. Then, he stepped up to her, grasping the swing's seat as he tugged her to him.

When the tip of his cock bumped against her creamy sex, she held her breath in suspense. Instead of just taking her, he nibbled her nape while he teased her. She tried to inch forward, but couldn't, as he tormented her, and she wound up dragging her tingling nipples against his hard chest, trying to hurry him.

"Enough," he barked as he swung her onto him.

She gasped, her sex milking at his thrusting cock. He held her there for a spellbinding moment, their bodies touching. Scorched where his body heat radiated into her, she was starting to adjust to the feel of his hardness pulsing inside her when he swung her away, making her cry out.

He gripped the edges of the swing's seat, controlling the pace as he swung her back tight against him again, thrusting deeper.

Gazing into his sultry brown eyes, she knew that she more than liked him. It was that simple, and had happened that fast. She couldn't deny it to herself. She moaned, holding on tight for the ride of her life. She refused to close her eyes, not wanting to miss a second of bliss as he took her.

"Come," he demanded, thrusting hard and holding her tightly to him, buried deep inside her.

She convulsed, wringing his cock with her tight spasms, her toes curling as she shimmered around him. Waves of pleasure wracked through her as she felt his release, his cock pumping. She watched the look of pure satisfaction that softened his rugged manly features, and knew that, come what may, she was glad she had him for the summer.

"I'd love to paint you in this garden."

"And so you shall," he said with a smile.

She didn't believe him, but it was kind of him to let her think so. She was only here to be his courtesan, not his portrait artist. Instead, she studied him, wanting to memorize him.

Chapter 6

Laura tried not to grumble as she sat in Nick's garden all alone three days later. He'd gone off to the city on what he'd said was urgent business, and she felt like a neglected wife, although she knew she wasn't. She had no claim on his love or attention, though he'd lavished a lot of both on her during their first days together.

Maybe he was tiring of her and thinking about replacing her. The thought brought her up short. She sighed and looked down at the sketch she'd been doing of him.

At least she'd have a little piece of him to take with her. She gazed forlornly at the drawing she'd made from memory. She was able to detach herself from the work to see that it was good, probably revealing more than she'd like about her growing feelings for him.

She was in love with her temporary Master. What a hopeless mess.

She'd drawn him as he'd looked in the garden before he'd made love to her on the swing—nude, sultry, and demanding all at the same time. Her lips twitched with humor as she gazed at his rampant form, wondering what he'd say about her drawing him that way. He was surprisingly conservative about some matters, especially when she'd made mention of going back to Madame Imogene's, not that she would. She didn't want to belong to another Master.

Nick was one-of-a-kind.

As if her thoughts had summoned him, she looked up to find him walking into the garden.

"I didn't hear you come in," she said, quickly shoving the drawing behind her.

"No," he said as if intrigued, watching her furtive movements. "You were too busy staring at the paper. Show it to me, Cherie."

She reluctantly drew the sketch out from behind her and handed it to him. "I told you I wanted to paint you in the garden."

Watching him breathlessly, she hoped he liked it. Pierre Gallo had wasted no time in telling her she didn't have any talent, but she refused to buy into that. Her mentor was angry because she refused to sleep with him. Nick's opinion of her work meant a lot more to her.

When a pleased smile lit his face, she felt a glow inside her. He liked it.

"I think you've captured me. You've got quite a talent, Laura."

She flushed, inordinately pleased by the compliment. "Mind you, it's only a sketch. Once I get home to the studio I plan to set up, I'll really be able to do you justice."

"You're already making plans for after you leave me," he said softly.

She thought she heard disapproval in his voice, but a glance at his stoic expression didn't reflect any reluctance to let her go. "A girl has to think about her future."

"I suppose you're right," he said, pinning her with a steady gaze.

She felt like he was trying to get a read on her feelings, and froze. If she let it slip that she loved him, he might let her go early. She couldn't let that happen.

"Thanks to the salary you're paying me, I'll be able to quit my temp jobs and kit out my studio properly."

"So, that's why you became my courtesan?"

She frowned, feeling like he was a detective digging for clues. "Why else?" she said, answering his question with one of her own.

"Why wait until you go home to paint my portrait?"

She smiled at the silly question. She didn't exactly have a paint set in her backpack. "Lack of equipment, for one thing. The mugger got all my—"

"Mugger?" he said pointedly.

She heard the 'got-you' note in his voice, and sighed. "I was mugged right before I signed on with Madame Imogene. He got everything but my backpack."

His eyes narrowed as a fierce look crossed his face. "Did he hurt you?"

She relaxed. "Just a few scrapes and bruises."

"Hopefully the police will catch him and recover your belongings."

"I didn't report it."

"Why not?"

"They wouldn't have believed me," she said, feeling his concern. There was no way she'd go back to the French police once they'd released her after rigorous questioning about the jewel theft. "Can we just drop this?"

"Yes, Cherie, we can drop it for now." He held out his hand. "Come, I have something to show you."

She walked with him deeper into the garden, intrigued. A small, but charming stone cottage sat at the far end of the property, surrounded by trees.

"What a pretty little cottage," she said in awe.

"I agree." He walked her up the flagstone path to the front door. "I like to come here sometimes to be alone." He opened the door for her, and ushered her inside.

She digested the fact that he was stressed. She was intrigued by the little glimpses he gave her of himself, and she liked what she saw. He was a complicated man, but fiercely loyal to those he loved. She let him usher her into the cozy cottage and stopped short when she realized he'd set it up as an art studio.

"I didn't know you painted."

"I don't," he said with a smile, showing her an easel with a fresh canvas on it. "This is for you."

She looked at him, stunned. "But you hired me to sleep with you. Not to paint your portrait."

He smiled, running a hand down her arm. "I hired you to serve my needs and I need to have my portrait painted by you. Will you accept the commission?"

She heated when his warm hand ran up her bare arm, and looked deep into his eyes, seeing sincerity there. He really wanted her to paint him. "I'd love to."

"Good," he said, dropping his hand. "Where do you want me, Cherie?"

"Against the stone fireplace, naked," she said instantly, and then blushed at his masculine smile. She was glad he was oh-so-willing to get naked for her. When he started to strip, she watched him bare his magnificent body, once again fascinated by him. She could never get enough of him, and she knew it.

When he was naked, he turned to her. "You too, Cherie."

Blushing at his order, she unzipped her dress and took it off, realizing it would be the first time she'd painted in the nude. It was kind of freeing. Besides, she usually slopped paint all over herself, and it would save her pretty new dress from getting ruined.

When she was naked, she warmed as his sultry gaze lingered on her. "Satisfied?" she asked, amused.

"Not yet, but you can satisfy me properly later." He leaned against the rough stone wall.

With his words ringing in her ears, she picked up a brush. She couldn't help being fascinated by him, and it inspired her. He was the perfect subject, his tanned skin contrasted against the rough stones. This composition was pure magic, and she wanted to capture the moment like trapping time in a bottle. Being Nick's courtesan was a once-in-a-lifetime experience, and she was going to enjoy it to the hilt.

Glancing lovingly at her Master, she started to paint.

"Tell me about your background," Nick said.

In the zone, she added another brush stroke, and said, "I grew up in a little lake town near Madison, Wisconsin."

"Ah, a Badger," he said, with a smile.

Now, how did he know she went to the UW—oh duh. The catwalk announcer at the auction. "That's right, I've got a degree in art history."

"Why art history?" he asked softly. "With your talent, don't you want to make a living as a fine artist?"

"My mother wanted me to have a steadier profession like working in a museum or teaching. Seeing as how she was kind enough to help with my tuition, I gave in to the pressure," she said absentmindedly as she captured his suddenly dark expression. He certainly was curious about her.

"Money was an issue," he said.

She smiled, thinking that someone rich like him could never understand what it was like to scrimp and save to go to school. "I got by."

"And you finally made the jump to Paris to start your fine art career."

"I did, but it's never going to happen now." She frowned as she thought about her nasty mentor. Bald, tanned, and always smelling of clove cigarettes, Pierre Gallo had a smarmy way with the rich women he painted. He'd taught her that talent and goodness didn't go hand-in-hand. The man could paint, although she found his technique heavy handed and cold. Who'd want to sit for her with a criminal record?

"Why?" Nick asked pointedly.

The brush trembled in her hand as she thought about the way her budding career had imploded before it had even begun, and swore when a blotch of paint splattered her right breast. "It's a good thing you made me get nude."

"Isn't it though?" he said. "Satisfy my curiosity, Cherie, and tell me why it won't happen now."

She sighed. There was his honesty bug working overtime, but it was just so humiliating to talk about.

"Fine, my reputation is in shreds after losing my job." She met his eyes, saw understanding there, and wanted to blurt the whole sordid business out, but what was the point? "I really don't want to talk about this," she said, focusing on her painting, getting lost in it.

The sun was beginning to set when she put down her brush and stepped back to gaze at her canvas.

When Nick walked over to her to look at the painting, she stood waiting anxiously, wanting him to like it.

His eyes widened. "I love it," he said in a tender voice.

She flushed, startled by the softness in his voice. "I'm glad that you like it. It's yours. I won't charge you."

His turned his head to pin her with an earnest look. "Artists should be paid. What about you?"

"You've already paid me more than amply. This is a gift from me. I want to give you something to remember me by, after..." She watched his mouth firm and didn't complete the thought. Was he just as troubled by their upcoming parting? God, she hoped so, because it hurt to be in love alone. Still, she kept silent, knowing that mentioning their parting always put him in a mood. Boys didn't like to share their toys, which was what she was to him.

Nick tugged Laura into his arms, irritated that she could speak so blithely about leaving him. He didn't want to let her go, regardless of the stupid contract he'd signed.

"You've already given me your greatest gift, your love," he said, the paint drops on her breasts smearing across his chest. "You have real talent, Cherie, and you belong here. Don't throw it away so easily."

He scooped her up in his arms and carried her toward the cottage's bathroom, feeling her suddenly keen gaze on him. She wouldn't be the first courtesan to have her contract extended and he wanted a long-term commitment from her, although he knew he was fighting an uphill battle.

Shit, she had big plans, and he didn't fit into them.

The knowledge pissed him off and made him even more determined to have her. He slapped on the rain shower and stepped under with her in his arms. And to think, he'd given his half-brother, Andre, a hard time when he'd married Simone, his former courtesan. Hell, he'd tried to talk him out of it, and now he was contemplating the same thing. Andre would no doubt laugh his ass off.

Nick's determined gaze locked with Laura's luminous one, and she sucked in a tremulous breath. His body hardened in response, his cock throbbing. What was the feisty minx thinking? The urge to kiss her was strong, but he knew he couldn't. Hell, she hadn't even allowed him past her defenses, why was he stupid enough to think she'd stay with him?

He let her go slowly, lowering her so that her sexy body dragged over his, as he set her on her feet in the steamy shower. When she leaned against him, trembling a little, her arms wrapped around him, and he opened his stance to take her sweet weight. Her mound pressed against his throbbing cock as her breasts pillowed against his chest. He held her for a moment, absorbing the sensation of her body against his before he reached for the soap. He slowly scrubbed her, soaping her breasts, finessing the nipples until they stood stiff for him and she was whimpering.

Only then did he move down to wash her pussy, feeling her tremble as he stroked her flesh. Her hips flicked forward when he did, and he ate up the show of unrestrained sexuality. His cock grew harder, pulsing with life, as she shimmied against him, inflaming him.

When he could stand it no longer, he picked her up, backed her against the stall's marble wall, and took her fast and deep. As his cock plunged into her wet heat, she cried out and clung to him. Her pussy rippled around him, driving him insane, as he gripped her ass tight and plunged into her time and again.

His heart was pounding, and her cries filled the steamy air as he twitched inside her, his balls growing tight.

"Come for me, Laura," he crooned.

She shivered around him, coming with a sob.

He stiffened, shouting as he exploded high and deep inside her, the after-spasms consuming him.

He stood there, trembling a little, holding her as she clung tightly to him, her arms and legs wrapped around him. As his pulse slowed in tandem with hers, it occurred to him that he'd abandoned the tight control he usually kept on himself.

Funny thing was, he kind of liked it.

Chapter 7

"Merde!" Nick roared into the phone in his study.

Laura looked down at him from her perch on the top of the library ladder. They'd fallen into a simple, seductive routine in the two weeks since she'd painted him. He hadn't said another word about her staying since he'd said she should and not waste her talent. She'd foolishly hoped he'd actually meant it, but was now forced to accept he'd been speaking in generalities. He thought she should remain in Paris, but there was no way she'd do that. Instead, she'd thrown herself into her role as his courtesan, determined to make the most of their remaining time together.

Aside from more sexy painting sessions, he had assigned her the fun task of cataloging his grandfather's vintage erotica volumes. She put down the antique book, noting Nick's tense body language as he hung up the phone. It'd been rather scandalous reading them aloud to him in the evenings and acting out the parts. She gazed down at him, concerned by his gruff manner.

"Bad news?"

"The worst," he said, looking up at her with a fond smile.

What could have him so outraged? He was usually in control, only allowing her occasional glimpses of his more vulnerable side. Wanting to help, she clambered down the ladder, and somehow put it in motion.

With a cry, she lost her grip on the darned thing and plummeted toward the floor.

An instant later, she dropped into Nick's strong arms.

"I've got you, Cherie."

She gazed up at him, impressed, as her racing heartbeat slowed. It only confirmed her thoughts that the man moved like a predator, fast and smooth. Something told her that Nick Renault hadn't always lived the life of a rich playboy. He'd been through his share of battles. She gazed at his sensual mouth, her self-protective shell melting. All she knew was that she needed him to kiss her.

"Would you please kiss me, Nick?" she asked breathlessly.

"I thought you'd never ask."

Her body went up in flames as she took in his victorious smile an instant before his lips touched hers. Shivering in anticipation, his dark irises contracted, and then his sensual mouth brushed against hers, hot, sweet, and demanding. She kissed him back, clinging to him as his mouth plundered hers. When he nipped her lower lip, she opened for him, letting his tongue surge into her mouth and mate with hers. Trembling with sensual overload, she clung to him. It was the intimacy she craved, and he seemed to be just as hungry for it. Her breasts swelled, pressing against him, and the spot between her legs grew dewy.

As if he knew her needs, he picked her up and carried her to the leather sofa, pulling her onto his lap. She whimpered, flaming inside, as his big hand shaped her breasts through her top, teasing the nipples to hard beads of readiness. When he bent to take one into his mouth, biting through the fabric, she let out a wild cry of pleasure. Her primal reaction shocked her because she knew she had to get at him. He was always in charge in the bedroom, but right now, she felt like the aggressor as she unbuttoned his shirt, snaking her hand inside to tease one flat male nipple.

She thrilled at his startled sudden intake of breath in response. He liked that. His rousing cock thumped against her bottom as she sat on his lap. Engendering such a primitive response in him gave her a feeling of pure female power as she nibbled his jaw while doing it again. Then she wriggled on his lap, earning a primitive growl from him and an arousing nip to her tight peak.

She shuddered at the brief pleasure/pain, but he quickly licked it away, making her squirm with need. She wasn't the only sexual aggressor in the room. His warm hand slipped up a bare inner thigh under her dress until he was touching the hot place between her thighs, caressing her through her panties. She gasped as his blunt fingertip unerringly pressed her swollen clit, and she came, muffling her shout of triumph into his mouth.

As she leaned against him in afterglow, there was a tapping on the library's door.

"Tell whoever it is to go away," she murmured, feeling sated.

Nick loved the feel of Laura snuggled in his lap. He smiled at her mutterings that he should send Bridges away, and turned to look at his butler standing stiffly in the doorway, but the butler's troubled expression gave him a feeling that something was wrong.

"What is it, Bridges?"

Bridges stepped into the room. "Inspector Henri Le Marche is here to see you, sir."

Laura stiffened against him at the name of the detective who'd nearly arrested her.

He bit back a curse. Damn it all, this was happening too fast. This wasn't the way he wanted to tell her about the investigation he'd started, and he hadn't anticipated Henri actually showing up here. It was a cue that something was wrong.

"Show him in," Nick said, keeping a firm arm around Laura when she tried to slip off his lap. Damn it all, he wasn't letting her go.

Laura shot a troubled look at him as Bridges left the room. "Henri Le Marche is the policeman who questioned me after I was accused of theft."

"I know." He took in her shocked look at his disclosure. He knew shock would soon turn to anger, and braced himself for it. Shit, he was losing her, and it killed him.

"But how?"

"Madame Imogene's report was incomplete, so I had you checked out." He shrugged as she narrowed her eyes.

"You really were afraid I'd steal the silver," she bit in outrage.

Her off-the-wall comment made him smile, despite his growing dejection. Here came her rejection, and he'd weather it, but he didn't want her to think he didn't trust her.

"No, Cherie, I never worried you'd steal from me. I knew that you were hiding something, and needed to find out what it was."

"Why?"

He felt her intensity as she studied him. He owed her the truth. "Call it a quirk. I have a little trouble with liars. My ex-wife, Yvette, lied and cheated on me."

"Oh," she said.

He wasn't quite sure how to interpret her new thoughtful expression. At least she wasn't glaring at him anymore.

"I figured you were innocent and wanted to prove it."

"Another one of your quirks," she said with a soft smile.

"Who told you that?" he asked, troubled that she could read him so well.

"Al happened to mention how you sprung him."

"The man gossips too much," he grumbled, hearing footsteps on the marble floor in the hall.

He glanced up to find his friend, Inspector Henri Le Marche, standing in the hall, gazing at them. He saw the twinkle in Henri's eye as he took in the intimate picture of Laura on his lap.

"Well, Henri, are you going to play Peeping Tom, or come in and talk to us?"

Laura's gasp made Nick smile. It was good to know he could still shock his courtesan.

Henri walked into the study and cast an amused look at Laura. "Mademoiselle Banks," he said, bending to kiss her hand.

"Get your own girl."

Henri gave him a Gallic shrug and settled into a leather wing chair. "I'm afraid I don't have the same effect on Laura. She ran off the instant I released her. My men were unable to follow or find her again."

"You tried to have me followed?"

Henri nodded. "I did, indeed. I was hoping you'd lead me to Pierre Gallo's treasure trove."

"Treasure trove?" she gasped. Her eyes narrowed. "Why would you think that?"

Henri shrugged again. "He hinted that you were intimate—"

"We were not. I wouldn't let that smelly, bald, sleazeball touch me."

Henri nodded. "I was skeptical at the time, but you wouldn't be the first protégé to fall into her mentor's bed."

She scowled at him. "If you're going to keep insulting me, why don't you just leave?"

Henri smiled and flashed an amused nod at Nick. "You've got yourself a wild one here, *mon ami*. Need a hand with her?"

"Not a chance in hell." Nick held tight to Laura as she shot them both go-to-hell daggers.

"Why are you here? To arrest me?"

"No, Mademoiselle Laura, have no fear on that account." Henri gave her an understanding smile. "I came to ask you to clear up a few loose ends in my case."

"Loose ends?"

"Yes, tell me how you came to be in Pierre Gallo's employ."

"That's easy," she said, leaning against Nick. "I answered an ad he placed in the student news. I'm an alumnus of the University of Wisconsin, and I did some occasional jobs for the art department. He was looking for a protégé, and the chance to travel seemed exciting to me. You know the rest."

"He flew you to Paris—"

"No," she said with a frown. "I drew out my savings and bought a ticket. Once I got here, he seemed more interested in putting the moves on me than mentoring. I also got the impression he thought I had money. When he learned that I was nearly broke and didn't go for his sexual advances, he told me I didn't have any talent, ignored me, and foisted the scrub work on me. A week later, Lady Davenport's diamond bracelet went missing, and everything fell apart."

"Ah yes, Lady Davenport. She was modeling for him in his studio on the sixth ward."

"Yes. They'd gone into his private quarters after the session, and I think they were fooling around. I'd just finished cleaning Pierre's brushes for the day when she screamed she'd been robbed. Before I knew it, I was accused, fired, and bundled off to the police station to talk to you. When you let me go, I knew you still suspected me. So, after I was mugged that night, I didn't dare come in to report it."

"You were mugged?" he said, his interest picking up.

"She was," Nick cut in gruffly. "I have my private detective running down leads, but all we've got to go on is her description—young, thin, greasy long brown hair pulled back in a ponytail, and probably strung out."

Laura frowned at the disclosure. "You are a natural-born snoop."

Henri bit back a laugh. "I do believe the lady's got your number, *mon ami*. I'll have one of my men drop off some mug shots for you to look at, Laura. Do you think you could identify him?"

She nodded and shuddered. "I'll never forget him. He had a knife. I'd just tucked my backpack under a park bench and was carrying my suitcases when he jumped me. He made off with everything but my backpack and the clothes on my back."

"Get him for me, Henri." Nick rubbed a soothing hand over Laura's trembling arm. If he laid a hand on the mugger, he'd be dead.

"I will do my best," Henri said, then turned to Laura. "I let you go because I knew you were innocent. Now that I know you're not an accomplice, I'm hoping you'll help me get Pierre Gallo. He's been implicated in such thefts before, and he's always had a convenient scapegoat."

"Rotten bastard," she bit out.

Henri's mouth twitched. "Quite. Now, the trick is to catch him at his own game."

"How?"

"You spent time with him," Henri said. "You could be invaluable in helping us find his stash of stolen goods."

"No," Nick said firmly as his old friend tried to drag Laura into this dangerous business. He could see by the keen interest on her face she was intrigued. "I'm not letting you put her in jeopardy, Henri."

Henri frowned. "I'll do all I can to shelter her from harm."

"Not good enough," he shot back.

Laura let out a growl. "Will you two stop talking over me like I'm a child? Henri, if I can be of assistance, I'd like to help. My dad was a sheriff, and I know how unsolved crimes can bring you down." She turned and gave Nick a tender smile. "I appreciate you trying to protect me, but I need to handle this. You know I'll be leaving soon, and I have to look after myself."

Nick stiffened at the reminder she was still thinking about leaving. "You're not going on some sting with Henri to catch Gallo, no matter how nicely he asks you. You still have a two-week contract with me, and I'm holding you to every moment of it."

He watched the flash of annoyance in her eyes and knew that he'd blown it.

"Relax, old friend, I wouldn't ask her to do anything dangerous," Henri said. "She doesn't even have to leave your estate. All she needs to do is answer my questions."

"Ask away," Laura said firmly.

Henri smiled. "Fine. You're familiar with his studio. Did you notice any hidden panels that might indicate hiding places?"

"As a matter of fact, one day I darned near fell into his cellar."

"Cellar?" Henri said, his brow arching.

"Well, not a true cellar like from back home. This was more of a root cellar with a trapdoor. He kept a rug over it so that I didn't know it was there, and the wood had rotted. I was carrying a load of art supplies for him and my foot went through it. He screeched like a little girl and went ballistic on me. It was only a few days later that he fired me."

"Is that enough to go on?" Nick asked Henri.

"It'll do for starters," Henri said, standing. "I'll let you know when and if I hit pay dirt. In the meantime, I wish you both much happiness."

***

Laura watched the inspector leave, still stunned by the fact Nick had known her secret all along and hadn't held it against her. He'd acted on his own to tried to clear her name, and it made her smile ruefully. It showed just how controlling he could be, but it also let her see his protective side. It touched her he cared enough to try to save her reputation.

She turned to look at Nick's enigmatic expression. He seemed to be waiting for her to blow up at him, but her quick anger had turned to warmth toward him.

She wrapped her arms around his neck, feeling his muscles flex under her. "Thank you."

"For what?"

"For believing in me, for starters, and going out of your way to try to take care of me." He'd gone about it in a totally Alpha male, take-charge way, but she still appreciated his efforts.

"Why shouldn't I take care of you?" he asked in surprise. "I do care for you, Laura."

It wasn't a declaration of love, but then, she wasn't expecting one. That she wasn't angry with him seemed to have loosened him up, and she liked the change.

"And I care for you too, Nick," she said softly, knowing she felt a whole lot more for him.

"Cherie," he murmured, nuzzling her neck.

She sizzled where his hot lips grazed her, and it was hard to keep her mind on what she'd wanted to discuss before the inspector had interrupted them. Oh yeah, his anger over the telephone call.

She pulled back to look him in the eye. "Now that you've solved my problem, I should do the same for you. Who was that on the phone, and what did they say to get you so riled up?" She watched him hesitate for a moment, and knew he was debating whether to let her in or not.

"The phone call earlier was my younger half-brother, Andre," he said with a smile. "He's the son born on the right side of the blanket."

"You two don't get along?"

"Au contraire, we get along very well, much to his family's displeasure. So much so, he's my second-in-command at Renault Corporation. He called to tell me our negotiations with the Lax Consortium have hit an impasse. We're trying to acquire their holdings in Asia in order to grow our market. On top of that, Andre passed along his wife Simone's suggestion that I host a party to wine, dine, and romance them into a deal."

"It worked with me," she said, remembering how he'd thoroughly seduced her.

The startled smile on Nick's face at her sassy rejoinder pleased her, but then he rolled his eyes.

"Women, you all think alike."

"We do not, but I think Simone's suggestion is a good one," she said as he gave her a thoughtful look. "Is she the sister-in-law whose sexy creations I've been wearing? The one who convinced you to buy me?"

"Not you specifically, because you were a last-minute entry into the market, and she didn't know about you. But Immy seemed inordinately pleased when it was you I chose to purchase. Simone told me I was in a rut and nagged me into going to Immy's. I actually hadn't planned on buying anyone, that is until a blushing feisty redhead stepped on the catwalk and stole my heart."

"I like her already," she said, wishing his words of love were true. She'd captured his interest, probably because she was so out of place, and stirred his lust. She was caught up in the same blazing fire.

He brushed a tendril of hair off her face as he gazed at her. "I think Simone would like you, too. You actually have much in common."

She thought she wouldn't have much in common with the French aristocrat who created these lovely, if scandalous, fashions, but nodded.

"Don't think your sweet talk is going to divert my attention from the party you should host." When he rolled his eyes again, she hid her smile, secretly glad she was able to push his buttons so easily. "You're the most devastatingly charming man I've ever known, and this is the perfect setting for a house party."

The corners of his mouth kicked up in a smile that made her melt.

"It used to be," he said. "My great-grandfather used it for orgies."

"So, that's where you get it," she teased, noting the wicked twinkle in his eyes.

"You're asking for another paddling," he warned huskily, one of his hands dropping down to rub her bottom.

"Can't wait." She burned where he touched her, and leaned in to nibble his ear. "Al and I can arrange for the food and drink, with Simone's input, of course. Bridges can be his usual stuffy self and intimidate them into behaving, and you can put on a tux and wow them. It'll work."

Nick growled with passion as he stroked Laura's body. "What am I going to do with you?"

"Love me," she said, wriggling against his burgeoning erection. "You don't have to take care of me, Nick, I'm a big girl. I don't want you pitying me."

He cupped her breast. "I feel a lot of things for you, and pity isn't one of them, witch woman."

She cried out, pressing her breast into his hand, giving him a passionate gaze.

Still, he couldn't help feeling annoyed she was so casually talking about leaving him. Didn't she care? He pulled her to him for a claiming kiss, his mouth slanting possessively over hers, his tongue mastering her. She quivered in his arms, going up in flames as he ravished her. He peeled off her sundress, baring her beautiful tits, squeezing one in his hand, feeling its weight.

She belonged to him.

"Yes," she breathed, pressing closer, her fingers flexing into his shoulder, kneading him.

He shuddered as his flesh tingled under her kneading fingers, his muscles flexing. His cock ached under her lush ass, waiting to be unleashed. When she unbuttoned his shirt to press her hot little tongue to his nipple, he let her, leaning back on the sofa to enjoy. Her secret was out, and she was dealing with it even better than he'd hoped.

"Position number one," he demanded in a sultry voice.

She shimmied off his lap to kneel at his feet and look up at him with excitement in her eyes.

He found himself captivated. "You're a natural-born tease, you know that?"

"It's your fault, Master," she shot back in a teasing, shivery tone that sent goosebumps down his spine. "You're the man who made me this way."

"Am I now? Tell me, Laura, do you enjoy teasing me?"

"You know I do. You've taught me the power of my femininity."

He smiled indulgently at her, charmed, despite her sassy answer. It was satisfying to know he was the man responsible for liberating her sexually. The dark thought that there might be others crossed his mind before he pushed it away.

"Take out my cock, Cherie," he commanded.

She rushed to obey, her fingers flying to the zipper of his chinos.

He groaned as her fingers trembled against his groin. It was enough to unman him. "Hurry, and pull them down," he said a bit gruffly.

She eagerly pulled down his zipper, making him moan when she compressed his burgeoning hard-on. He noticed her stealing furtive looks his way, wondering if he was going to have to rein her in, and he tried not to smile.

"Use your teeth, my sassy courtesan," he ordered in a firm tone. He watched the blush that crept up her beautiful body, satisfied he'd shocked her with the new command.

She blushed and leaned in to comply, catching the edge of his briefs in her teeth, her nose brushing his groin. Her hot breath tickled him, tortured him. He was more turned on than ever, and desperate to sway her from taking up with another Master. She tugged his briefs down with her teeth, and he lost his train of thought. His cock sprang out, hot and pulsing.

"Open your mouth and suck, Cherie."

She made a yummy noise and flicked her tongue at him, bathing the tip of his cock.

"Suck," he commanded. "Show me you know who your Master is."

He growled when she drew his stiff cock into her mouth. She bobbed up and down, driving him out of his mind. When she took him deeper into her throat, he groaned.

"Good girl." His fingers twined into her fiery locks, holding her head fast, her hair tumbling over his lap, teasing him, too.

"When I come, swallow it all, or else," he bit out, surging into her mouth.

He could feel her excitement at his words, and she sucked harder, making his cock tighten, twitch. He came, spurting into her mouth in salty streams. She drained him.

When he pulled back to look, a few drops of his cum were glistening on her beautiful breasts.

"I spilled," she said, biting her lip.

He could feel her arousal, her curiosity about what he had planned for her. She'd be punished, but how?

He stood, zipping up his pants. Now it was her turn.

"Come," he ordered, walking toward her, around to the high padded arm of the sofa. "Bend over the arm, my sassy courtesan," he ordered.

He felt her watchful gaze on him as she went over with a sigh.

"That's right, my love, face and tits down," he said softly, his eyes eating her up. "Bottom up, high in the air," he added.

He saw the heated blush that radiated right down to her ass, intrigued by his modest tease. She awaited his pleasure or his punishment, her pretty ass arched high and out for him, her face partially hidden by the sofa cushions. She trembled, and he felt the motion transfer into his stirring cock. His courtesan was in the perfect spanking position, and she'd have to hold still for it, without restraints—something he hadn't asked her to do yet. It would be a true trial of her willingness to serve him.

"Cherie, this is your second submissive pose," he said, running a hand over her butt. "Your head is down respectfully, your bottom is out for my correction." Her skin heated under his palm, and he felt the little shiver that went through her, inflaming his own passion.

He walked over to the desk, smiling when he saw that she was peeking over her shoulder at him, eyeballing him, as no true sub would do. She was a fiery minx and he enjoyed trying to tame her. He pulled out the lube he'd slipped into his top drawer for just this occasion, and turned to her.

He walked up behind her, his hand running possessively down her sleek spine. "You're beautiful, Cherie."

"I'm glad you think so."

He pressed against her, his cock suddenly on fire for her. She was burning him up where he stood, melting into him with a needy sigh. God, he needed her. He didn't want to think about the end of summer when he might lose her.

Smiling against her skin, he bent to press kisses down her neck. "You are so good for me, Cherie," he said, his erection pressing against her.

She laughed, then groaned as he reached around her to cup her breasts, his hands holding them and squeezing slightly. "Thanks...that is, I don't know..."

He froze at the subtle confirmation she was going to leave, and sighed when his randy cock brushed against her. "We'll discuss this later. For now, we can let our bodies do the talking."

"If you say so." She gasped as he tweaked her nipples.

"I do," he said, stroking her ass. "Is it lubed for me, Cherie?"

***

Laura felt a burst of mingled arousal and apprehension go through her as Nick stroked her bottom. "You know it is, Master," she said with a pout.

He gave her a stinging spank in retribution.

She let out a whimper when heat telegraphed through her bottom, making her ass and pussy ripple.

"None of your sass," he said firmly.

She melted when he cupped the globes of her bottom and then stroked the puckering flesh between. Hell yes, she was lubed as instructed, and wore her butt plug every day. She knew that he was just toying with her. He stroked her deeper and her knees weakened. So far, he'd been nothing but a tease. If only he'd stop teasing about taking her ass and just do it.

Risking another smack, she said, "So far, you've been nothing but a tease, Master."

"Now you know how I feel, Cherie. You make me crazy for you, and for this tight little ass." He teased the lubed opening with a swirl of his fingertip. "I burn to open it with my cock."

Her anus pulsed around his teasing finger as she absorbed his words. It pleased her that he was just as hot for her. It gave her back a little power in their relationship.

"First, your punishment." He picked up the paddle.

She bit back a cry of need, knowing it was far from punishment to her warped mind. He was going to make her pay for her pleasure with strokes from the paddle. When he drew back his hand to give her left cheek a rapid smack, she gasped, stifling her cry against her palm, not wanting Bridges or Al to overhear.

"Very nice," he said, stopping to stroke her red bottom.

She went still when he drew back the paddle again and brought it down on her right cheek. Heat flooded her sex and her ass. Throbbing, she bit back a moan, trembling as he played the paddle up and down her hot bottom, making her spasm. Her sex creamed, misting her inner thighs with her juices. She arched her hips out, leaning into the strokes.

"You're mine," he said, with a final smack.

She couldn't help but agree. She didn't want anyone else.

"I'm yours." She melted as he dropped the paddle.

He stepped behind her, his stiff cock touching her ass.

"Are you hot for me to take your tight little rosebud, Cherie?" he asked, nibbling her ear.

"Blazing," she admitted before she let out a rueful laugh as he pressed against her.

"Good," he said. "We'll have to go paddle shopping online so that you can pick out an assortment."

"That's right, paddle me, Master Nick, that's the key to my heart," she said with a hiss as his cock touched her ass.

"But first, I've got something to give you, if you want it," he teased.

She pressed back against him. He was so close, but not taking her yet.

"Ah, yes. You know I want it," she said with a needy groan.

"Good." He pushed against the ridge of her sphincter.

She cried out as he started to enter her, the broad head of his cock easing into her. He was so big, slowly but relentlessly filling her. She forgot to breathe for a moment, so stunned by his possession.

He lay still inside her, his abs pressed against her paddled bottom. She moaned, adjusting to the feel of him inside her tight back passage. After a moment, her muscles began loosening a bit.

He growled, and bent to kiss her nape. "This is mine, and only mine."

Heat flooded through her at his possessive words. Did he really mean them?

He started to move inside her, driving all rational thought from her. She moaned as her ass rippled around him, milking at his driving cock as her pussy clenched.

He groaned. "Easy, Cherie, relax and let me love you."

She could only pulse around him as he slowly pulled back and surged inside. Filled completely, she was turned on beyond belief. She met his thrusts, gasping as her pussy and ass both clamped down, tugging at him.

"Slowly, Cherie," he said, grasping tighter to her hips to control the pace.

She wanted to fight his slow pace at first, but gave up with a moan as he thrust, building a relentless driving rhythm that made everything inside her tighten as she cried out. She rocked back against him, his balls slapping into her as he took her harder, deeper.

"Come for me, Cherie," he said, reaching down to circle her clit.

She let out a cry as her body tightened, her ass and pussy pulsing hard, and she came with a shriek.

"That's it, Laura, come for me." He exploded inside her.

She whimpered, his climax setting off another within her, her eyes rolling back in her head, her toes curling, almost losing consciousness as she collapsed, sandwiched between the sofa arm and Nick's hot body.

Chapter 8

The next morning, Laura woke up and yawned. She stretched, and only then realized she was in the wrong room.

Nick hadn't sent her back to her bedroom as he usually did. Precedents were being broken all over the place. She couldn't believe she'd let him kiss her last night, but she wasn't sorry she had.

A big hand cupped her left breast and her nipple budded, tingling against his warm palm. His cock pressed against her ass, his semihard manhood nestling between the cheeks of her bottom.

She quivered against him, remembering when he'd taken her, and her body heated in response. Her breath caught as she felt his manhood grow bigger against her. He'd pleasured her three times during the night, and was still hungry for more. He was insatiable, and she was just as hot for him.

Arching toward him, she tantalized herself, rubbing against his cock. She pushed back against him harder, whimpering with pleasure when his stiff cock rode between her cheeks. His hand closed firmly around her breast, his finger finessing her nipple.

When he didn't make another move, she froze. Was he awake? It certainly wasn't like him to just lie there and let her set the pace. It wasn't his style. No, he had to be asleep.

Carefully lifting his hand off her breast, she turned to gaze at her naked lover. He was still sound asleep, and reminded her of a resting beast, all coiled muscle, ready to spring at the least provocation. She couldn't help being impressed or losing her heart. Their summer of love was almost at an end, and she'd be leaving soon. It pained her just thinking about it because she didn't want to go.

Was he having regrets, too? It would explain his extra strict behavior toward her of late. She reached out to lightly touch his chest, running her hand down his warm, resilient skin. The covers were down low around his hips. Her finger slicked over his washboard-flat abdomen to swirl around his navel.

Giving in to temptation, she inched the covers lower to expose the part of his anatomy that tempted her so. His cock was fascinating, a steel column covered with tanned silky skin. It stirred as she watched, suddenly pulsing with life. She reached out to touch the hot velvety head, testing it gently with her fingertips. It jerked, swelling even more. Intrigued, she wrapped her hand around the shaft, feeling it pulse with life.

He woke with a groan, and thrust into her hand.

She blushed as he locked gazes with her. "Good morning."

"Finish it, Cherie," he said with an indulgent smile. "Before I take you over my knee."

She didn't need further urging to lean over and taste him, flicking her tongue over his cock's slit, savoring him. And then she was lost in the act, sucking him hard as his hands stroked down her body, his fingertips pinching her nipples. She whimpered and sucked harder, making his cock jerk inside her mouth.

"My turn," he said, urging her up.

She gave him a pouting mew, not wanting to let him go, and then finally relented. The moment she did so, he rolled her onto her back and kissed his way down her trembling body. He sucked first one hard nipple and then the other into his mouth, making her squirm. When she was out of her head, he moved lower until his hot rough tongue was stroking her weeping sex. She cried out, trying to surge off the mattress, but he held her still as he teased her with his tongue and sucked her clit.

Everything inside her tightened and she started to come. Only then did he surge up her body and thrust home. He waited until her after-spasms subsided and rolled onto his back, taking her with him. Sitting astride him, still joined, she felt him pulse inside her.

"Ride me, love, and make it good," he said.

She let out a pleasured laugh and rode her stallion, setting a rhythm that soon had them both gasping for air. When he tightened and came inside her, it set off a tidal wave that had her tightening around him, crying out his name.

***

Laura bustled around the ballroom later that day as she helped Al lay out the silver. The party would be starting soon, and she was both excited and worried. What did she know about society affairs like this?

"Anybody home?" a woman's sultry voice trilled as she walked into the room.

Laura took one look at the slinky, drop-dead gorgeous blonde, and felt about as sophisticated as Bozo the Clown.

"Well, I see you finally showed up," Al said.

Laura heard his gruff, but affectionate tone and looked at him, wondering who the beauty was. Her contract was about to run out, maybe Nick was already calling in replacements.

"Hello there," the blonde said, striding over to her. "I'm Simone. You must be Laura."

Laura felt chagrined by her jealousy. "Nice to meet you," she said. "I love your collection."

Simone passed an approving glance over the challis print sundress Laura was wearing. "You wear it well."

The compliment made Laura relax and smile at Nick's sister-in-law.

"What can I do to help?" Simone asked.

"You tell me. I've worked at a few faculty teas, but that's the extent of my party experience."

"I was in your shoes last year," Simone said. "Don't worry, you're doing well. I almost made a mess of our engagement party, but Al rescued me."

Laura glanced at Al, who was flush with embarrassment.

Beside her, Simone chuckled as he left the room. "It's easy to fluster the poor dear, is it not?"

"It is," Laura agreed with a smile, adding, "but I have to admit, I've never thought of him in those terms."

"He's a lovelorn fellow," Simone said confidentially. "If only he and Imogene would loosen up and see that there could be a future for them, all would be well."

Laura gaped at her. "Al and Imogene are attracted to each other?"

"But, of course. They are perfect for one another. You met Immy and seen how kind she is."

"You know her pretty well, do you?"

"I ought to, I was one of her courtesans," Simone said.

Laura stared at her in shock. The fact that there could be a life after her contract was through had never occurred to her.

Chapter 9

That night, Laura glanced at the blue silk dress laid out on her bed. Her thoughts naughty, she dressed for the party. She wished Nick could see her slithering into it, but he was in his study, meeting with his brother and other key employees. She hated resenting his work, but she wanted Nick right here, staring at her, smoothing his hands over her, spanking her.

Her face heating, she slipped on the gown. As she smoothed it over her champagne-colored bustier, she knew she looked as sexy as she could. The form-fitting dress matched her eyes and was low-cut, displaying her cleavage, nipped in at the waist, and fell over her hips to swirl around her calves in a handkerchief hem. The sensual gown left no doubt about her sexuality. Time with Nick had made her blossom into a sexual person.

She wanted to make him proud to have her on his arm, and she was nervous. Knowing she couldn't put it off any longer, she left her bedroom and headed downstairs.

Simone, Nick's designer sister-in-law, was in one of the bedchambers getting ready, but Laura didn't give in to her desire to get more reassurance. She could do this. Even if the others guessed that she was a courtesan, she didn't care. She'd never see any of these people again. Her time with Nick was up tomorrow.

Biting her lip at the thought, she started down the staircase, wanting to be in place before the first guest arrived. She hesitated for only a second before striding into the ballroom, casting a glance over the buffet. The caterers, under Al's direction, set out delectable canapés. A bar had been put at the end of the room, and three bartenders were laying out crystal stemware. A band warmed up on the dais.

She let out a sigh of relief. Everything was proceeding as scheduled. She wanted the night to be a success for Nick's sake.

She heard his distinctive footsteps and turned around to find him standing there. He leaned against the doorjamb, looking her up and down. He v was drop-dead gorgeous in his tux, and her heart skipped a beat.

"Hey there, handsome."

Nick grinned as his brother passed by and stopped, glancing at him.

"Yeah, pretty boy," Andre teased. "I'd better go change before you show me up."

Nick gave him a grin. "Yeah, you'd better."

She waited as Andre went upstairs. He was a younger version of Nick, and she could see that he and Simone were made for one another.

"I like your kid brother," she said.

"He's not bad." He smiled, turning to her.

Hearing the tension in his voice, she wondered if he was worried about the evening. "I'm sure you'll win over the Lax Consortium."

"You might be right," he said. "But even if I don't, I'm still glad we're having the party. You look beautiful."

The sound of guests arriving made her straighten. "They're here."

"I've got something to tell you first."

She looked up at him, bemused. "What?"

"Pierre Gallo has skipped town. When the police arrived to arrest him, he was gone, but they did find some contraband in his hiding place."

"The bracelet?" she asked.

It was the first bit of good news she'd heard in a while. But Nick's serious expression made her wonder.

"No, your things. The suitcases the mugger took from you."

She looked at him, shocked. "But, how would…"

"How do you think?"

"He sent that guy to rob me and rough me up, but why? My things weren't worth much to anyone but me."

He shrugged. "Maybe he did it to make sure you ran home fast and didn't talk."

"What a creep." She scowled.

"On the plus side, you are no longer a suspect," he said.

She beamed at him, throwing her arms around him. "You cleared my name. Thank you."

He claimed her mouth for a fast, hot kiss, and then drew away. "You are most welcome, my Cherie amour."

She smiled and leaned against him for a moment before the guests intruded.

***

Later that evening, Nick stopped chatting with Mike Reynolds from the Lax Consortium and turned to walk toward Laura. She was like an exotic butterfly attracting a lot of troubling admirers.

"Let's dance," he said, holding out his hand.

"I'd love to."

He burned when he waltzed her across the floor, her soft body pressed against his hardening one. He pulled back before he embarrassed himself. He gazed down at her, and the last piece of his reserve melted. He wanted her and he meant to keep her. Now, he just had to convince Laura. She was the key to his other half, even if she didn't understand it.

A noise caught his attention, and he looked to see Andre looking at him pointedly. Shit, business was the last thing on his mind tonight.

"I think your brother wants you," Laura said.

"I see him," he grumbled, not letting her go. "We need to talk."

"Can't we do that later?" she said, sensing his urgency.

He whirled her into a secluded corner. "I want to extend your contract. I'll have my attorney speak to Immy in the morning."

She looked up at him, stunned. It was what she'd longed to hear, and yet it was incomplete. There was no declaration of love, only ownership. She needed to own him just as surely as he possessed her. But she loved him. She wanted him to love her, too. Then she'd truly be his. Completely.

"I can see that you're surprised," he said, watching her.

"Flabbergasted, actually," she said, finally pulling herself together.

She moaned when he took her silence as agreement and pulled her into his arms for a blazing kiss. His mouth slanted across hers and she opened for him, pressing against him with need. Maybe being owned, even without his love, won't be so bad. Her nipples hardened instantly, and her sex got creamy.

Then he pulled away, breaking the kiss.

"I'll meet you out in the garden as soon as I can get away." He gazed resolutely down at her.

She nodded, glad to have time alone to contemplate her future. She watched him go, her body still aroused, her thoughts troubled. But she already knew if an extended contract was all he was offering, she'd jump at it. Anything to stay with him.

With a sigh, she turned and made her way to the French doors leading to the garden, her feet aching in her new shoes. She stepped out into the garden, took a breath of the perfumed air, and walked over to sit on the bench. She kicked off her shoes, wiggling her toes in the cool grass with a sigh.

Just then, the overpowering and familiar scent of cloves wrinkled her nose, reminding her of Pierre Gallo and his potent cigarettes. She turned a glance toward the garden and froze when she saw him standing in the shadows.

Inspector Le Marche had said he was missing, but why would he come here?

Before she could react, he morphed from the dark, a gun in his hand.

"Don't scream," he said, his hand shaking.

Scream? She could barely breathe as she stared sickly at the gun. If she moved, he'd shoot her. She had no doubt of it. He seemed out of control, desperate.

"Where is it?" he hissed.

She gulped, managing to ask, "It?"

His eyes narrowed. "Don't play dumb with me, Laura Brooks. I want your backpack. Get it now."

Why would he want her ratty old backpack? She gaped up at him like he'd lost his marbles. Unless he'd hidden something inside it? That might explain his bizarre demand, but she hadn't noticed anything new in her raggedy old satchel.

"I don't have it with me, as you can see," she said, glancing down at her beaded silk evening dress. "It would clash with my dress."

"This is no time for jokes," he barked.

He was so right. His hands twitched. She had to play for time. Surely, one of the guests would wander out into the garden, see her, and sound the alarm.

"Don't even think about calling for help," Pierre said, glancing at the partygoers through the window. "If anybody gets in the way—say, Nick Renault—I'll kill him."

She trembled, her hands knotting impotently in her lap. She winced when she heard a seam rip, but a ruined gown was the least of her worries. She stared at Pierre's glare and believed he'd shoot. The fact he knew about Nick chilled her.

"The backpack is up in my room," she said, slipping away from him to stand. She took a half step toward the house, saying, "I'll have to go inside to get it."

He closed the gap between them, whispering, "We'll go together. I'll blend in with your guests."

That was why he'd dressed in formal wear. He was a clever crook. She'd have to be smart to defeat him. She led the way into the house, leaving her shoes behind, and shivered when Pierre closed in behind her, jabbing his gun into her spine. To a casual observer, they'd look like friends, maybe even lovers. She shuddered at the thought. She didn't want another lover but Nick, even if it meant only being his courtesan. Too bad she hadn't told him that when she'd had the chance. Hopefully, if she played this out right, she'd get a second chance.

Once they stepped inside the hallway, she hesitated and glanced toward the ballroom. The band was playing and there was the animated sound of partygoers having a good time. At least the party had been a success. There was no way she'd take the crazy man behind her through the party, even though it was the fastest way to her room. She couldn't risk Nick intervening and possibly getting shot. He was tough, but he was no match for a bullet.

Pierre grunted his disapproval at her hesitating and jabbed the gun into her back.

She glared at him over her shoulder. "We can go up the back stairs."

"Then move," he hissed. "No more of your tricks."

Hell, he hadn't seen anything yet. She still had her mace in her backpack. And there were a few bondage restraints she could grab. Busy coming up with a plan, she took Pierre past the kitchen on her way to the back stairs, and stifled a groan when she saw Al working at the stove.

Please don't let him scare Pierre and get shot, she prayed, but he barely glanced up as they passed. She let out a shuddering breath, both relieved and scared out of her mind.

Then they were at the back staircase, and she knew she couldn't hesitate anymore. "This way," she said, heading upstairs.

It was just possible he'd leave if she handed over her backpack, but she didn't think so.

The tinkle of Simone's laughter and her husband's low voice came from their room.

Laura closed her eyes.

Shit, not more people in the line of fire.

"Come on," she said, rushing down the hall to her room, making Pierre grumble and rush after her.

"If you think..."

"Shut up," she said, tearing open her bedroom door and leading the way inside. She turned to glare at her pursuer.

He was sweating, his eyes darting around the room like a frog on speed. He slammed the door behind him and her heart raced.

Nick walked out into the garden to meet Laura, hoping she'd come to accept his contract extension offer, and frowned when he realized she wasn't there.

Shit, maybe in trying to keep her, he'd made her run. The sense of despair that ran through him at the thought made his heart stop.

Then he noticed her shoes lying on the grass and his trampled flowerbed, and felt his gut twist in alarm. Something was very wrong.

He tore inside, bumping into Al. "Have you seen Laura?"

Al gave him a troubled look. "Yeah, about ten minutes ago. She was giving some guy a tour. Why?"

"Describe him," Nick bit out, having no time for explanations.

"Bald, over-tanned, about fifty, in a rented tux."

"Shit," Nick said as he recalled Laura's description of her crooked mentor. "It's Gallo."

"They headed toward your study," Al said.

Nick tore that way with Al at his heels, and stopped when his foot crunched on a blue crystal. He picked it up and fingered the small gem in his hand. "It's a bead from Laura's dress."

"Smart lady." Al nodded in approval.

"*My* lady," Nick said proudly, and grimly followed the trail she'd left him.

Pierre Gallo was a dead man if he dared touch her. Behind him, Nick could hear Al talking into his cell phone to Detective Le Marche, but didn't let it distract him. When the trail of beads suddenly turned and went up the back staircase, his gut twisted. She was up there alone with that maniac.

Damn, this was his fault, and it was too late to fix it. He should have sent her home the moment he knew Gallo was at large. Now, he'd just have to pick up the pieces.

He prowled silently up the staircase with Al at his feet. As they passed Andre and Simone's room, Andre poked his head out.

"What's going on, guys?" Andre smiled. "Are you playing spy or something?"

"Shh," Al said, and spoke to him in low tones.

Nick kept moving quickly and quietly all the way to Laura's door.

The beads stopped there.

"Stop stalling and get me the damned bag, you stupid whore," Pierre said.

"I'm getting it," Laura shot back. "Just take what you came for and get your stinky butt out of here."

"One more word, and I'll shoot, bitch."

Ice encased Nick's heart at the mention of a gun.

He gave Al and Andre a look, and they slipped into his bedroom. The two rooms shared an adjoining bath, and it would give them an element of surprise. He leaned on the door just as there was the sound of ripping canvas and a low-pitched screech.

He burst into the room to see Pierre rolling on the floor rubbing at his tearing eyes and howling. Laura's backpack lay shredded on the floor, and she stood over Gallo, holding a diamond bracelet.

"I think this is what he was looking for," she said, rushing into Nick's arms.

He shuddered, holding her, as Al and Andre stormed the room. He barely noticed when the two men pounced on Pierre because Laura was shaking so badly.

"Shh," he murmured, trying to soothe her. "It's all over now."

She sniffed back tears. "I got him."

"I noticed," Nick said, pulling back to gaze at her. He noted the bruise on her face and winced, glaring at Gallo. Tears were flowing down the man's cheeks. "You used your mace."

She nodded. "Seemed like a good idea at the time."

"Al said you walked by the kitchen and didn't say anything," he added with a frown.

"I didn't want the loser to hurt anyone I love."

Nick felt like smiling as the words slipped from her sexy mouth. "You love Al?"

She frowned at him. "I care about Al. I love you, you idiot. Call Madame Imogene and sign me up for a long-term contract."

Her fierce tone made him laugh.

"What are you laughing at?" she snapped at him.

"You, my feisty little courtesan," he said, holding her tight. "You don't tell a man you love him by calling him names."

"Oh yeah?" She snuggled against him. "And how would you tell a woman that you loved her?"

"Simple," he said, beaming down at her. "I love you, Laura. Now about that contract, how about signing up for a lifetime with me?"

"That could be arranged," Laura said, before kissing him.

Chapter 10

Laura smiled when Nick carried her into the bedroom two weeks later. The room glowed with candlelight. Jasmine petals covered the Persian carpet and the four-poster bed. Her husband was a romantic at heart, even if he was a dominant one. The heady bouquet hung in the air, making her dizzy, or maybe it was the man whose arms she was in. He'd made their wedding perfect, flying in her family and even making peace with his father's family in an effort to include them.

She clung to him, still shocked that she was married to such a hunk, and that things had worked out so perfectly. "I love you, Nick."

"And I love you, Laura."

She shivered with delight when his eyes darkened with passion, and she knew he meant the words.

He set her on the floor in front of the bed, and she trembled in reaction. She wanted him badly, but he was making her wait.

She watched, fascinated, as he started to peel off his clothes, shedding his jacket and untying his tie. She started to unbutton the row of tiny pearl buttons on the front of her strapless wedding dress.

He shook his head. "That's my pleasure, Cherie."

It so reminded her of his words on their shocking first morning together, that she blushed. Then she saw his wicked smile and gave him one in return as he finished stripping. As always, she was struck anew by his muscular strength, and when his cock sprang free, she couldn't help but focus on it.

He stepped up to her slowly, unbuttoning her gown. It was one of Simone's creations and fit her like a glove. When his hands brushed against her breasts, she shivered, arching toward him. His teasing smile told her he knew exactly what he was doing to her.

She slowed her breathing, making herself stand still as he worked his way down to the last button. By the time he got there, she was quivering. He knelt at her feet, gazing up at her with hooded eyes. The dress fell off her to pool gracefully around him on the floor, and per her Dom's instructions, she wasn't wearing underwear. Standing there, nude in front of him, she felt as vulnerable as she had on their first encounter. Her mouth watered at the sight of him at her feet. He was all the man she'd ever want or need.

He took off her slipper and placed a damp kiss on the arch of her foot, and she melted where she stood. Then he did the other foot, and she wobbled against him, hearing him chuckle. It annoyed her for a second, but then he kissed her inner thigh and she gasped, her sex creaming helplessly. He urged her to spread her legs a little farther, and when she did, he touched his hot tongue to her clit. She muffled her cry in her hand, not wanting their guests, her family and his, to overhear.

He growled and did it again, lapping at her clit and then gently nipping it. She came with a cry, collapsing against him. He laid her back on the bed and plunged into her wet heat. Quivering as her sex milked at him, she shuddered as he took her hard and fast.

"Come for me, Cherie," he demanded, grinding against her.

She tightened around him, stars exploding behind her closed eyes as she came, giving him all her passion and receiving his in return.

CHECK OUT MORE ROWAN PROSE ROMANCES!

Julie Castle has always had a love affair with the written word. As a child growing up in a small town, she loved visiting the local library, a converted gilded age mansion, and getting lost between the pages of a book. The drafty old mansion could be a spooky place, but she still loved it. She enjoyed poking into behind the scenes areas she wasn't supposed to venture into. She's still the same way, which is why she loves writing romance with an edge, paranormal, suspenseful, super sexy, or just laugh your pants off funny. She is an award-winner, and resides in Wisconsin with her family.